"I'd like to make love to you."

"Is that *all* you want…?" Alexandra asked skeptically.

"I'd take you to a little inn up the coast," Chase answered. "We'd lie on a soft rug in front of a roaring fire and I'd undress you slowly and watch your pearly skin blush from the heat of the flames. Then I'd kiss—"

"I wasn't asking for a description," Alexandra broke in breathlessly. She'd allowed herself to imagine the erotic scene for far too long. "We both know your real priority is not my pearly skin but rather, convincing me Willie is your nephew."

His eyes moved to the scooped neck of her jacket. "It might have started out that way, but—"

"It doesn't matter how good you are in bed," she insisted. "You won't change my mind."

Chase smiled mischievously. "You might at least let me try…."

Dear Reader,

May is a time of roses, romance...and Silhouette Special Edition! Spring is in full bloom, and love is in the air for all to enjoy. And our lineup for this month reflects the wonder of spring. Our THAT SPECIAL WOMAN! title, *Husband by the Hour*, is a delightful spin-off of Susan Mallery's HOMETOWN HEARTBREAKERS series. It's the story of a lady cop finding her family... as well as discovering true love! And Joan Elliott Pickart continues her FAMILY MEN series this month with the frolicking *Texas Dawn*—the tale of a spirited career girl and a traditional Texas cowboy.

Not to be missed is Tracy Sinclair's warm and tender *Please Take Care of Willie*. This book is the conclusion to Tracy's CUPID'S LITTLE HELPERS series about matchmaking kids. And speaking of kids... *The Lady and the Sheriff* is Sharon De Vita's latest heartwarming installment of her SILVER CREEK COUNTY miniseries. This story features Louie, the kid who won readers' hearts!

May is also the month that celebrates Mother's Day. Cheryl Reavis has written a story that is sure to delight readers. Her FAMILY BLESSINGS series continues with *Mother To Be*. This story is about what happens when an irresistible force meets an immovable object...and deep, abiding love results.

Finally, we round off the month by welcoming historical author Barbara Benedict to Silhouette Special Edition. She makes her contemporary debut with the lighthearted *Rings, Roses...and Romance*.

I hope you have a wonderful month of May!

Sincerely,

Tara Gavin,
Senior Editor

Please address questions and book requests to:
Silhouette Reader Service
U.S.: 3010 Walden Ave., P.O. Box 1325, Buffalo, NY 14269
Canadian: P.O. Box 609, Fort Erie, Ont. L2A 5X3

TRACY
SINCLAIR
PLEASE TAKE CARE OF WILLIE

SPECIAL EDITION®

Published by Silhouette Books
America's Publisher of Contemporary Romance

SILHOUETTE BOOKS

ISBN 0-373-24101-1

PLEASE TAKE CARE OF WILLIE

Copyright © 1997 by Tracy Sinclair

Printed in U.S.A.

Books by Tracy Sinclair

TRACY SINCLAIR,

author of more than forty Silhouette novels, also contributes to various magazines and newspapers. An extensive traveler and a dedicated volunteer worker, this California resident has accumulated countless fascinating experiences, settings and acquaintances to draw on in plotting her romances.

MY FAVORITE THINGS
by Willie Clark

1) Teddy the bear—he's my best friend.

2) Ice-cream cones—chocolate, yummy, yummy, yummy!

3) King the dog—he's funny.

4) Birthday parties—with lots of fun surprises!

HAPPY BIRTHDAY

5) Going to the circus...they've got B-I-I-I-G ELEPHANTS!

6) Alex and Uncle Chase—I love them the bestest, next to my mommy.

(as told to Alexandra)

Prologue

Chase Mainwaring would always remember what he was doing on the day Brenda Clark disappeared.

The day began uneventfully enough. Chase arose early, even though he'd gotten in late the night before. He led an active social life, but that never interfered with business.

He went to his office, high up in the Alcoa Building with a breathtaking view of the San Francisco waterfront. It would have been a distraction to most people, but not to Chase. His desk was piled high with work, and he had the usual board meetings and conferences scheduled.

His secretary hovered in the doorway for a moment before he noticed her. Linda Hooper was a happily married woman, but she could still appreciate a superior male when she saw one. And Chase was definitely that. His patrician profile could have graced an old Roman coin—straight nose, high cheekbones and a firm jaw. He even had the autocratic expression of one of the emperors of old, but the expensive suit draped over his impressive frame placed him in the twentieth century.

When he glanced up, his secretary said, "There's a woman named Brenda Clark on the phone. She insists on speaking to you. I asked her what it was about, but she wouldn't tell me. She says it's personal."

"I don't know anybody by that name. She's probably selling something," he said dismissively. "Get rid of her."

"I tried, but she was very persistent. She said she has something important to tell you and this might be the last chance she'll get."

Chase frowned. "It's some kind of sales gimmick, no doubt. I'll take care of it." He reached for the phone. "Chase Mainwaring here. You wanted to speak to me?"

"Yes, it's about your brother, Bill," a soft voice said. "I'm afraid I have bad news for you."

A muscle twitched at the edge of Chase's square jaw. "You've seen my brother? Where is he? Did he tell you to call me?"

"I wish there were some easy way to tell you this, but there isn't. He's…he died two days ago."

Chase gripped the phone so tightly his knuckles turned white. "Who the hell are you?"

"My name is Brenda Clark. I guess I'm your sister-in-law. Bill and I were married five years ago."

"Now I know you're lying," Chase said harshly. "My brother's name is William Mainwaring."

"I didn't know that when I married him. Bill had been in some kind of trouble and he changed his name. He didn't tell me his real last name until after we were married. He used to talk about you and your mother, though. I think he missed you both very much," she said softly.

"That's a very touching story, but hardly believable. How gullible do you think I am? You could easily have found out I have a brother named William, who left town years ago. Why don't you get to the bottom line and tell me what you really want?''

"Nothing! I called to tell you about Bill because he would have wanted me to.'' She hesitated for a moment. "And for another reason, too. We have a son named William. William, Jr. I call him Willie. He's four years old.''

"Now we're getting someplace.'' Chase's expression was cynical. "This child is supposed to be my long-lost nephew, and you need money to take care of him.''

"No, I don't want anything. I can't blame you for being suspicious, but I'm not trying to extort money from you. I just wanted to tell you about your brother. I'm sorry it has to be over the phone. I know this is very sad for you, and I thought you might like to ask me some questions and to have the signet ring he always wore. But certain things have made it impossible for us to meet, so this will have to be our only contact. Bill did something foolish and I'm afraid that—'' She paused before continuing. "Willie and I are going away. I only told you about him because you're all the family he has. If anything should happen to me, I'd like you to take care of him.''

"What do you think might happen?''

"Nothing, I hope. But just in case it does, please take care of Willie. No matter what arguments you and your brother had, Willie is his son, your nephew.''

Chase was silent for a long moment. "I'm not saying I believe your story, but I'm willing to keep an open mind. If you don't want to come to the office, I'll meet you somewhere.''

"No, there isn't time. I'm sorry you had to find out about Bill this cruelly. Try to remember him with love, the way I will,'' she said in a choked voice. "Goodbye, Mr. Mainwaring.''

"Wait! Don't hang up!'' It was too late. The line went dead.

Chase sat motionless at his desk for long minutes. Was

it possible that the woman was telling the truth? If so, then Bill was dead. A sharp pain slashed through him at the thought. That's the way she wanted him to react, he told himself. These con artists played on people's emotions. And yet…she knew about Bill's signet ring, the ring Chase had never known him to take off.

That was hardly conclusive, Chase thought impatiently. It wasn't even very imaginative. Thousands of men wore signet rings. She had to be pulling some kind of scam and this was the opening gambit. Her next phone call would set the hook more firmly, and then she'd ask for money. That had to be it.

He walked over to the window to gaze out at the Golden Gate Bridge, a bright span between the dark clouds overhead and the rough water below. Brenda—if that was truly her name—hadn't offered any real proof to support her outrageous story, so why was he letting it upset him? If she thought she'd snared herself a pigeon, she was in for a rude awakening.

Chase's jaw set and he strode over to his desk. Switching on the intercom he said, "Get Commissioner Grimsby on the phone. And bring me the file on Shoreham Oil. I'm having lunch with their CEO at the Pacific Union Club today and I want to have my facts straight."

His momentary uneasiness was put to rest. Chase was once more in charge.

Chapter One

Alexandra Reynolds was talking on the telephone when a young woman and a small boy entered the Jet Away Travel Agency.

"I'll be right with you," Alexandra said.

The woman waited impatiently, not even glancing at the colorful posters depicting glamorous vacation spots. It was the small boy who was attracted to them. He was a beautiful child, with blue eyes and curly golden brown hair almost the same color as the teddy bear in his arms.

"Is that where we're going, Mommy?" he asked eagerly, pointing to a poster of a sun-drenched Caribbean island. "I like it. It's pretty."

"Yes, it is, darling." The woman's tight mouth relaxed. "Maybe we'll go there some day, but not this trip."

Alexandra concluded her call. "Sorry to have kept you waiting. I'm Alexandra Reynolds. How may I help you?"

"We're going to London, just Mommy and me." The little boy answered before his mother had a chance.

"That's very exciting." Alexandra smiled at him. "You'll have lots of fun. Have you ever been there before?"

"Can we get on with this?" the woman interrupted. "I'm in rather a hurry."

"Of course. What can I do for you?" Alexandra's businesslike tone didn't betray her curiosity.

The woman wasn't a typical Jet Away client. Most people were filled with enthusiasm at the prospect of a trip to Europe. They couldn't wait to discuss their travel destinations and what they wanted to see when they got there. The difficulty was pinning them down to the subject of departure dates and hotel reservations. This woman acted as if she was doing a necessary chore, like picking up the laundry or going to the grocery store.

"I need plane tickets to London," she said.

Alexandra indicated the chair on the other side of her desk. "Please have a seat while I jot down some information for our files." She picked up a pencil. "May I have your name and address?"

"My name is Brenda Clark and this is my son, William." Without giving her address she said, "We'll need two tickets."

"No, *three*, Mommy. Don't forget Teddy." He held up the stuffed bear to show Alexandra. "He's my friend."

"Please, Willie, let Mommy finish here." Brenda's curt tone softened when she spoke to her son.

"He's an adorable child," Alexandra said. "How old are you, Willie?"

"I'm four." He held up four dimpled fingers.

"Would you like to look at some pictures while I talk to your mommy?" She led him over to a chair next to an end table piled with magazines and travel brochures.

After Willie was happily occupied, Alexandra said to his mother, "Now then, what date would you like to leave?"

"Right away," Brenda answered. "Tonight, if possible."

"I'll see if anything is available." Alexandra tapped some keys on the computer. "I must warn you that if I do get you seats, it's going to be quite expensive. The cheaper fares always require an advance purchase."

"It doesn't matter. I want to go first class."

"That might make it even harder on such short notice. First-class seats are very limited."

"Are you telling me you can't get me out of San Francisco?" Brenda's voice was shrill. "You're a travel agent, aren't you? Isn't that what you do?"

Alexandra was startled by the woman's sudden loss of control. What was the urgency about getting to London? The illness of a loved one—or perhaps something even worse? That would account for the tension she seemed to be under.

"Do you have a special reason for wanting to get to London?" Alexandra asked slowly.

"Nothing that concerns you," Brenda answered tautly.

"I only asked because the airline might make an extra effort if it was an emergency."

Willie had picked up the panic in his mother's voice. He came over to lean against her and look searchingly into her face. "Is something wrong, Mommy?"

"Not a thing, darling." She hugged him. "Go back to your picture books and I'll be through here in a few minutes. Then we'll go and get an ice-cream cone. Would you like that?"

"Yes!" His cherubic face lit up.

Brenda gave Alexandra a tentative smile. "I'm sorry if I sounded impatient. It's going to be a long trip for Willie and I just want to get it over with."

"I understand. Traveling with a small child is never easy." Alexandra looked at the computer screen. "There's nothing available tonight, but I can get you on a flight that leaves San Francisco at nine o'clock tomorrow morning. Unfortunately you'll arrive in London in the middle of the night, because of the time change. Do you want to do that?''

"I suppose I have no choice."

"You could wait for an evening flight tomorrow and fly all night. It might be easier on Willie. He could sleep most of the way."

"No, I have to leave immediately. I'll take the nine o'clock in the morning."

"All right, now when do you want to return?"

"I haven't really decided. Perhaps I'd better buy one-way tickets," Brenda said casually.

"It will be a great deal more expensive in the long run. I could write you two open-ended tickets. That means all you'll have to do is call the airline office in London and request seats when you decide to come home."

"No, I think it will be simpler to make my own arrangements from there." Before Alexandra could try to change her mind, she said, ''If you'll tell me the amount, I'll pay you."

Alexandra shrugged. Evidently money was no object. "Whatever you prefer. Would you like me to make hotel reservations for you?"

"No, I…uh…we'll be staying with friends."

Alexandra didn't believe it for a minute. The woman's hesitation indicated she was lying. Why? Alexandra couldn't help being curious, but it wasn't any of her business.

After being told the sizable cost for the airline tickets, Brenda said, "I'll have to go to the bank."

"That won't be necessary. I'll be happy to put it on your credit card. Or you could give me a check. I'm sure you have proper identification," Alexandra said tactfully.

"I prefer to pay cash." Brenda rose and turned toward

the door. "Oh, no!" she exclaimed. "It's raining and I didn't bring an umbrella."

"I left mine at home, too. It was supposed to clear today," Alexandra said. "But I might have a rain bonnet around somewhere."

"I'm not worried about myself, it's Willie. He's just getting over a cold."

"No problem, you can leave him here with me."

"I couldn't do that," Brenda said firmly.

"He won't be any trouble," Alexandra assured her. "Willie and I will get along fine. Won't we?" she asked the child.

He wasn't so sure. "I want to go with you, Mommy."

Brenda hesitated, clearly reluctant to leave her son but concerned about his well-being. "You'll get awfully wet if you come with me. Maybe you would be better off here. I won't be gone long, honey."

Alexandra took some colored pencils out of a cup and held them out to the little boy. "If you stay here you can draw pictures and we'll put them up on the wall."

He let go of his mother's hand and came over to the desk. "Do you have a red one? That's my favorite."

Brenda looked at Alexandra gratefully. "I'll be back as soon as I can."

"No problem, take all the time you need. I'll take care of Willie."

After his initial objection to being left behind, Willie was perfectly happy with Alexandra. He sat across the desk from her, filling sheets of paper with stick figures and a lopsided square topped by a peaked roof and a chimney.

"That's my play school," he explained. "And this is Stevie and Brittany, my friends. And this is Mrs. Thompson's cat. She's our teacher."

"It must be a very nice school." Alexandra smiled at the look of absorption on his angelic face.

"Yes," he answered, starting to draw a larger figure. "This is Mommy. She took me to the movies and then we had dinner in a restaurant. I liked that."

"Did your daddy have dinner with you, too?"

"No."

Alexandra regretted her innocent question. Perhaps his mother and father were separated or divorced.

"Sometimes Daddy makes Mommy cry," Willie remarked unexpectedly.

"I'm sure he doesn't mean to," Alexandra said. "Why don't you draw me a picture of Mrs. Thompson's cat?" she asked, to distract him. "What color is he?"

"It's a girl cat. But I can't draw her because I don't have an orange pencil. That's what color she is."

"I'll show you a little trick I learned when I was your age. First you color with a red pencil, then you draw over it with a yellow pencil. See? Now you have orange."

"I wanna do that!" Willie exclaimed delightedly.

When he eventually tired of drawing, Alexandra gave him a box of paper clips to play with and showed him how to make a chain. It was intricate work for small fingers and kept him busy for quite a while. She was able to take care of business almost as if he weren't there.

One of the many phone calls to the office was from Tina Hamilton. She was the travel agent Alexandra had hired when her former partner, Mandy, left to get married.

"How are you getting along without me?" Tina asked. "I feel terrible about leaving you there to cope all alone."

"Don't worry, everything's running smoothly. I can see you got your phone connected," Alexandra commented. Tina was moving into a new apartment and she'd needed the day off to wait for her utilities to be turned on.

"Yes, the man just left. The gas and electric people were here, too. That's why I'm calling. I can come in now, if you need me."

Alexandra glanced at her watch. "Don't bother, it's almost quitting time. I'll see you in the morning."

She hung up, frowning. The time had passed so quickly that she hadn't realized how long Brenda had been gone. The banks were closed by now. What could have happened to her?

"I want an ice-cream cone," Willie said. "Mommy said she was gonna buy me one. When is my mommy coming back?"

"She'll be here soon," Alexandra said reassuringly. "How would you like a cookie?"

"What kind? I don't like coconut."

"I think these are chocolate chip. Let's find out." She led him to the small area they'd converted into a lunchroom. "Yep, they're chocolate chip. Would you like one?"

"Okay." He gave her a sunny smile. "But when Mommy gets here I still want an ice-cream cone."

Alexandra was grateful for the distraction. She didn't want Willie to start clamoring for his mother. He'd been so good up until now.

As the minutes inched by, Alexandra became more and more uneasy. Finally she called her friend Mandy.

"You mean, the woman just dumped her child on you and took off?" Mandy exclaimed, after Alexandra had explained the situation.

"No, I'm sure she wouldn't do a thing like that. She seemed like a very devoted mother." Alexandra slanted a glance at Willie and lowered her voice. "I'm concerned that something might have happened to her."

"Like an accident, you mean? Then you'd better call the police."

"I don't like to do that. It could make things awkward if she just got delayed somehow."

"Doing what? The banks are closed by now. You said that's where she told you she was going, although it sounds fishy to me. Why would she want to pay for her tickets in cash? What's wrong with a credit card? That's what everybody else uses, especially for such a large expenditure.''

"I got the impression that she's running away from something, maybe an abusive husband. If she used a credit card, he'd know where to find her.''

"What a bummer!''

"Yes, the poor thing was really stressed out. She got very upset when I told her I couldn't get her on a plane tonight. I thought it was strange, but it makes sense if he's right on her tail.''

"You think he caught up with her?'' Mandy asked slowly.

"I don't know what to think. I only know she wouldn't abandon her son. If you'd seen how gentle and loving she was with him, you'd agree with me.''

"Then you have to call the police.''

Alexandra hesitated. "I hate to jump the gun. Maybe she has a reasonable explanation for being gone so long. I don't want to make even more trouble for her.''

"Well, it's up to you. You're the one who's stuck with the boy.''

"I don't mind that part of it. He's a darling child, so well adjusted. Whatever Brenda's problems are, she hasn't let them affect Willie.''

"I hope everything turns out all right. Let me know. I'm really interested.''

"I'll call you,'' Alexandra promised. "With all that's going on, I forgot to ask how you're feeling.''

Mandy was pregnant. That was the reason she hadn't returned to the agency after her marriage. Both Mandy and her husband were ecstatic about the baby.

"I feel wonderful! I keep telling Connor that, but he treats me like a fragile piece of china. He won't let me lift a finger around here.''

"If you're looking for sympathy, forget it!''

"I wasn't. Connor is the dearest man in the whole world,

and I know how lucky I am," Mandy said softly. "I only hope you find someone just as wonderful."

"That makes two of us, but my love life isn't very promising right now. There isn't a keeper in the bunch."

"I felt the same way until I met Connor. You'll meet somebody when you least expect to."

"I'll take your word for it," Alexandra replied. "Right now I have other things on my mind."

Alexandra became increasingly concerned as time passed and Brenda didn't return. Willie was starting to get anxious, too. He wouldn't accept her assurances for much longer.

Finally Alexandra knew she had to call the police.

She began to have misgivings when the squad car pulled up in front of the travel office and two uniformed men got out. They were both large and imposing, although not intentionally. Their manner was polite. Only a hint of admiration was visible as they gazed at Alexandra's long, shining blond hair and thickly lashed hazel eyes. The younger policeman was especially careful to appear professional.

"I'm Officer Torelli," he introduced himself. "And this is my partner, Officer Greenleaf. You reported an abandoned child?"

"His mother left him with me," Alexandra said carefully. "I didn't say she abandoned him."

"How long has she been gone?"

"She left to go to the bank a couple of hours ago and she hasn't returned."

The two officers exchanged a glance. "Was she carrying a large amount of money?" Greenleaf asked.

"I don't know. She did intend to draw some out. Do you think she could have been mugged?"

Willie sensed something was wrong. His happy smile had vanished, replaced by an anxious expression. "Where's Mommy? I want to go home now."

"In a little while." Alexandra tried to soothe his budding fears. "I just have to talk to these nice men for a few minutes."

It was difficult to explain what had happened, with Willie listening to every word. He stayed by her side, refusing all her attempts to send him into the inner office to play.

"You said you'd never seen the woman before," Officer Greenleaf said. "How did she happen to come here?"

"I don't know. Maybe she just picked our agency out of the phone book."

"Did she give you her address?"

"No. I asked her, but we started to talk about airline schedules and she never did give it to me."

Torelli looked at Willie. "Do you know where you live, sonny?"

"Uh-huh." The child nodded. "In a great big house with lots of rooms. It has a restaurant where me and Mommy have dinner and there's a little store that sells candy bars and stuff, only it doesn't have any door."

"It sounds like he's describing a hotel," Greenleaf remarked to his partner.

"Do you know the name of the house?" Torelli asked Willie.

"No."

"How about your daddy's name?"

"It's Bill. Mommy calls him that, but I call him Daddy."

"Do you happen to know his telephone number or where he works?"

When the little boy shook his head, Torelli said to Alexandra, "We'll try to track down the hotel where he and his mother were staying. If she has any relatives, they'll have to be notified."

"You agree with me, don't you?" Alexandra asked. "Mrs. Clark didn't desert her child."

"It's too soon to say, miss. We'll investigate all the possibilities.'' The officer flipped a page of his notebook. ''Can you give us a description of her?''

Willie tugged on Alexandra's sleeve. ''You said Mommy was coming back soon. Where is she? I want to see her *now!*'' Tears were starting to gather in his big blue eyes.

This was what Alexandra was afraid of. How could she reassure him, when she didn't have any answers?

Officer Greenleaf tried to do it for her. He hunkered down in front of the boy, but even then he towered over the child. Willie shrank back and pressed against Alexandra.

''How would you like to go for a ride in a real police car, sonny?'' Greenleaf asked in a coaxing tone. ''As soon as we're through talking to this lady, we'll give you a ride to the police station. Won't that be fun?''

Alexandra gave the man a startled look. ''You can't take a four-year-old to a police station! That's no place for a child.''

''What do you suggest we do with him, miss? You're the one who called us.''

''Yes, but I didn't think you'd take him away.''

''We don't have any other choice. Don't worry, he'll be fine.''

''That's a matter of opinion,'' Alexandra snapped. ''He can stay with me until you find out what happened to his mother.''

''We can't let him do that,'' Torelli said. ''We have to take him into custody.''

''You're talking as if he's a criminal!'' she exclaimed.

''I didn't mean that the way it sounds. Believe me, he'll be well taken care of.''

''By whom?'' she demanded.

''Children's Services will see that the boy is all right.'' Greenleaf's soothing tone was the same one he'd used on Willie.

''I'm sure they're very competent, but I told Mrs. Clark

I'd take care of her son until she returned. That makes me responsible for him. All I want you to do is find her."

"We're going to do our best, but we still have to take the boy," Torelli insisted. "He'll be placed in protective custody for now. If or when we find his mother, she'll have to convince the court that she's fit to take care of him."

Alexandra was aghast at what she'd set in motion. The two policemen were only following procedure, but Willie's whole life would change. He'd seemed such a happy, secure child. Now he'd be placed with strangers, taken away from everything that was familiar to him. It was bound to leave a mark on him.

"Can we finish up here, miss?" Torelli asked with a touch of impatience. "You were going to give us a description of the missing person."

That sounded so impersonal. As if Brenda were just a statistic, instead of a loving mother in some kind of trouble. Alexandra knew she couldn't stop the policemen from taking Willie. They'd do it forcibly, if necessary, and that would be even more traumatic for the child. Her mind raced, looking for some way to persuade them to change their minds. And then she thought of one.

"I'll give you Mrs. Clark's description in a minute," she said. "First I have to make a phone call."

"I don't like this any better than you do," Greenleaf said mildly. "But it will be better all around if we get it over with."

"I know you're right, but I really do have to make a call. I was so busy with Willie all afternoon that I didn't have time for anything else. I have to phone a client before he leaves his office." Without waiting for the men to object, Alexandra went into her private office with Willie trailing close behind.

She tapped out a number and waited breathlessly for her friend Mandy's husband to answer. Connor Winfield was a

very important man in San Francisco. He knew a lot of
influential people. If anyone could help her, it was Connor.

"Thank heaven you're still there!" she exclaimed when
he came on the line. "It's Alexandra, and I really need
your help."

"Of course, Alex. What's the problem?"

She explained hurriedly, lowering her voice so the men
in the other room wouldn't hear. "You know all kinds of
influential people. Is there anyone who can convince the
police to let me take Willie home with me tonight?"

"I suppose so, but have you thought this through?" he
asked slowly. "There's no telling how long it might take
them to find his mother."

"I'm not worried about that. He's no trouble."

"It sounds like you're getting very involved here. You
mustn't become too attached to this child," Connor
warned. "Even if the worst happens and his mother never
shows up, he undoubtedly has relatives who would claim
him."

"That's what I'm hoping for. I know I can't keep him
permanently, but I can spare him a lot of misery. Willie is
a scared little boy. He won't understand why two big,
strange men want to take him away. Just imagine how
frightened he'll be when they take him to some impersonal
place and dump him with more strangers."

"It isn't a happy situation," Connor admitted.

"Exactly! And it's so unnecessary. He's comfortable
with me, so why not let me keep him temporarily? What
if his mother shows up in the morning with some explanation we haven't thought of? The poor child will have
been traumatized for nothing."

"I wish I had your optimism about his mother. I don't
like the sound of all this."

"But you have to admit it's a possibility," Alexandra
insisted.

"I suppose anything is possible," Connor agreed grudgingly.

"Will you help me, then?"

"I guess I could call the police commissioner. I play handball with him."

Alexandra laughed delightedly. "You can't go much higher than that. I knew you could help me!"

"I can't guarantee anything, but I'll tell him what you told me. Can you stall the two cops for a short time while I get in touch with Wesley?"

"Don't worry, I'll manage."

As soon as she hung up, Alexandra dialed another number. She really did have business calls to make, although they weren't as pressing as she'd indicated. It was a practical way to gain precious minutes.

The two officers didn't have unlimited patience. They paced the outer office, looking with disinterest at the travel posters on the wall. Finally Torelli came over to stand in the doorway.

"We have to finish up here, Miss Reynolds," he said in a firm tone of voice.

"Of course. I'll be right with you." Alexandra decided not to push her luck. She concluded her call and joined him in the outer office. "I'm really sorry, but you can't get some people off the telephone. Of course, it's understandable. They have a lot of questions about their trip."

He brushed that aside. "You were going to give us a description of the missing woman." He looked at his notebook. "Brenda Clark?"

"Yes. Well, let me see. Her hair is a little lighter than Willie's and she's very attractive. She was wearing a designer suit that was just gorgeous, especially on somebody with her figure. The suit was beige with a straight skirt and one of the new shorter jackets." Alexandra threw in every detail she could think of, to stall for time. She was about to add more, when Torelli interrupted her.

"About how old would you say she was and what color were her eyes?"

"She had on dark glasses, so I don't know what color her eyes were."

"She didn't take them off inside?"

"No, but that isn't unusual. Some people are very sensitive to light. One woman I know—"

"How tall was she and how old?" Torelli asked doggedly.

"About twenty-five, I'd guess, and medium height."

After a few more questions he put away his notebook. "Okay, that about does it. If you think of anything else you can call Officer Greenleaf or myself." He held out a card. "We'll take the boy now."

Phil Broderick, the daily *Tribune's* crime reporter, was idly shooting the breeze with the desk sergeant at the station house. It was a quiet night and they had plenty of time to discuss the basketball scores and speculate about who would win the division championship.

"Well, I guess I'd better nose around somewhere else," Broderick remarked finally. "I'm not going to get a story around here tonight."

"Doesn't look that way," George Dunbar, the sergeant, answered. "Unless you want to write about that woman who left her kid in the travel agency."

"Give me a break! That's a television plot, not a news story."

"Sorry, but we're fresh out of serial murderers tonight," Dunbar said dryly.

"I'll settle for less," the reporter said, starting for the door. "Let me know if anybody comes in to report seeing Elvis or a UFO."

"I thought you wanted an *unusual* story." Dunbar chuckled as the phone rang.

Broderick paused at the door when the other man's tone

of voice changed. The sergeant also sat up straighter in his chair.

"Yes, *sir,* Commissioner," he said. "What can I do for you?" After listening for a few minutes he shuffled some papers around on his desk until he found the right one. "Officers Greenleaf and Torelli went out on that call. It was half an hour ago, though. They might be on their way back now with the boy. That's standard procedure in a case of child aband—" The sergeant sat up even straighter as he was cut off in midsentence. "Yes, sir, I understand. I'll get in touch with them right away."

Broderick drifted back to the desk, looking curious. "What's going down? Was that the police commissioner you were talking to?"

"Yeah, just what I need! He's taking a personal interest in the kid who was left at the travel agency. He wants us to keep hands off." Dunbar was rapidly punching out a pager number.

"What's his connection?"

"I wasn't about to ask him, but you can bet this is no ordinary kid."

The reporter's interest quickened. "Maybe there's a story here, after all. I'll pick up a photographer and get over there." He glanced at his watch. "Hot damn! There's time to make the morning edition."

"You didn't hear anything from me," Dunbar warned, before speaking rapidly into the phone. "Torelli? I'm glad I caught you. Here's what I want you to do."

Back at Jet Away's office, Alexandra was trying to reason with the two policemen.

"Please, Miss Reynolds. I know you don't want to upset the boy, so don't make us carry him out of here," Officer Greenleaf said patiently.

"No! I don't want to go with them," Willie howled, clutching Alexandra tightly. "Don't let them take me!"

She spoke soothingly to him while shooting an indignant glance at the policeman. "This is all so unnecessary. If you would just call the police commissioner as I asked, he'd tell you it's all right for Willie to stay with me."

"We're just street cops, lady. We don't know the commissioner personally," Torelli drawled.

"I'm not asking you to invite him over for dinner," she snapped. "Just make the damn call!"

Alexandra was about to lose the argument when Officer Torelli's pager beeped. While he was on the phone with his precinct, two men came through the front door, Phil Broderick and his photographer, a man named Tony.

"That must be the kid," Broderick said, and Tony snapped a rapid succession of flash photos.

"What do you think you're doing?" Alexandra exclaimed angrily. "Who are you and why are you here?"

Instead of answering her question, the reporter fired several staccato ones of his own. "What's your connection with the police commissioner? Are you or he any relation to the boy? How long has his mother been missing?"

"I don't know who you are, but—" she began indignantly.

"Phil Broderick of the *Tribune*. Why did this—" he paused to look at his notes "—Brenda Clark leave her kid with you? Where's the father? Who *is* the father?"

"You're making a big deal out of nothing," Alexandra protested, with a sinking heart. This whole thing was mushrooming out of control. Without ever meaning to, she'd gotten poor Brenda into a mountain of trouble. "Willie's mother will be back for him. She's just been unavoidably delayed."

"Then why did you call the police?"

"It was a mistake," Alexandra answered carefully. "I was concerned and I overreacted."

"So, you've heard from his mother? You know where she is?"

"Well, not exactly, but—" She took a deep breath. "It's a private matter and I'd prefer not to discuss it. Will you please leave?"

"Do you suspect foul play? Is that why the commissioner is taking an interest? Who *is* Brenda Clark, anyway?"

Alexandra turned to the two officers, who had their heads together conferring in low tones. "Will you please ask these men to leave?"

After exchanging a few more words, the policemen came over to join her. They nodded to the other two men, whom they evidently knew.

"We just got authorization for you to keep the boy, Miss Reynolds," Torelli said. "Children's Services will be contacting you, but he can stay with you for now."

"Thank heaven!" she exclaimed.

"No hard feelings, I hope. We were only doing our job. Just between you and me, I'm glad it turned out the way it did." Torelli's official manner relaxed and he gave her a friendly smile.

"You'll keep looking for Willie's mother?" Alexandra asked anxiously.

"Count on it. And we'll let you know as soon as we find out anything. Why don't you take the boy and go home now? We'll call you if anything turns up."

Phil Broderick had been listening and taking notes. Suddenly he said, "Look this way, Miss Reynolds."

She complied automatically and a flashbulb went off, dazzling her.

As Alexandra exclaimed in annoyance, Greenleaf said, "Come on, guys, give the lady a break." He and his partner urged the other two men out the door.

It seemed very quiet in the office after they had all left. Willie knuckled the tears out of his eyes with a small fist. "I don't like them. I'm glad they went away."

"I am, too, darling." Alexandra hugged him close. "Come on, let's go home and have some dinner."

"No, I have to wait here for my mommy."

It took all of Alexandra's ingenuity to convince him that his mother would want him to stay with her, but she finally succeeded.

"But she'll come for me tomorrow, won't she?" he asked anxiously.

"We'll get up bright and early and come back here," Alexandra promised, evading the issue.

There was no point in telling him the truth and upsetting him all over again. Things looked grim right now, but who knew what tomorrow might bring? She was determined to keep a good thought.

Chapter Two

Chase had put in a busy day and a stimulating evening. By the time he arose the next morning, Brenda and her disturbing story were just a vague, unpleasant memory.

He showered and dressed rapidly before going into the kitchen of his penthouse apartment to pour himself a cup of coffee. He rarely used the kitchen for anything else.

While standing at the counter, he opened the morning newspaper to scan the headlines and leaf quickly through the front section. He glanced in passing at a picture of a small boy on the third page, then his eyes swung back as the name in the heading registered: Police Seek Missing Mother, Brenda Clark.

The accompanying article told how a little boy named Willie Clark had been left at a local travel agency by his mother, who hadn't returned to claim him. The police refused to speculate about whether it was a case of child abandonment or if the mother, Brenda Clark, had met with foul play. They were asking anyone who had information about her disappearance to please contact the police.

Chase's eyes were bleak. If that part of Brenda's story was true—that she was afraid something might happen to her—then there was a distinct possibility that the rest of her story was also true. It was hard to accept the fact that his brother could be dead. Chase faced the sobering thought for long, saddened minutes. Then his expression hardened. One thing was sure, he was damn well going to find out what happened.

Alexandra went to her office early the next morning, in case Brenda reappeared—or at least tried to contact her. Someone was indeed waiting for her, but it was a man rather than a woman.

Chase's tall, broad-shouldered frame made him formidable looking at any time, and the scowl on his face added to her uneasiness. Alexandra instinctively put her arm around Willie.

"If you're waiting to get into the travel agency, I'm sorry but we won't be open for another hour," she said.

Chase ignored her. He was staring at Willie with a mixture of emotions. "So you're Bill's son," he said softly.

"I assume you saw his picture in the paper this morning," Alexandra said. "Do you know something about his mother?"

"No, but I knew his father. He was my brother." Chase hunkered down in front of Willie, gazing at him poignantly. "You look like your dad."

Willie showed no sign of recognition. He leaned against Alexandra, intimidated by yet another big man.

"I'm not doubting you, Mr. Clark, but—" she began.

"It's Mainwaring, not Clark. Chase Mainwaring. My brother evidently changed his name when he left town years ago."

"*Evidently?* Don't you know?"

"Unfortunately, I didn't. It's a long story, and it doesn't concern you."

"That's where you're wrong!" Her hazel eyes flashed dangerously. "Everything about Willie concerns me."

"According to the article in the paper, you're a complete stranger to the boy. I'm grateful to you for keeping him, but I'll take over now."

"You're out of your mind if you think I'm turning this child over to you! You show up out of nowhere and claim to be his uncle, but it's obvious that Willie doesn't know you. I have no idea what kind of game you're playing, but you won't get away with it. Leave us alone or I'll call the police."

People were hurrying by on their way to work. Some of them slowed to look curiously at the angry couple and the small troubled child.

One man stopped and said, "Hey, isn't that the kid whose picture was in the paper this morning?"

As people started to gather, Willie tugged on Alexandra's hand. "I want Mommy. You told me she'd be here."

"Did they find his mother yet?" a woman asked.

"Must we stand out here on the sidewalk like a sideshow at the circus?" Chase asked impatiently. "Hasn't the child been through enough?"

Alexandra wasn't wild about letting him into the office, where they'd be alone. But all the curious attention was upsetting Willie, and Chase clearly didn't intend to leave without further argument. She reluctantly brought out her key and opened the door.

When they were inside, Alexandra tried to hide her trepidation. Chase seemed to fill the room. She'd be physically powerless against him, if the situation turned sticky.

He didn't look like a common thug. His suit was custom-made and he patronized an expensive barber. Still, you never could tell. His firmly set jaw and the determination in his narrowed blue eyes made her uneasy.

Raising her chin, she said coolly, "If you have any proof that you're Willie's uncle, I'd like to see it. Otherwise I want you to leave."

"Gladly," he scowled. "But when I go, I'm taking the boy. His mother phoned yesterday and asked me to take care of her son, if anything happened to her. Evidently something has. That's why I'm here, to carry out her wishes."

"How do I know you didn't have something to do with her disappearance?"

"Are you out of your mind?" Chase exclaimed.

"There has to be a reason why Brenda didn't return. I got the feeling she was running away from something or somebody. Maybe it was you."

"That's nonsense!" he said heatedly. "I'm a well-known business man. I've never had anyone question my word before. I'm telling you this is my nephew. He's coming with me, where he belongs!"

"And I'm telling *you*, he's staying with me!"

"Why are you being so obdurate?" He gave her a comprehensive look for the first time, noticing her lovely face and softly curved body. "You don't look like one of those frustrated women who goes around snatching other people's children. I'm sure you could have one of your own. You might even enjoy the search for a suitable father," he drawled.

Alexandra felt the impact of his masculinity, even as her temper threatened to flame out of control. When he wasn't being obnoxious, this man must be a master at seduction. There would always be women willing to overlook his autocratic manner for the pleasure that lithe body could bring. But she wasn't one of them.

Gritting her teeth, she said, "If you're not out of here in one minute, I'm calling the police."

"Good idea. Call them. If you don't, I will. Maybe *they* can talk some sense into you."

* * *

Danny Riker didn't usually rise until noon. When his telephone rang around eight that morning, he buried his head under the pillow to shut out the noise. But the ringing continued.

Finally he swore fluently and fumbled for the phone. "Who the hell is it?"

A male voice said, "You really blew it. Have you seen the morning paper?"

"I'm still in bed, for chrissake! What's so important in the paper?"

"Brenda left her kid with somebody and took off. You were supposed to grab her. How the hell did you let her slip through your fingers?"

Danny sat up and reached for a cigarette. He was in his late thirties, the kind of man who played a car salesman in movies or maybe a crooked politician. He was nice looking, but there was something slightly shifty about his eyes.

"Jeez, Nate, it wasn't my fault," he whined, in answer to the other man's question. "I was right on her tail all afternoon, waiting for a chance to get her alone someplace where there weren't a lot of people around."

"Did you think she was going to walk down a dark alley just for your convenience?" Nate asked sarcastically.

"Well, what did you expect me to do? Snatch her off a busy street, where somebody might jump me and yell for the cops? Then we'd really be in trouble."

"What makes you think we aren't already? The boss is having a fit. He wants to know what happened."

"I thought I had it made when she dumped the kid and took off alone. I tailed her to a bank, but it was crowded and she gave me the slip. One minute she was there and the next minute she just disappeared. I guess she went out another door."

"That's just great!" Nate said disgustedly. "You let an amateur put one over on you."

"It's just a temporary setback. I knew Brenda wouldn't come back for the kid while I was hanging around the place, so I figured I'd pick up her trail again at the hotel. She doesn't know I found out where she's staying."

"You can bet she didn't go back there." Nate told him about the article in the morning paper. "You really loused things up. Now the cops are looking for Brenda, too."

"If we can't find her, they can't."

"Do you think that's going to make Karpov feel better?" Nate asked dryly.

Danny licked his dry lips. "Come on, Nate, give me a break. It could have happened to anybody."

"Well, you better finish the job, and quick. Only this time, play it smart. Instead of running all over the place looking for Brenda, let her come looking for you."

"How do you figure I pull *that* off?"

"Simple. What's the only thing she cares about, now that Bill is dead? The boy." Nate answered his own question. "If we have him, she'll come."

"It's a neat plan, but how do we get him? Somebody else already has the kid. Why would they give him to us?"

"Not us—you. This is what you're going to do," Nate said.

The two policemen who responded to Alexandra's call were different from the day before. Officers Martinson and Wallace were trying to be impartial in a difficult situation. They had been briefed at the station house and were disposed toward Alexandra, since the police commissioner had taken an interest in her. But they were unprepared for Chase. The Mainwaring name was well-known in San Francisco, and Chase's forceful manner validated the image of money and influence.

"We believe your story, Mr. Mainwaring," Officer Wallace said carefully. "But it would help if you could give us some proof that you're the boy's uncle."

"See? I told you so!" Alexandra crowed.

Chase glared at her. "Has anyone ever told you that you're a very annoying woman?"

"No, you're the first," she said blandly.

"You must know some very wimpy men," he muttered. "I wouldn't put up with you for five minutes."

"I wouldn't want you to," she countered, tilting her head to stare up at him pugnaciously.

Before he could answer, the bell over the front door jingled and Tina Hamilton came in.

She looked wide-eyed at the two policemen. "What's going on?"

"I'll explain it to you later," Alexandra said. "Will you take Willie into the inner office?"

"No! I want to stay with you," the little boy said, clutching her skirt.

Alexandra knelt down and put her arms around him. "It's all right, honey. I'll be right out here. Tina is very nice. She'll play games with you."

"Is this the child I read about in the paper?" When Alexandra nodded, Tina held out her hand and gave him a big smile. "How would you like to fool around on the computer, pal? I have a game that plays music."

He was torn between interest and reluctance. "Mommy has a computer at home, but I'm not allowed to touch it."

"Ours is different," she said. "I'll teach you how to type on it. Do you know the alphabet?"

"Yes." He nodded proudly, taking her hand. "Well, not all of it, but I know some."

The adults were silent until Tina took Willie into the inner office and closed the door.

"He's a nice little boy," Chase said in a husky voice.

Alexandra was surprised to find herself thawing slightly toward him. His face held such sadness. Was it possible his story was true? The momentary weakness passed. Chase might simply be a very good actor. She'd need a lot more proof, before she turned Willie over to him.

"Well, now," Officer Martinson began, and then the doorbell interrupted them again. They all turned to look at the man who entered.

Danny Riker was medium height and well-dressed, although his suit didn't have the quiet elegance of Chase's. He smiled pleasantly, not appearing to be surprised by the presence of two policemen.

"I'm sorry, but we aren't open yet," Alexandra said.

"I'm not here on business." Danny introduced himself. "I came about the boy."

"You know something about his mother?" Martinson asked as the others waited tensely for his answer.

"Yes, she's my fiancée. I came to get Willie." Danny looked around the room. "He's here, isn't he?"

Alexandra ignored the question. "Where is Brenda? Why didn't she come herself?"

"It's a long story and I'm in rather a hurry. Where is the child?"

"I don't know who you are, but you're not taking him anyplace," Chase said grimly.

"We'd like to ask you a few questions, Mr. Riker," Wallace said. "If you have information concerning Mrs. Clark's whereabouts, we want to hear it."

"This is very awkward," Danny said. "You see, Brenda and I had a little misunderstanding."

Before he could continue, Willie came running out of the inner office. "Can I have a doughnut?" he asked Alexandra. "Tina said they're not good for me, but I had one before. Can I, huh, Alex?"

She looked for some reaction from Danny. When he didn't register any emotion, she said to Willie, "Don't you want to say hello to Mr. Riker?"

Willie glanced at all four men without enthusiasm. "Huh-uh."

"Do you know which one Mr. Riker is?" Alexandra persisted.

"Huh-uh," the child repeated. "Can I have a doughnut?"

"You can have half of one, with a glass of milk." She waited until he'd gone back to Tina. "This man should be prosecuted for attempted kidnapping, at the very least," she told the policemen indignantly.

"I think you have some explaining to do, Mr. Riker." Martinson looked at him without expression. "Can you tell us why the boy didn't recognize you? That seems a little strange, if you were Mrs. Clark's fiancé, as you claim."

Danny sighed. "I didn't want to tell you the whole story, but I can see I'll have to. Brenda and I haven't known each other very long, but it was love at first sight for both of us. I didn't ask her anything about herself, because I didn't care about her past. I just knew she was the girl for me."

"That's very touching," Chase said sardonically. "But where does Willie come in?"

"We discussed our future together, and I stupidly told her I didn't want children. I only meant for the first year or two, because I wanted Brenda all to myself before we took on responsibilities. I never would have said it, if I'd known she already had a child. Of course I'll love the little fellow, but I never got a chance to tell her that. The last couple of days, things started to go wrong between us. Suddenly we quarreled a lot and I didn't know why. Finally, yesterday morning, Brenda just disappeared. I realize now she thought a clean break would be less painful for both of us, since our relationship wasn't going anywhere."

"If she decided to cut you out of her life because of Willie, why would she leave him behind?" Alexandra demanded.

"The poor girl was very upset," Danny explained. "Maybe she just needed to get away by herself for a little while and think things out. Or maybe something happened to her. She could have been hit by a car crossing the street. My poor Brenda could be lying in a hospital right now, not knowing who she is."

"We checked all the hospitals," Officer Wallace said. "She wasn't in an accident.

"Thank God for that!" Danny said. "Then I know she'll come back to me."

"That's the damnedest story I ever heard," Chase said disgustedly. "It isn't even a good fairy tale."

Danny frowned. "Who the—who are you?"

"Mr. Mainwaring claims to be the child's uncle," Martinson said.

"I don't *claim* to be," Chase said forcefully. "I *am* his uncle!"

Alexandra looked thoughtful. "If your story is true, Mr. Riker, you're not especially fond of children. Why would you want to take Willie?"

"I like kids," Danny protested. "That's what I want to prove to Brenda. I know she'll come back for Willie, and when she sees what good care I took of him, we'll patch up everything between us."

"You're not using my nephew to make points with your girlfriend," Chase stated.

"At least I knew his mother," Danny said. "She never mentioned *you.*"

"There seems to be a lot you didn't talk about," Chase drawled.

"Neither of you are very convincing," Alexandra observed.

"My credentials are as good as his," Danny said. "I'm a prominent businessman in this town."

Martinson produced a notebook. "What do you do, Mr. Riker?"

"I own the Time Out. It's a restaurant on Powell Street. We've been in business for years."

"Isn't that a bar?" Chase asked.

"It's a sports bar," Danny admitted reluctantly. "But it also includes a very fine restaurant. We're crowded every night."

"That means you work nights. What did you plan on doing with Willie while you're working?" Alexandra asked.

"I...well, I'll hire somebody to take care of him."

"Don't bother, because you aren't getting him," she said.

"That's one thing we agree on," Chase said. "I wouldn't have thought it was possible."

"It's the *only* thing!" She turned to the officers. "I'm not handing Willie over to anyone but his mother, so would you please tell these men to leave?"

A muscle twitched in Chase's square jaw. "I don't like to bring in my attorney, but I will if you persist in being obstinate."

"Is that supposed to frighten me?" Sparks were almost visible as Alexandra and Chase faced each other angrily.

"If you were a man I'd break you in half," he growled.

"Isn't your vocabulary up to a verbal battle?" she taunted.

Wallace cleared his throat. "There's no need for anybody to get excited here. We're all concerned about the boy's welfare. As I see it, the problem is what to do with him." As the three combatants all started to talk at once, his partner intervened.

"We don't have the authority to make that decision," Officer Martinson said. "The child was left in Miss Reynolds's care, and that's how it will have to remain for now. If you gentlemen feel you have a claim to the boy, you'll have to work it out in court."

"I don't have time for that!" Danny exclaimed. When the others looked at him speculatively, he modified his tone. "I mean, what if Brenda comes back for Willie? I want to show her I care about him."

"You don't seem too concerned about her disappearance." Chase stared at him with narrowed eyes. "Could it be because you already know what happened to her?"

"Hey, you're not going to hang this thing on me! I'm a lot more interested in finding her than you are."

"We'll contact all of you as soon as we find out anything," Wallace promised. "Well, I think that about wraps things up."

Chase looked dissatisfied, but there was nothing he could do at that moment. "You'll be hearing from me," he told Alexandra.

"I can hardly wait," she answered sweetly.

He took a step toward her. "Don't push me too far, Miss Reynolds. I can be a good friend or a bad enemy." His voice was very soft, which didn't detract from its menace.

She stood her ground, although a little chill rippled up her spine. "With any luck we won't meet again, Mr. Mainwaring, so I don't have to make the decision."

"Oh, we'll meet again, Miss Reynolds." His smile wasn't reassuring. "You have something I want very badly."

The room was quiet after Chase left. He seemed to take a lot of the vitality with him.

"I certainly wouldn't want to trust a child to a man like that," Danny remarked self-righteously, breaking the small silence.

Alexandra looked at him blankly, still vibrating from Chase's impact. She had no doubt that Chase would be a bad enemy. The question was, how good a friend would he be? Could a man like that ever be friends with a woman? Or would he always need to dominate—even in lovemaking? Yet she didn't doubt that he'd satisfy his partner totally.

"Miss Reynolds?" Officer Martinson repeated.

Her cheeks warmed as she realized he'd been trying to

get her attention. "I'm sorry. I was thinking about Willie," she answered hastily.

"We're leaving now. If Mrs. Clark contacts you, please call the police immediately."

"Yes, of course I will. I hope you find her soon."

"We're doing our best. Mr. Riker?" The officer opened the front door and stood aside for the other man to precede them.

Danny had no choice. He turned to smile at Alexandra. "I'm not going to threaten you like Mainwaring did. I'm not that kind of guy. I know you're only doing what you think is best. I just want you to understand that I am, too."

"Goodbye, Mr. Riker," Alexandra said, without voicing an opinion.

Tina came out of the inner office as soon as they'd all gone. Willie stayed behind, still engrossed in the computer. "I've been bursting with curiosity," Tina exclaimed. "What was that all about?"

Alexandra filled her in on everything that had gone on, both that morning and the day before.

"What do you think? Are either of these guys on the level?"

"I doubt it. They both told such incredible stories."

"Why would they lie?"

"I don't know, but at least one of them is," Alexandra said. "Probably both."

"It makes you wonder. What's so different about Willie? He's a cute kid, but two men couldn't see his picture and suddenly decide they had to have him. Two men who never even knew he existed before. It doesn't make sense."

"Chase thinks Willie is his nephew. If he really believes they're family, there could be a good reason," Alexandra said grudgingly.

"I wouldn't mind being related to him." Tina grinned. "He's drop-dead gorgeous."

"Really? I didn't notice."

"Come on, who are you trying to kid? Any woman with a pulse would notice that fantastic bod. I wonder what he looks like without the expensive Armani suit."

"You have my permission to find out—just don't tell me about it."

"I'm starting to worry about you, Alex," Tina teased. "You don't recognize a real man when you see one. What could you possibly find wrong with him?"

"He has a nasty temper, for one thing. He practically threatened me!" Alexandra said indignantly.

"With two cops listening in? Maybe you just imagined it. Did they say anything to him?"

"Just yes, sir, and no, sir. They were so disgustingly polite, you'd think he was the governor!"

"Well, the Mainwarings are pretty hot stuff in this town. What they don't own, they have a controlling interest in."

"That doesn't give Chase Mainwaring the right to try and intimidate me." Alexandra's eyes were stormy with remembered annoyance. "He's going to find out he can't always get his own way."

"I'll bet he doesn't hear that from women very often." Tina laughed.

"Then it will be good for his character."

"Don't get complacent. I have a feeling he has plenty of ammunition. When he finds out you don't scare easily, he might switch tactics."

"I don't doubt it for a minute. Winning is a macho thing with men like Chase, but he still won't get Willie," Alexandra said stubbornly.

"I'll bet a guy like that could turn the heat up pretty high."

"It wouldn't surprise me. That would be typical male mentality."

"It probably worked in the past."

"What does that tell you about him?" Alexandra asked scornfully.

"That it makes me wish I was in your shoes." Tina laughed.

Chase was still fuming when he reached his office. "Hold my calls and get my attorney on the phone," he snapped as he swept by his secretary's desk on the way to his private office.

A few moments later he was telling his lawyer and long-time friend, David Madison, about the events that morning.

"This is incredible, Chase. You didn't know your brother had a son?"

"I didn't even know he was married. Bill left town more than five years ago, after he got in trouble over that horse-racing debacle."

"I felt very badly that I couldn't get them to drop the charges. If it had been a first offense..." David's voice trailed off.

"You did everything you could. How often could you bail him out of trouble?" Chase sighed heavily. "Bill thought he could get away with anything. It was kind of a game to him. I tried to straighten him out, but after Dad died he was completely out of control. I could never get through to him."

"It must have been tough being the older brother."

"It was. Bill counted on me to clean up his messes, yet at the same time he resented me for it." Chase's eyes were bleak. "Maybe I should have let him face the music the first time he had a brush with the law. If he'd had to appear before a judge and perhaps been forced to perform some community service, he might have realized he wasn't immune to punishment."

"It's pointless to second-guess yourself. You did what you could. Now it's time to move on. Are you sure this boy is Bill's son?"

"Positive. You would be too, if you saw him. He's the image of Bill at his age. Before that, I was skeptical. I thought it was a scam of some sort and Brenda would ask for money. But all she wanted was for me to take care of her son—my nephew. And that's what I damned well intend to do.'' Chase's jawline hardened with determination. "I want you to get a writ or a subpoena, or whatever the hell you need."

"It's not that cut-and-dried, Chase. You have no actual proof that the boy is your nephew, only your word that you had a phone call from a woman who said she was his mother and your sister-in-law. That isn't the most compelling evidence in the world."

"Are you telling me there's nothing you can do?" Chase demanded.

"I didn't say that. There's a lot I can do, but not right now, this morning, which is what I think you want. You'll have to be patient—although I know that's not one of your strengths." David laughed.

"What am I supposed to do while you're shuffling papers around? I want to take the boy home and get to know him. Do you realize what this will mean to Mother?"

"Have you told her about Willie?"

"Not yet. I wanted to be sure it wasn't a cruel hoax before I told her she has a grandson. Damn it, David, I'll do anything to get that boy." Chase gripped a pencil so tightly it snapped in his fingers. "I can't wait for a court to move in its customary glacial manner. I have to *do* something!"

"Then I suggest you mend fences with the young woman who has temporary custody of Willie. That way, maybe you can at least see him while we're petitioning the court. She might even let you take him to visit your mother."

"Fat chance! We took an instant dislike to each other—only in my case it was justified. She's the most irritating, combative woman I've ever met."

"You can still make nice. She'll come around. I don't have to tell *you* how to soften up a woman."

"My reputation in that department has been greatly exaggerated."

"Like your penchant for only taking out beautiful women?" David chuckled.

Chase smiled unwillingly. "They're prettier than homely ones."

"It won't kill you to date a plain Jane for a change."

"What makes you think Alexandra is plain?"

"I just assumed...you mean, she isn't?"

"Far from it. She's a honey blonde with hazel eyes, a straight little nose and skin like a camellia blossom. Her figure is pretty spectacular, too."

"But none of those things appeal to you," David commented dryly.

"Not when they come with an attitude. We took an instant dislike to each other."

"Of course, you were the soul of tact."

"Whose side are you on?" Chase demanded. "I'll admit I was pretty emotional when I saw Willie and realized he was Bill's son. I told Alexandra about Brenda's phone call, but she acted as if I was trying to abduct the child. The woman is positively paranoid!"

"It's too bad you two got off on the wrong foot. I'm sure Alexandra is as difficult as you say, but you have to butter her up if you want to get to know your nephew anytime in the near future. Do it for your mother's sake, if nothing else."

"I honestly don't know what I can do to change her mind about me."

"That's not the Chase Mainwaring *I* know." David chuckled. "You'll think of something."

Danny was as frustrated at the way things had turned out as Chase was. He was also extremely uneasy when he was summoned to Los Angeles, to the office of his employer. It was too bad the boss had to find out about Brenda's disappearance. That fink, Nate, probably couldn't wait to fax him the article in the San Francisco paper.

Victor Karpov was a big man with heavy eyebrows and a black beard to match. He had cold eyes that never lit up—not even when he smiled, which was seldom. His expression wasn't encouraging as he looked at Danny across his wide polished desk.

"You screwed up, Riker," he said in measured tones. "I don't like that."

"It's just a temporary glitch, boss. I'll find her. Brenda is still in San Francisco."

"How can you be sure? The newspaper said she was last seen at a local travel office. What makes you think she didn't get on a plane? She could be anywhere by now."

"Brenda wouldn't leave town without her kid. She's hanging around, waiting to go back for him. And when she does, I'll grab her."

"Why should I believe you? You loused it up before."

"I just needed a little more time, that's all." Danny whined. "She never went out without the kid. I couldn't put the arm on her with him around. He would have screamed bloody murder and attracted a crowd. People walk right past a mugging, but they decide to be heroes when a kid is involved."

"I'm not interested in your comments on human behavior," Karpov said bitingly. "I want my merchandise back."

"You'll get it, boss."

"How? The police are looking for her now, and after that description they put out half the town will be, too."

"Yeah, but I got a plan," Danny said eagerly. "This time I won't have to go looking for Brenda. She'll come to me." He didn't say the idea was Nate's.

"How convenient. And will you guarantee she has the diamonds on her?"

"Well, maybe she sold a couple of the stones to finance her getaway," Danny said uneasily. "But she wouldn't know how to unload the whole shipment. I don't think you have anything to worry about.''

"I'm not the one who should be worrying." Karpov stared at him impassively. "You've always had a thing for Bill's wife. Why do I get the feeling that this whole disappearing act could be a scam you cooked up with her? The two of you could live pretty well in some foreign country on that little bag of diamonds."

"That's crazy!" Danny could feel sweat breaking out on his forehead. "I'd never cross you, boss. You know you can count on me."

A smile that was more of a facial tic lifted the corners of the other man's mouth. "What have you done for me lately?"

"Give me another chance," Danny pleaded. "I've got a foolproof scheme to flush Brenda out of hiding." He told the other man about the plan that would deliver Willie into his hands.

Karpov looked dissatisfied. "While you're romancing the broad, I'm out a couple of million dollars." His frown deepened to a scowl. "I can't believe Clark was stupid enough to think he could get away with ripping me off."

"I can't either, boss. Maybe his wife put him up to it. She's the one who ended up with the stones."

"Find her," Karpov snapped. "And after you get the merchandise back, waste her."

Danny looked uneasy. "That's not really my specialty. Maybe it would be better if Nate took care of her."

"You don't think you can handle it?" The older man gazed at him without expression.

"Well, sure, but none of our activities have ever been traced to my sports bar. We don't want to jeopardize our operation."

"The only way that could happen is if you foul up again. In which case, you'd be out of business anyway. I trust we understand each other?"

"Yes, sir." Danny was sweating freely now. "I won't let you down. You'll be hearing from me."

"Make it soon."

Chapter Three

Things were just starting to calm down at the travel office when a messenger arrived with a ribbon-tied florist's box for Alexandra. Inside were a dozen long-stemmed white roses and a small square envelope.

"I wish I had a romantic boyfriend," Tina commented. "Who are they from?"

Alexandra opened the envelope. "He isn't a boyfriend. They're from Chase Mainwaring."

Tina read the note aloud. "'Please forgive my conduct this morning. It was inexcusable. I can only hope you're as generous as you are lovely.' I'd say that was a very handsome apology, wouldn't you?"

"Not really. Have you ever heard the saying, beware of Greeks bearing gifts? He only sent these to butter me up."

"You're too suspicious. If that was his only purpose, he could have thought of something a lot cheaper. These long-stemmed babies cost a bundle."

"Chase has plenty of money—that's what worries me.

If he unleashes his staff of lawyers on me, I don't have the resources to fight back."

"That sounds as if you're planning to keep Willie," Tina said slowly.

"Just until this mess is straightened out. I'd be willing to give custody of him to any relatives, if they turned up. But I want to be sure they really *are* relatives."

"Meaning, you don't think Chase is?"

"I can't imagine sweet, little Willie having an uncle like Chase." Alexandra's generous mouth thinned with remembered annoyance. "He's rude and arrogant, and he'd be a terrible influence on a child."

"Come on, he isn't all bad. He did apologize. It isn't like you to be so unforgiving."

"Okay, I forgive him," Alexandra said impatiently. "Now, can we get some work done? The Hendersons' itinerary has to be printed out and mailed to them, and we have to confirm hotel rooms in Tahiti for the Wallensteins."

When she was alone at her desk, Alexandra examined her feelings toward Chase. Why *did* he arouse such strong emotions in her? Was it because she knew instinctively that she'd met her match when it came to strong wills? That was ridiculous! Some of the men she knew were quite forceful. She'd never been attracted to wimps. Not that she was attracted to Chase. He was undoubtedly a dazzling specimen of manhood, but their chemistry was all wrong. They were like gasoline and matches—an explosion just waiting to happen.

Alexandra put Chase firmly out of her mind as she made up a folder for a new client.

It was a couple of hours later that Chase telephoned. Alexandra really had succeeded in forgetting about him, and she was caught off guard.

"Oh...well, hello. I got your flowers. Thank you."

"They were my way of hoisting a white flag of surrender,'' he said with a smile in his voice. "I'd like to be friends.''

Alexandra had succeeded in pulling herself together. "I don't want to open hostilities again, but I know exactly what you want from me and it isn't friendship.''

"That's the curse of being such a beautiful woman." He chuckled. "Men can't resist you.''

"You didn't have any trouble this morning.''

"I was a little preoccupied." His voice sobered for a moment, then he continued in a light tone, "You made quite an impression, though. I've been thinking about you all day. I'd like to see you again.''

"Me—or Willie?''

"Both of you. Will the two of you have dinner with me tonight?''

"I'm sorry, but he's a little young for fancy restaurants. I assume that's what you had in mind.''

"You persist in misjudging me. I'd be perfectly happy at a pizza parlor or a hamburger joint, if that's where you think we should go.''

"You'd have to take off that Italian suit first.''

"Not on a first date." He laughed. "We haven't even kissed yet.''

"I was sure we had," she drawled, hiding her annoyance. "Perhaps I have you mixed up with some other slick talker.''

Chase's jaw tightened for an instant, then his eyes started to brim with amusement. "I could never confuse *you* with anyone else.''

"I'm not quite sure how to take that," Alexandra said.

"The way it was meant—as a compliment," he answered smoothly. "You're a very unique woman. I've never met anyone quite like you.''

"Are all the women you meet instantly compliant?" she asked tartly.

"Your opinion of me is flattering, but quite erroneous.

I'd like a chance to change your mind. I'm really quite a nice fellow when you get to know me."

"That may be true, but you're wasting your time. I'm still not going to let you take Willie."

"You've made that abundantly clear," Chase said curtly. He swiftly covered his momentary show of annoyance. "So you must realize my interest in you is personal."

"Why would it be? We argued bitterly at our only meeting. You threatened me!"

"You got in a few good licks yourself." He laughed. "We were both a little emotional at the time. I apologize, though. I'm usually very gentle with women."

"If you say so." Alexandra didn't sound convinced.

"I'd be happy to demonstrate," he answered softly.

His seductive tone irritated her. She was clearly supposed to imagine herself in his arms, her passion rising as he stroked her body tantalizingly and parted her lips for a deep, arousing kiss.

"I'm very busy right now," she said abruptly. "You'll have to excuse me."

"Of course. I'll let you get back to work if you agree to have dinner with me tonight."

"I'm sorry, I don't think that's a very good idea."

"Are you sure you won't reconsider? I'd really like to be friends. It's so much more civilized than snapping at each other—or worse yet, getting attorneys involved."

Alexandra hesitated. Chase's voice was casual, but his underlying message was clear. He would use any means to take Willie from her, and he had a lot more resources than she had. If she appeared to cooperate, maybe he'd back off.

"All right, I'll have dinner with you." When that sounded too reluctant, she added, "I'd really like to get to know you better. But we wouldn't be able to talk with Willie there. Let's make it just the two of us instead."

"Who's going to look after him?"

"He can stay with my former partner, Mandy. She and

her husband have a darling teenager. Willie should be very happy there. Dee Dee has every computer game known to man.''

Chase paused for a moment, then decided not to argue. ''Whatever you say. What time would you like me to pick you up?''

''I'm really swamped with work. I won't even have a chance to go home and change. Why don't you pick a restaurant and I'll meet you there?''

Chase wasn't fooled by the excuse. He knew she didn't want to be alone in private with him. But again, he didn't argue. ''How about Johnny O's in the Park Westfield?'' It was a trendy restaurant in a posh hotel. ''Is that public enough for you?'' he asked dryly.

''That will be fine,'' she answered, without taking the bait. ''What time?''

After they'd concluded the arrangements and hung up, Alexandra phoned Mandy. She hoped her friend wouldn't mind baby-sitting. Chase would never believe Mandy had previous plans. He'd be sure it was just an excuse for not going out with him.

''I'll be happy to look after the little fellow,'' Mandy said. ''I can't wait to see him.''

''Poor little kid,'' Alexandra said. ''He's pretty confused about what's going on, but I don't think he'll be any trouble.''

''Not to worry, he'll be fine. You can leave him here overnight.''

''Are you sure? I can pick him up after dinner.''

''No, he'll be asleep by then. We might be, too, if this guy turns out to be a winner.'' Mandy laughed.

''There's no chance of that. He only wants one thing from me.''

''So, how does that make him any different from all the others?''

"Chase isn't like any man I've ever met," Alexandra said soberly.

"He sounds interesting, at least."

"Not to me. I have to go, Mandy. I'll see you in the morning."

Alexandra didn't notice the unobtrusive tan car that followed her when she drove Willie to Mandy's apartment after work. She was preoccupied with how the child would react to being left with strangers. He'd formed a strong attachment to her in a very short time, since she was now the only stable figure in his life.

Willie was shy and clung to her at first, but he warmed up almost immediately to Mandy's teenage daughter, Dee Dee. When the young girl suggested going upstairs to play computer games, he left Alexandra with scarcely a backward look.

In spite of what she'd told Chase, Alexandra went home to change clothes. She felt grubby after a day at work, she told herself. It had nothing to do with wanting to look nice for Chase.

A quick shower left her time to spend on her makeup. She started with green eye shadow to accentuate the predominant green in her hazel eyes. Mascara lengthened her naturally long lashes and lip gloss over coral lipstick made her mouth luminous.

Her face took so long that she didn't have time to do anything to her hair except brush it until it shone like a shining length of pale satin.

The choice of an outfit required some thought. Alexandra didn't want Chase to think she regarded their date as a special occasion. But the idea was to soften him up, so she didn't want to look too businesslike, either. Finally she settled on a white suit with a scooped neckline. The short jacket was embroidered all over with swirls of matching ribbon, and the slim skirt called attention to her long legs.

As she sprayed herself with perfume while looking in the mirror, Alexandra was satisfied with her appearance. She looked poised and in command. The little ripples chasing up and down her spine weren't evident. What was causing them? Apprehension? Anticipation? Certainly not the latter, she told herself as she grabbed her car keys and went out the door. This date was an obligation, not a pleasure.

There was no reason for Alexandra to notice the black car parked across the street with a man at the wheel. She didn't know him. There was nothing unusual, either, in the fact that he started his motor when she pulled away from the curb.

Chase was waiting for her at the crowded bar that ran along one wall of the restaurant. He was with another couple, evidently friends. Chase was smiling at something the woman said, and Alexandra was struck by the difference in him. Could he be the same person who had appeared so menacing?

This man was the ultimate sophisticate in a thousand-dollar suit. If she didn't know better, Alexandra would have thought he was the sort who never raised his voice.

When Chase caught sight of her, he excused himself and came over immediately. The expression on his face was wholly male as he got a better look at her.

"How lovely you are," he said.

Alexandra couldn't help responding to his warmth. "I left my horns and pitchfork at home," she joked.

"Not a wise move. You might need the pitchfork to discourage me."

"I'm sure a man like you knows when not to be insistent," she said lightly.

"Don't underestimate yourself. I have a feeling you've driven more than one man to lose control."

But not Chase, she told herself. It would be so easy to

believe he was really interested in her. Before she could answer, the maître d' came over to them.

"Your table is ready, Mr. Mainwaring," he said.

It was a choice table in a corner of the room where it was relatively quiet. The man presented them with menus and left.

"I'm glad you decided to come," Chase said.

Alexandra could have told him he didn't leave her any choice, but instead she said, "You made a lot of sense. Civilized people can resolve their differences if they really try."

"How far are you willing to bend?"

"You cut right to the chase, don't you?" she asked wryly.

"I'd like to get our business dealings out of the way so I can concentrate on the personal." His enigmatic expression changed to a melting smile.

"You don't take off your clothes on a first date and neither do I," she answered.

He laughed. "I didn't mean *that* personal—although I wouldn't complain."

"I believe in setting the record straight right from the beginning. It saves misunderstandings later on."

"Now that we've established what you *won't* do, can we move on to what you will?" He grinned. "I'd like to know what to expect."

"As little as possible. That way you won't be disappointed."

"I don't think you could ever be disappointing," he said in a smoky voice.

The candle flame was reflected in his eyes, making them incandescent. Alexandra felt an answering warmth in the pit of her stomach. This man was awesome! He could awaken a woman's sexuality without even touching her.

Their waiter provided a diversion. "May I bring you a drink?" he asked.

Chase looked inquiringly at her. "What would you like? How about a champagne cocktail to celebrate our detente?"

"That would be nice." When the waiter left she said hastily, before Chase could pursue their former conversation, "Shall we look at the menu? I can't stay out too late."

"Are you tired of me already?" he teased.

"How could I be when you're being so charming?"

"Then why do you have to leave early?"

"Tomorrow is going to be a hectic day. I have to get up early to go over and pick up Willie. He's spending the night at Mandy's. Then sometime during the day I'll have to go shopping for him. The only clothes he has are the ones he had on when Brenda brought him to the office."

"That proves she intended to come back for him. When I spoke to her on the phone, she indicated that she was afraid of something—or someone. I only hope she's still alive," Chase said somberly.

"Don't even say such a thing!"

"You have to be realistic. We both agree that she wouldn't leave her child behind. But if she was in an accident, the police would know it by now. What else could have happened to her?"

"I just don't know," Alexandra said in a muted voice. "I've been going through hell, because if she was harmed it was my brother's fault."

Alexandra sighed. "Yes, I got the impression that she was running away from an abusive husband."

Chase gave her a surprised look. "That wasn't what I meant. Bill would never hurt her. From what Brenda said, I gathered they loved each other very much."

"Then how could it be his fault?"

Chase paused while the waiter served their cocktails, then took their dinner orders.

When the man left, Chase continued with what he'd been saying. "Bill was the one you'd pick for most likely to succeed. He was handsome and charming. Everybody liked him. He was one of those rare people who had everything. Maybe it all came too easily for him. Perhaps that's why he began testing the boundaries, seeing how much he could get away with.''

"Like what?" Alexandra asked when Chase didn't continue.

"It began with underage drinking and drag racing at horrendous speeds, among other things. The sort of trouble a lot of reckless kids get into. He was arrested once, but Dad had the charges dropped. In retrospect maybe that was wrong, but what parent would do any differently? I can't fault my father, because I was guilty of providing Bill with the same kind of crutch after Dad died. The difference is, Bill's misdemeanors escalated into more serious trouble.''

"Is your brother older or younger than you?"

"He was four years younger," Chase said heavily, realizing that by using the past tense he had accepted the fact that his brother was dead. "Finally he got into trouble that even our money couldn't buy him out of. He was facing a possible prison term when he decided to skip town instead. That was over five years ago and we haven't seen or heard from him since. I didn't even know he'd gotten married until Brenda called me yesterday.''

Alexandra didn't know what to think. Would somebody make up a story like that? "Why would she suddenly call you after all these years?" she asked tentatively.

"To tell me that Bill was dead."

"I'm so sorry," Alexandra said in a hushed voice.

"Yes, it's hard to take." Chase toyed with the food the waiter had brought while they were talking. "I keep thinking I should have done more for him.''

"It sounds as if you did everything you could."

"Maybe." He seemed unconvinced. "In any case, it's too late to help Bill, but at least I can provide for his son. That's why I want Willie so desperately. And for my mother's sake, as well. Bill's child will help ease the pain of her loss. You do understand what Willie means to us, don't you?''

"It's a very sad story," Alexandra said haltingly.

"But you don't believe a word of it."

"I didn't say that!"

"You don't have to. I can tell." His jaw tightened as he stared at her with narrowed eyes. "What does it take to convince you?"

"I want to believe you, but you haven't given me a shred of proof. I have only your word for it that Brenda called you or that she was ever married to your brother."

"At least you believe I have a brother," he remarked sardonically. "I suppose that's something."

"If you care about Willie you should be glad that I'm being supercautious. I have to take everything into consideration. Like Danny Riker, for instance. I can't ignore his claim."

"The man's a clown! His story is laughable."

"It does sound unbelievable, but sometimes truth really is stranger than fiction. Why else would he want Willie?"

"I have no idea," Chase said impatiently. "Maybe for the publicity value. Or maybe he's just a nut."

"That's what I have to find out."

"It strikes me that you have a lot of authority, for a person who has absolutely no ties to the boy."

"His mother left him with me," Alexandra said stubbornly. "I can't allow myself to be swayed by emotion."

Chase leaned back in his chair and gazed at her without expression. "It seems the line has been drawn in the sand. The question is now, where do we go from here?"

Alexandra knew where *he* was going—straight to his attorney. She hadn't handled this evening very well. All the lightheartedness and pretense of interest on his part were gone. This was the real Chase. Too bad. She had to admit she'd enjoyed their cessation of hostilities, even the feeling that he was attracted to her. But she had more pressing things to worry about. Like how to placate him. That was the object of this meeting—not date—and she'd allowed herself to be charmed into forgetting it.

"I know you think I'm being cold and unfeeling," she began carefully. "I'm really not. I still hope Brenda will turn up, but if she doesn't, I hope you can prove your claim. I think Willie would be lucky to have an uncle like you."

"Now who's buttering up whom?" Chase asked dryly.

"It may sound like that, but it's the truth. You might not be completely trustworthy where women are concerned, but I think you'd be an excellent father figure."

He raised a dark eyebrow. "What makes you think I'm a danger to womankind?"

His potent male appeal, for one thing. But Alexandra wasn't that blunt. "I wouldn't put it that strongly, but you're very persuasive. I think you could talk a woman into almost anything."

"I don't seem to be having much success with *you*," he said wryly.

"Our case is different. I was referring to a male, female relationship."

His eyes wandered appreciatively over her delicate face. "I'm sure ours would be a memorable one."

"That husky tone of voice is very effective, but it doesn't work when I know you want something from me," she said matter-of-factly.

"I'll admit it freely. I'd like to make love to you."

"Is that *all* you want?" she asked skeptically.

"How much more fortunate could a man be? I'd like to take you to a little inn I know up the coast, where the surf pounds against the beach. I'd build a roaring fire in the fireplace and we'd lie on a soft rug in front of it. I'd undress you slowly and watch your pearly skin blush from the heat of the flames. Then I'd kiss—"

"I wasn't asking for such a graphic description," Alexandra finally broke in breathlessly. His deep voice was so hypnotic that she'd allowed herself to imagine the erotic scene for far too long.

He smiled mischievously. "I thought you were checking out my technique."

"We both know your real priority is Willie, not my pearly skin," she said tartly.

His eyes moved over the scooped neck of her jacket. "It might have started out that way, but you're enough to distract any man."

"It doesn't matter how good you are in bed, that still wouldn't change my mind about Willie."

"You might at least let me try," he grinned.

"This isn't getting us anywhere," Alexandra said impatiently. "We both tried making nice and it didn't work. We just don't trust each other."

"I never said I didn't trust you. I simply think you're misguided."

"Whatever. The question is, what are we going to do about it?"

"You're really asking what *I'm* going to do," he said.

"Yes."

"I'm a hardheaded businessman, Alex. Why would I tell you my game plan?"

"This isn't a game we're playing," she said sharply. "No matter what we think of each other, a little boy's future is at stake. I don't want him dragged through the court system—and if you care about him, you shouldn't want that either. What if they take him away from both of us and he winds up in a foster home?"

His face was austere. "That will never happen."

"You've had experience with the justice system. You know that money can't buy everything."

Warring emotions made Chase look uncertain for the first time. "What are you suggesting? That I sit back and do nothing? That's completely unacceptable!"

"I'm just asking you to have a little patience. Don't do

something that will start an avalanche you can't stop," she said urgently.

"Shall I ask my mother to be patient, too? How do I tell her she has a grandchild, but she can't see him?"

"What if you raise her hopes, and for some reason Willie isn't her grandson?" Alexandra countered. "I know you're convinced, but Brenda might have concocted that story about being married to your brother. Just like Danny might be lying about being engaged to her now. Everything is so murky. I honestly don't know what to believe."

"Poor Alex." Chase's voice was unexpectedly gentle. "You didn't ask for this mess."

For the first time, she believed his sympathy was sincere. Or was that what he wanted her to think? "I'm a pretty strong person," she said. "I can handle it."

"Just my luck. Why couldn't you have been one of those indecisive women I could push around?"

She returned his smile. "You can't say you didn't try."

The waiter came to clear the table and present dessert menus. They both ordered coffee, but declined dessert.

After the waiter had left, Chase said, "So, where do we go from here?"

"I guess the ball is in your court. What do you plan to do?"

"I've been thinking about what you said, and it makes a lot of sense. I'm willing to be reasonable. Providing you are, too."

"I'm not quite sure what you mean," she replied warily.

"I want to be allowed to see Willie, to get to know him. You don't have to tell him I'm his uncle. It would probably be too confusing for a child his age. But I won't be cut out of his life any longer."

Chase's steely gaze told her the point wasn't negotiable. But there was no reason to refuse. "I have no objection to your spending time with him. As long as I'm there when you do," she added.

"Do you think I'm going to kidnap him?" he demanded.

"Perhaps. If you thought it was in his best interests."

"You really have a rotten opinion of me, don't you?" Chase shook his head with a mixture of amusement and annoyance.

"I wouldn't say that. The first impression I got was that you're a very strong man."

"Is that so bad?"

"You've always gotten your own way," she said, avoiding a direct answer. "I'm not sure you accept the fact that you'll have to bend a little this time."

"You haven't left me any option. Either I agree to chaperoned visits or I don't get to see my nephew."

"It won't be so bad." Alexandra stirred the coffee the waiter had brought. "After Willie gets used to you, I'll try to leave you two alone together as much as possible."

Chase leaned back in his chair and looked at her with a little smile. "It suddenly occurs to me that if Brenda doesn't show up we're going to be spending a lot of time together."

"Nothing in life is perfect," she remarked lightly.

"I wasn't complaining. In fact, it's a very interesting development."

"I don't see it that way. The only thing we have in common is Willie."

"You can't really say that until we find out. Tell me about yourself."

"There isn't that much to tell. I had a happy childhood in Phoenix, where I grew up. My family still lives there. I came to San Francisco to attend college and I liked it here so much that I stayed on." Alexandra smiled. "You see? My life isn't very exciting. Maybe that's why I got into the travel business—to live vicariously."

"I'm sure that's not true. You aren't the kind of person who can sit on the sidelines watching the game."

"Not by choice, anyway," she said wryly. "But so far,

my partners have had all the excitement. They each left to marry wonderful men.''

"I'm sure your turn will come next."

"That isn't what I'm looking for. I'll admit I'd like a little more stimulation in my life, but I'm not really interested in getting married."

"Some lucky man will change your mind." Chase smiled. "You're much too lovely to spend your life alone."

"Why haven't *you* ever married? At least, I assume you're still single." Alexandra looked at him uncertainly, realizing she knew very little about him.

"You assumed correctly. I'm a card-carrying bachelor."

"You must know a lot of eligible women. What are you looking for in a wife?"

"I guess I'm like you. I'm not really looking. I don't think it would do any good, anyway. You don't go shopping for a wife like you do for a suit. If I ever do meet the right woman, I'll know it."

"How?"

He paused to consider. "By the chemistry between us, for one thing. She'll have an instant impact on me. I don't mean violins will play or the sun will break through the clouds. I'll just know she's different from any other woman I've ever known."

"That only happens in the movies or romantic novels. And even there the hero and heroine don't fall in love instantly. Their relationship is explosive and they have a lot of misunderstandings."

"It sounds like us, doesn't it?" He smiled.

"Exactly. Which goes to prove you can't rely on instinct. Could any two people be worse suited to each other?"

"I wouldn't say that. We had a rough beginning, but look how well we're getting along now."

"Until I refuse you something you want," Alexandra said cynically.

He gave her an amused look. "I've been turned down before. I don't sulk and I always accept no for an answer."

"I wasn't referring to sex," she said curtly.

"Maybe we should consider it. Think how good we'd be together," he teased. "We could channel all that negative energy into something positive."

"Positive for which one of us?" she asked dryly.

"It would be a privilege to make love to such a beautiful woman." His amusement died and his eyes took on a glow. "I'd try to make it as memorable an experience for you as it would be for me."

Alexandra didn't doubt his ability. He was blatantly virile. Although he didn't touch her, she could almost feel his hands on her shoulders, urging her closer. She stared at his firm mouth, her own lips parting unconsciously.

"You feel something, too, don't you?" he asked softly.

Her first impulse was to deny it, but Chase was too experienced with women to be fooled. He knew exactly what buttons to push for the desired result.

"It's perfectly normal for a woman to be attracted to a handsome man," she said in a dispassionate tone of voice. "It doesn't mean any more than having an urge for a hot fudge sundae or a jelly doughnut—something you have no intention of indulging in."

"Are you in the habit of denying yourself simple pleasures?" He smiled.

"You're not talking about something simple—but the answer is, yes. If I know they're bad for me."

"And you think I would be?"

"Let's just say I don't trust your agenda. I'd want to be a man's first priority, not simply a means to an end."

"If a man did have an ulterior motive, he'd forget it the moment he took you in his arms. You don't know how enchanting you are. But I can tell I'm not going to convince you of that tonight."

"Or any other night," she said firmly.

"We'll see." Chase smiled as the waiter came over to ask if they wanted more coffee.

"No more for me, thank you," Alexandra said. "It's been delightful," she told Chase formally. "But I have to leave."

"You can bring the check," he said to the waiter, without trying to dissuade her.

When they were outside, waiting for the valet to bring Alexandra's car, Chase said, "When can I see Willie?"

"I guess you can come over tomorrow night after work," she said, trying not to show her reluctance.

Alexandra didn't want to get involved with Chase under these circumstances. But what other choice did she have? A few uncomfortable evenings would be worth it, if she could keep him placated. And he couldn't very well get romantic with Willie around.

"What do you propose to do with him while you're at work?" Chase asked.

"I'll take him to the office with me. He's remarkably well behaved for such a little fellow."

Chase frowned. "I don't care how good he is. You can't keep a child cooped up in an office all day."

"I'll buy sandwiches and take him to the Marina Green for lunch. He can run around and watch the sailboats in the bay. Kids love that. The park is always full of them."

"It won't make up for the hours of sitting around an office. He's just a child!"

"It's only a temporary arrangement. Willie will be fine. Tina and I will take turns keeping him amused. Here's my car." Alexandra got in before he could argue further.

Chase was obviously not satisfied, but there was nothing he could do about it at the moment. "I'll see you tomorrow night," he said, bending down to speak to her through the open window. "What time?"

"Anytime after six." She drove away, ending the discussion.

* * *

Alexandra couldn't make up her mind about Chase. She tried to weigh all the pros and cons as she drove home. Did he really think he was Willie's uncle? The anguish on his face when he told her about his brother was genuine, she'd bet on it. Nobody was that good an actor. Besides, what other motive would he have for wanting the child? His concern for Willie was praiseworthy—but the way he was trying to get the boy was not.

Chase would take her to bed in a minute, if it would accomplish his purpose. That was really underhanded! Alexandra tried to work up some indignation, but all she could think of was his hard body covering hers, moving erotically against her while his mouth drove her to distraction.

She tried to put him out of her mind when she reached home. There were plenty of other problems to occupy her— Willie, for one. Chase was right about him. The child was bound to get bored and cranky at the office after awhile. When she went out to replenish his wardrobe, she'd have to pick up some coloring books and little toys to keep him busy during the day.

Alexandra went into the bedroom, trying to figure out when she'd have time tomorrow to do all that shopping. She took off her watch and the jade ring she'd worn, then unfastened her gold earrings. They'd been a birthday present from her parents, and she always kept them in the little jeweler's box they'd come in.

The box wasn't in the right-hand corner of the dresser drawer where it always was. Somehow it had worked its way to the back of the drawer. That was strange. She always kept it in the same place.

Her frown cleared as she took off her suit and hung it in the closet. With all she had on her mind, was it any wonder she put things in the wrong place? But the frown returned when she removed her high-heeled pumps and reached up to put them away.

Alexandra kept all of her shoes stacked on a shelf in their original boxes. After getting dressed earlier, she'd replaced the empty box on top of the stack. How could she be mistaken about a thing like that? But now it was on the bottom of the stack, as if someone had taken down all the boxes and replaced them in a different order. A little chill rippled up her spine. Had somebody been in her apartment?

The front door hadn't been tampered with. There were no scratches or gouges, and she hadn't had trouble turning the key. Alexandra moved swiftly to her dresser again to look for her jewelry box. She had a few nice pieces, nothing terribly valuable, but things she would hate to lose. The box was in the drawer and everything was still there.

"You're turning into a nervous Nellie," she scolded herself.

Still, she couldn't shake off a feeling of uneasiness. To prove to herself that she was being foolish, Alexandra went through the apartment looking for signs of an intruder. Her concern grew as she found more disturbing evidence.

The bedspread was slightly bunched up on one side and some desk drawers in the living room weren't completely closed the way they were usually kept. Even the kitchen showed signs of being searched.

Alexandra recalled having heard that sometimes people hid their valuables in the freezer compartment, so she opened her freezer. The contents had definitely been moved around. All of these things couldn't be absentmindedness on her part. But what could she possibly have that somebody wanted?

Once she'd accepted the fact that an intruder had gotten in, Alexandra started to wonder if it was just a crime of opportunity. Or had someone known she'd be out tonight? Somebody like Chase. Had he asked her to dinner just to get her out of the house?

But that was crazy! Why would he want to have her apartment searched? Possibly to find something that would prove she was unfit to take care of a child—erotic love letters, perhaps, or provocative photos. Would Chase go to those lengths?

When she remembered how steely his gaze could get and the way his jaw set like granite, the answer was yes. But there was the other Chase, the caring man who grieved for his brother, the man who was concerned about a little boy. Or was she just being gullible?

Alexandra was suddenly worried about Willie. She had no doubt that whatever was going on revolved around him. If somebody would break into her apartment, there was no telling what else they might do! She looked at her watch. It was a quarter to eleven, not too late to call Mandy. They didn't go to bed this early.

Mandy's unruffled voice was reassuring. "Did you call to give me a rundown on your date? That sounds promising."

"No, I called about Willie," Alexandra said. "Is he all right?"

"Everything is fine here. He and his teddy bear ate a big dinner—at least, Willie did. Teddy wasn't very hungry. They've both been asleep for hours."

"He and that bear are inseparable." Alexandra smiled. "He wanted Brenda to buy an airline ticket for his stuffed toy."

"Willie undoubtedly thinks of him as a live friend. Any news on his mother?"

"Nothing so far, but I'm still hoping. It hasn't been that long yet."

"You'd better start thinking about what you're going to do with him. I read somewhere that if a missing person isn't found within forty-eight hours, they might never be heard from again."

"Brenda didn't desert her son," Alexandra said stubbornly.

"All the more reason for you to make a decision. I hate

to think something bad happened to the poor woman, but it's a possibility. If that does turn out to be the case, it would be ideal if Chase Mainwaring is really his uncle. He could give Willie every advantage.''

''Monetarily perhaps, but what does he know about children?''

''Roughly the same amount as you do,'' Mandy answered dryly.

''A woman has more of an instinct for mothering. Chase probably runs around with a different woman every night. He didn't perfect that line of his sitting home alone.''

''Oh? That sounds interesting. Did he come on to you?''

''Only because of Willie. To soften me up. Chase isn't attracted to me. That's what made his performance so annoying.''

''You sound disappointed,'' Mandy teased.

''Not at all,'' Alexandra answered coolly. ''We don't get along very well. One minute we're arguing and the next minute he's telling me how he'd like to—well, never mind. Take my word for it, I'm only putting up with him because I have to. He's a very irritating man.''

''It sounds to me like the beginning of a beautiful romance.'' Mandy chuckled. ''Did he ask you for another date?''

''No, he asked to see Willie. I had to agree because it was a package deal. If I let Chase spend time with Willie, he won't try to get custody until we sort things out.''

''That sounds like a fair trade.''

''I suppose so. But it means I'll have to let Chase come to the house.''

''What's wrong with that?''

''Funny things have been going on.'' Alexandra told her all the evidence she'd found that her apartment had been searched.

''That's terrible! Are you sure? Maybe with everything

that's happened, you just haven't noticed that things were disarranged. You said nothing was taken.''

"I don't think it was a simple burglary. I think whoever did it was after something specific. I don't know what, but it seems strange that it happened tonight when I was out with Chase.''

"Surely you don't think Chase was behind it!'' Mandy exclaimed. "He comes from one of the finest families in San Francisco.''

"Good trees can have an occasional rotten apple,'' Alexandra said darkly. "I'm not accusing him, but I intend to be on my guard.''

"Maybe you're getting in over your head,'' Mandy said slowly. "You did the right thing in keeping Willie, but that was when there was a reasonable expectation that his mother would come back for him. Now it appears there's a lot more involved in her disappearance. Perhaps it's time to let the authorities take over.''

"How can I do that to a little child?'' Alexandra protested.

"I don't like it any better than you do, but he'll have people watching out for him. That's more than I can say for you. I'm worried about you, Alex.''

"I'll be fine. I've been letting my imagination run away with me. Unfortunately, break-ins aren't unusual in a big city. It was probably just a coincidence that I got hit while all this other stuff was going on.''

"I suppose it's possible,'' Mandy said doubtfully.

"I'm sure of it.'' Alexandra put aside her own doubts for her friend's sake. "Thanks for keeping Willie for me. I'll be by first thing in the morning to pick him up.''

"I've been thinking about that. You can't get any work done with a child around. You're welcome to leave him with me during the day. He's no trouble.''

"I appreciate the offer, but that would be an imposition. Willie isn't your responsibility.''

"What are friends for? Don't argue, it's late and my husband wants me to turn off the light." Mandy laughed softly. "Have I told you how terrific marriage is?"

Alexandra hung up slowly, thinking how nice it must be to curl up in bed with someone you loved and forget all your problems. Would she ever be that lucky? she wondered wistfully.

Chapter Four

Alexandra decided not to tell the police that her apartment had been broken into. Since nothing was taken, they might think, as Mandy had at first, that it was her imagination. Was it possible that it was? She wasn't normally either nervous or absentminded, but her life wasn't usually as eventful as it had been lately.

Alexandra was catching up on her bookkeeping when the police phoned later that morning. Willie's picture in the newspaper had brought results. The manager of a hotel on Nob Hill called to say Willie and his mother had been staying there. They were still registered, although he hadn't seen either of them in days.

The police examined her room and its contents, and they now had some clues to Brenda's past. The labels in her clothes and Willie's were from various stores in Los Angeles. That was the good news. The bad news was that her room had already been searched before they got there, presumably after her disappearance.

"Everything was thrown all over the place," Officer Torelli told Alexandra. "The perps didn't make any effort to cover their tracks."

"What do you think they were looking for?" she asked.

"It's hard to tell. Jewelry, maybe, or cash. Mrs. Clark seems to have been rolling in it."

"Past tense?" Alexandra asked apprehensively. "You think she's dead?"

"We have to consider all the possibilities, but so far there's no evidence of foul play. We're hoping to find some leads in Los Angeles. I have to tell you, though, Miss Reynolds, this is shaping up to be more than a simple case of child abandonment. I really think you should consider turning the boy over to the authorities."

"I'm hoping you'll locate some of Willie's relatives, someone we're sure is a relative, and then that won't be necessary." Alexandra was glad she hadn't mentioned the intruder in her apartment. Torelli might be even more insistent. "Will you let me know what you find out?"

"You can count on it," he promised.

Alexandra was still thinking about the puzzling aspects of the case when Danny phoned.

"Have you heard any more about Brenda?" he asked.

"Not directly, but the police just called." She told him what the officer had told her. "Tracing Brenda to L.A. might clear up some of the mystery surrounding her. It might give them a clue as to why she disappeared."

After an imperceptible pause, Danny said, "I certainly hope so. How is the boy doing?"

"He asks for his mother, naturally, but I try to keep his mind off her."

"I'd like to help. Why don't I take the two of you to lunch today? I called last night to see how you were getting along, but nobody was home," Danny said.

"I was out, but there was no message on my answering machine when I got home."

"I didn't leave one. I hate talking to a machine."

"I don't think anybody likes them, but they're necessary evils," she answered, wondering if he was telling the truth.

Or had Danny seen her go out and decided it would be a good time to search her apartment? Maybe it hadn't been Chase, after all. But what could either of them have been looking for?

He changed the subject. "So, how about lunch? You and the boy."

Alexandra didn't want to tell him that Mandy was taking care of Willie for her. Maybe she was being overly cautious, but it was better than being too trusting.

"I'm sorry, but I'm really swamped with work," she said. "I don't get as much done with Willie around."

"I can imagine. Well, then, why don't I take him off your hands for an hour or so," Danny suggested casually. "The little fellow and I will have a great time together."

"That would be lovely, but Willie seems afraid of strange men. I guess it's understandable after all he's been through, but it makes things a little difficult. He won't let me out of his sight."

"The kid has good taste." Danny chuckled. "Well, if we can't have lunch, what if I come over to your place tonight? To see Willie," he added hurriedly.

"I'm sorry, but tonight won't be convenient, either."

"Listen, you don't own that kid!" Danny's geniality vanished and his voice became harsh. "I have as much right to him as you do—more actually. Brenda and I were involved in a loving relationship."

"That might be your opinion, but it doesn't appear to have been hers," Alexandra replied crisply.

"I explained about our misunderstanding. What do you want from me?"

"Only that you stop bothering me, Mr. Riker."

He took a deep breath. "Look, Alex," he said more moderately, deliberately using her first name to get back on a friendly footing, "I'm sorry I blew my top, I was way off base, but this thing with Brenda has got me crazy. She's all I think about. You don't know how much I want to find her. My whole future depends on her!"

He sounded so anguished that Alexandra relented. Danny hadn't been very perceptive with Brenda, but he seemed to be trying to make amends. "I know this must be difficult for you, and I'm not trying to keep Willie away from you," she said more gently. "I really am busy tonight, but you can come by tomorrow night if that's convenient."

Danny hesitated. "Yeah, okay, if you're sure we can't make it any sooner. I could meet you for a drink after work. Just to see the kid and talk about his mother."

"I really can't."

"Then I guess I'll have to wait until tomorrow night," he sighed.

Alexandra left work early so she could go shopping for clothes for Willie, as well as dinner, before picking up Willie at Mandy's house. The market was crowded and it seemed to take ages to select what she needed and then get checked out. Willie would be waiting for her, and she was also in a hurry to get dinner started so he would be fed by the time Chase got there. Whenever that was. Alexandra wished they'd set a time. Maybe this mad rush wasn't necessary.

Mandy wanted her to stay and visit for a while, but Alexandra explained why she had to go home. She was juggling a large bag of groceries and searching in her purse for her door key when Chase's voice startled her.

"Let me hold that for you," he said.

"What are you doing here so early?" she blurted out.

"You said any time after six." He looked at the thin gold watch on his wrist. "It's six-ten."

"I'm not ready for you yet," she said helplessly.

His eyes sparkled with amusement. "You don't have to

slip into something sexy for me. I find you irresistible, just the way you are.''

Alexandra was conscious of her windblown hair and less than glamorous blouse and skirt. ''You know what I mean,'' she answered curtly, allowing him to take the bag. ''I have to make Willie's dinner.''

''I'll help you,'' Chase said as he followed her into the living room. ''We both will, won't we?'' He smiled at the little boy.

Willie was losing his fear of strange men, after being with so many of them. He looked up at Chase with interest. ''I don't know how to cook,'' he said.

''Don't tell Alex, but I don't either.'' Chase laughed.

She couldn't help smiling. ''We're a fine group. I'm not exactly a gourmet chef, myself.''

''I think I'd better take both of you out to dinner,'' Chase said.

''No, I fought my way through the supermarket. Now you have to suffer, too.''

''Am I invited to dinner?''

''I can't very well let you sit here and watch us eat. You and Willie can get acquainted while I see what I can whip up.''

''I want to help,'' Willie said.

''All right, you can set the table. And you can make us a drink,'' she told Chase.

''That's a job I can handle.'' He grinned.

''I thought that might be your field of expertise,'' she remarked dryly.

''Where do you get these scurrilous impressions of me?'' he complained. ''I'm just an ordinary guy.''

''Sure, just your average millionaire playboy.'' Alexandra unwrapped a package of chicken breasts and arranged them on a broiler pan.

''I can't help being rich, but I object to being called a playboy. I'm a hardworking businessman.''

"Maybe so, but somehow I can't see you sitting home every night after work, watching television."

"I doubt if that's the way *you* spend your time, either. Does that make you a playgirl? Forgive me for being politically incorrect, but somehow playwoman doesn't sound right." He was opening cabinets in search of her liquor supply.

"Can we have this discussion later, when I can concentrate better?"

Chase seemed to fill her small kitchen. Everything she needed was either in a cupboard or a drawer that he was blocking. She ducked under his outstretched arm to reach for a can of paprika on the spice rack.

"I'll never get dinner ready if you don't stop distracting me," she complained.

His arms lowered and he placed his palms on the counter, forming a cage around her. He didn't touch her, but she was pinned just inches from his lithe body. "I didn't think it was possible to distract you. I've been trying without much success to get your attention."

If that was his intention, he had it. Alexandra was keenly aware of her proximity to Chase's lean body. Her eyes were drawn to his firmly chiseled mouth. She had an almost irresistible urge to feel it moving over hers.

"You said I could set the table, Alex," Willie reminded her.

"I'll get the silverware and place mats for you," she said as Chase's arms dropped. "And you can go in the living room and watch TV," she told Chase firmly.

"I wanna watch TV, too." Willie was easily distracted by something that promised to be more fun.

"Good, I can use the space," Alexandra muttered.

As she turned toward the sink, Chase gave her long hair a playful tug and leaned down to murmur in her ear, "It's always more fun to share it."

"Are you gonna kiss Alex?" Willie piped up unexpectedly. "Daddy used to kiss Mommy sometimes when she was making dinner."

Chase's mischievous expression sobered instantly as he turned to the small boy. "Tell me about your daddy. Did he ever talk to you about your grandmother?"

Willie nodded. "She's a nice lady and she lives in a great big house. Daddy says someday he'll take me to visit her."

Chase struggled with strong emotions. "Did he ever mention his brother?"

"Yes, he wishes he could tell him something. I forget what, but he looked real sad when he said it. Most of the time Daddy laughs a lot."

"At least he was happy," Chase said in a barely audible voice.

Alexandra's heart twisted with compassion for this strong man who looked so desolate and vulnerable suddenly. She wanted to put her arms around him and comfort him. Instead, she put her hand on his arm in a silent show of support.

Chase squeezed her hand in acknowledgment, but his attention was focused on the boy. "Did you live in a nice house with a backyard for you to play in?"

"We lived in a bunch of different houses," Willie answered. "Mommy said she felt like a gypsy, but she laughed when she said it. What's a gypsy?"

"It's a person who moves around a lot," Alexandra explained. "Were all of these houses in Los Angeles?"

"I don't know. I guess so. I wanna watch television now."

When he went into the other room to turn on the set, Chase said to Alexandra, "Why did you ask him about Los Angeles?"

She told him about Officer Torelli's call.

"I can't believe Bill was living so close and I never knew it!"

"He could have moved there recently. Willie said they

lived in a lot of houses. Some of them could have been in other cities, even different states.''

"I suppose you're right. But wherever he'd been all these years, I have a feeling he was working his way back home. If only he'd contacted me! I might have been able to save his life.''

Chase's expression was so tortured that Alexandra followed her impulse this time and put her arms around him, comforting him like a little child. "Just remember that he had a happy life with a loving wife and a darling child. That's more than a lot of people ever have.''

Chase held her tightly and buried his face in her hair. "I'll try, but it won't be easy.''

"You're the strong one in the family, remember?''

He drew back slowly and took a deep breath. "I'm sorry I went to pieces on you.''

"It just proves you're human, like the rest of us.'' She smiled gently. "I'm glad. Supermen make me uncomfortable.''

"Then you should be very relaxed with me,'' he said wryly.

"I am, but you're still in my way. Go and watch television with Willie.''

As she boiled water for the frozen broccoli and took salad ingredients out of the refrigerator, Alexandra realized her attitude toward Chase had changed. She no longer regarded him as an adversary, a man with some secret agenda. Chase might not really be Willie's uncle, but he honestly believed he was. And she couldn't help believe it, too—or at least keep an open mind.

But it was too soon to turn Willie over to the Mainwarings. Was that because it would mark the end of her relationship with Chase? a nagging voice asked. Alexandra firmly ignored it. She didn't deny being attracted to Chase, but Willie's welfare was uppermost in her mind.

Dinner was a relaxed affair in the little dining nook adjoining the kitchen. Willie talked about his day at Mandy's.

"I like it there," he said. "They have a whole bunch of stairs. Dee Dee slides down the banister, but she won't let me do it."

"Your grand—" Chase paused and glanced at Alexandra before continuing, "My mother has a two-story house. Maybe we could go there for a visit some day, if Alexandra says it's all right."

"Say yes, Alex! Can I slide down *her* banister?" he asked Chase.

"Certainly not," she answered before Chase had a chance.

"Did you think I was going to give my permission?" He grinned.

"It wouldn't surprise me. You're a pushover for that child."

"I'm an easy mark for all the people I'm fond of," he answered, gazing at her meltingly.

Willie was watching them with keen interest. "Are you in love with Alex?" he asked Chase.

"Where did you get an idea like that?" she gasped.

"Mommy and Daddy looked at each other funny like that. When I asked her why, she said 'cause they were in love.''

"It was different with them," Alexandra explained carefully. "They were married."

"Do you have to be married before you get to love somebody?"

"Let's see you get out of that one," Chase murmured.

She shot him an annoyed glance before saying to Willie, "Not necessarily. There are all different kinds of love."

"Like what?"

"Well..." She couldn't mention family, because he didn't have any that she knew of. Then Alexandra had an inspiration. "You love Teddy, don't you? That's one kind of love."

"He's my best friend." Willie reached down to pat the teddy bear beside his chair. "He got losted and I cried. I couldn't find him anywhere, but Daddy found him for me."

"I know that made you both happy." Alexandra was glad the subject had been changed. To be sure it stayed that way, she said, "Finish your dinner, so we can have dessert. I bought cookies and ice cream."

"You tried to lead us astray about your culinary skill," Chase commented. "The dinner was excellent."

"I guess anybody can broil chicken and cook frozen broccoli," she said dismissively.

"Then it must be the company I enjoyed so much," he said, giving her a melting smile.

When they'd finished dessert, Alexandra said to him, "You don't have to stay. You probably have plans for the evening."

"Are you picturing a sexy redhead or a glamorous brunette?" he teased.

"Whatever turns you on," she answered lightly.

"That would be a blonde with hazel eyes. Or are they green?" He cupped her chin in his hand and gazed into her eyes. "Sometimes they're golden and sometimes they're the color of a meadow bathed in sunshine."

"That's very poetic," she said, sitting back in her chair to dislodge his hand. "What do you tell *blue*-eyed blondes?"

"You're a very hard sell." He laughed, without denying he was handing her a line.

"I keep hoping you'll realize it and give up." She stood and carried some plates into the kitchen.

"Don't count on it," he called. "I enjoy a challenge."

Alexandra turned to find him right behind her, bringing more plates. "You don't have to do this," she said.

"You cooked dinner, so I should do the washing up. It's only fair." He began to roll up his sleeves.

Chase had removed his jacket and tie, so those were safe. But his pale blue shirt with an unobtrusive monogram on the cuff was made of imported Egyptian cotton. His slacks also looked custom-made and even more expensive.

"You'll get your clothes all dirty," she protested.

"This is the second time you've suggested I get undressed." He grinned. "I'll be glad to oblige, but don't you think we should wait until Willie is in bed?"

"I don't want to go to bed," Willie stated, saving her the necessity of a reply.

"You can play in the bathtub for a while," Alexandra promised. Turning to Chase, she said, "If you really want to be helpful, you can supervise his bath."

"I'll be glad to," he said meekly, observing the set of her chin. He lifted the little boy onto his shoulders. "Come on, champ, we've both been banished from the kitchen."

Willie chortled with glee as he anchored his fists in Chase's thick hair. "Daddy used to give me rides like this. When is my daddy coming home?"

"I don't know, honey," Chase said in a husky voice. "But I'll be here to give you rides—and anything else you need."

"You aren't my daddy," the little boy said doubtfully.

"No, but I can be your uncle. You can call me Uncle Chase."

Willie considered it briefly, then said, "Okay. I want my rubber duck and my plastic ball in the bathtub with me. Alex says I can."

"She's the boss." Chase chuckled.

Alexandra had finished cleaning up the kitchen by the time Willie was out of the bath. When he was tucked into bed with his ever-present teddy bear, she and Chase returned to the living room.

"Would you like another cup of coffee?" she asked.

"Don't bother," he said. "You've done enough."

"It's no trouble. I'd like another cup, myself."

Chase carried the tray into the living room and placed it on the coffee table. They both sat on the couch in front of it.

"This is nice." He put his head back and sighed happily. "I'm beginning to understand why people get married."

"Tonight was a highly sanitized version of marriage," she said dryly. "Willie wasn't difficult, dinner was edible if not gourmet, and best of all you get to go home to your spacious apartment and sleep late tomorrow if you feel like it."

"I'm an early riser, but that's a minor point. Why are you so down on marriage?"

"I'm not. I'm just more realistic than you. I know it isn't always the Cleaver family or Donna Reed—those old TV shows about picture-perfect families. In real life children get cranky sometimes and the plumbing stops up. Husbands and wives snap at each other occasionally, which is understandable. It must be hard to work all day and then come home to more responsibilities."

"There have to be compensations. People don't flock to the altar for no good reason."

"I guess that's where love comes in—and blind faith."

He turned his head to look at her curiously. "This is the second time you've bashed marriage. Do you know of some really bad ones?"

Alexandra was as puzzled as he. She believed in Cinderella stories and happy endings. So why did she keep giving Chase the opposite impression? Was it because she felt he wasn't serious about making a commitment to any woman? Chase was simply playing the devil's advocate. If she argued *for* marriage, he'd argue against it.

"Actually my two best friends have wonderful marriages," she said. "They're divinely happy."

"Then I don't understand why you're so adamantly opposed."

"I don't think I'm adamant about anything," she protested. "I like to think I keep an open mind."

"Have you been known to change it?"

"Frequently."

"That's encouraging. It means we might become lovers one day." He grinned.

"That's entirely possible," she said calmly, refusing to let him ruffle her. She'd decided the best way to handle Chase was to give him back some of his own medicine.

It worked. His teasing tone disappeared and he stared at her in surprise. "Are you serious?"

"Completely. But I must warn you, I'm very possessive. If we become lovers, I'd expect to be the only woman in your life."

"I can't conceive of wanting anyone else," he said in a sensuous voice, as he traced the contour of her ear erotically.

"That's what I needed to hear," she murmured.

"Sweet, little Alex." He kissed the corner of her mouth.

She turned her head so their lips grazed tantalizingly. "I know you want me, but do I really mean something to you, Chase? I'm terribly attracted to you, but it has to be more than sex for me. Am I different from all the rest?"

"Darling Alexandra, I can truthfully say you're unlike any woman I ever met before."

"Oh, Chase, I can't believe this is happening!" She looked at him adoringly.

"I can't, either." His lips slid down her neck to the opening of her blouse.

She tensed for a moment, then continued in the same eager voice, "I only played hard to get because I thought you were just interested in a brief fling. But everything's different now that we've made a commitment to each other."

He raised his head to look at her. "You're a beautiful woman, Alexandra," he said carefully. "I'd like very much to make love to you, but I'm not asking you to make a commitment."

"I want to, darling. I've been searching all my life for someone like you. Someone to spend every night with and every weekend. We'll share everything together. I don't want there to be any secrets between us."

Chase drew back, looking slightly dazed. "Don't you think a relationship like that would be a little smothering?"

"How can you say that? I'm beginning to think you don't really care about me," she pouted. "It was all just an act."

His eyes narrowed on her for a moment, then he started to laugh. "Like the one you're putting on now?"

Alexandra dropped her love-struck pose. "Don't you like having a woman come on to you?" she asked dryly.

"I get your message—belatedly—but I scarcely came on that strong," he protested.

"Maybe not, but you weren't exactly easy to discourage."

"I suppose it's useless to tell you I really am attracted to you."

"Don't you ever learn?" she exclaimed.

"I'm being honest, whether you believe it or not. I don't expect anything to develop between us, because you made it quite clear just now that the attraction is one-sided. I just wanted you to know why I was persistent. Too much so, although I didn't realize it at the time."

"I guess I could have said something without going overboard," she said grudgingly.

"It wouldn't have been as effective. I've never been put in my place so decisively." Chase didn't look angry. His powerful body was relaxed and he wore an amused expression.

He could be covering up, though. Men had fragile egos,

especially over rejection. "I was just trying to cut through all the phony baloney so we can be friends," she explained.

"I think it would be safer than being lovers," he agreed, his blue eyes sparkling mischievously. "I wouldn't want to disappoint you. Knowing you're already critical of me might inhibit my performance. I've never made love when I thought I was being critiqued."

Alexandra didn't rise to the bait, although she couldn't imagine that splendid body failing to satisfy. "I'm glad we're still on good terms."

"Absolutely. Now that that's settled, what do platonic couples talk about?"

She couldn't help laughing. "I know it's a strain. You don't have to stick around."

"I'm trying to be friends," he said reproachfully. "Work with me."

"Okay. Well, let's see. We could talk about the weather, but that's pretty boring. How about movies?"

"I rarely go to movies."

"All right, restaurants, then. What's the best meal you've ever eaten?"

"Let's see," he mused. "It's a tough call, but I'd have to say it was the *lasagne di carnevale* I had at a little café in Venice, around the corner from the Gritti Palace. Do you know that section of the city?"

Alexandra shook her head. "Unfortunately I've never been to Venice."

"What a shame. It's one of the most romantic cities in the world. Even the parts that tourists flock to, like Piazza San Marco. But the real Venice is in the winding streets away from the piazza, where fountains splash in little plazas and women visit from their balconies across narrow streets."

"It sounds very colorful," she said wistfully.

"There's no place quite like it. I try to spend at least a day or two there every time I go to Europe."

"Do you go frequently?"

"About once a year, sometimes more than that. I'm a director of several companies that have their headquarters overseas, so I combine business with pleasure."

"Where do you go for a vacation?"

"That depends on what time of year it is. The French Riviera is lovely in the spring, and of course the skiing is superb in Switzerland in the winter."

Chase told her about all the glamorous places she only knew about from sending other people. But he wasn't an ordinary tourist. He knew all of the "in" places, the pleasure spots of the rich and famous.

When he noticed her rapt face, he said teasingly, "If we were more than just good friends I'd take you with me."

"It would be nice to go with someone who's so knowledgeable," she answered matter-of-factly. To keep him from becoming personal again she said, "Your coffee must be cold. Would you like me to heat it up?"

"No, I'd better get going. I'll carry this into the kitchen for you." He stood and picked up the tray. As they both walked toward the other room he said, "Thank you for dinner. Will you let me return your hospitality tomorrow night? We can eat early—anywhere you think is suitable for Willie."

"I'm sorry, but I'm going to be busy tomorrow night."

"Oh?" He didn't question her in so many words, but his rising inflection did it for him.

Alexandra told herself she didn't owe Chase an explanation, even though he was clearly waiting for one. "I do have a life of my own," she finally said grudgingly.

"Not much of one lately, I'll bet. Becoming an instant mother must have really complicated your life."

"Oh, well, I don't really mind. It's only temporary."

"Still, it creates problems. Your male friends don't have the interest in Willie that you and I share. I doubt if they'd want him along on a date."

"Willie is a darling little boy," she said evasively, not wanting him to know Danny was the reason she was busy the next night.

"You don't have to convince *me.* But I have a special feeling for him. What I was leading up to was a suggestion. I'd be happy to baby-sit for you tomorrow night."

"I couldn't ask you to do that," she said quickly.

"Why not? He's comfortable with me now. It will be a lot easier than bringing in a stranger to sit with him."

"I wasn't going to hire a sitter."

"You intend to take him to your friend Mandy's again? Even if it's true that she doesn't mind, it's very disruptive for Willie. The poor little kid doesn't know what bed he's going to sleep in next."

"You talk as if I'm neglecting him," Alexandra flared.

"I didn't mean to imply that."

"It certainly sounded that way. Besides, I only left him there to go out with *you.*"

"I offered to take him along. In fact, I urged you to. But I didn't mean to start an argument. I'm simply offering my services so you won't have to go to all that trouble."

"I appreciate the offer, but it won't be necessary." When Alexandra could see that he wasn't willing to let it go at that, she added reluctantly, "You needn't worry about Willie. I plan on staying home tomorrow night."

"Your date is coming here?" Chase stared at her incredulously. "Why didn't you say so in the first place?"

"I didn't think it was necessary," she answered coolly.

"I'm not trying to pry into your personal life," Chase said impatiently. "My concern is for Willie."

Alexandra knew that, but it was a timely reminder. There had been moments tonight when he'd made her forget his real purpose in being here. "Now that you don't have to be concerned about Willie, you can go out and enjoy your usual type of evening tomorrow night," she said in a crisp voice.

"I'm sorry if you got the impression that I didn't enjoy *this* evening. I did, very much."

"It's nice of you to say so."

He gave her a dissatisfied look. "I'm not just being polite. I had a very good time—and not only because of Willie. I'm sorry if it sounded that way."

Alexandra shrugged. "It doesn't matter. We both know our only mutual interest is Willie."

"I wouldn't say that," Chase murmured. "I think we established a couple of other interests."

She wasn't falling for that line again. "I believe you said you had to leave," she remarked pointedly.

He gave her a perplexed look. "We were getting along so well. I don't like to leave feeling I've said or done something to make you angry."

"You didn't," she said quickly. "I'm just a little tired. It's been a long day."

"I understand. It must be hard to work all day and then have to come home and cook. I shouldn't have stayed for dinner."

"You weren't any bother. I had to make dinner for Willie and myself, anyway."

"Why don't you let your date take you out tomorrow night?" Chase urged. "Make it as easy on yourself as possible."

"Maybe I'll do that."

"Good. What time will he be here?" He smiled at the startled look on her face. "Don't worry, I'm not planning to intrude. I only asked because I promised Willie I'd bring him a fire engine he saw on television. It has all kinds of gadgets, a siren and a ladder that goes up and down. I'll drop it off before your date arrives."

"No, don't do that!" Alexandra didn't know what time Danny would get there, and she certainly didn't want the two men to meet. "I mean, it would be better if you brought it by when you can show him how it works."

"It can't be that complicated. You can do it."

"It's your gift. I think you should be the one to show him," she insisted.

"I'd be happy to, but I told Willie I'd get it for him tomorrow. I don't want to break my promise."

"He'll probably forget all about it by morning, but if he doesn't I'll tell him I told you not to come until the next night."

"It would be a lot simpler for me to simply drop the thing off and leave." Chase frowned. "Unless you think I might stick around too long. Is there some reason you don't want your date to see me?"

"Of course not! Why should I mind?"

"That's what I'd like to find out. He might be the jealous type, but why wouldn't you come right out and tell me so? I'd make sure to leave promptly." Chase's jaw set firmly. "There must be some other reason. Who do you have a date with tomorrow night, Alex?"

"I don't have to tell you," she said, with equal determination.

"That's true. I can simply come over and find out for myself."

"You have no right to harass me like this! My personal life is my own."

"You're perfectly right—if this was a personal matter. I don't think it is. I believe it has something to do with Willie." He stared at her with narrowed eyes. "Are you tired of taking care of him? Are you turning him over to the social-service people rather than letting me have him?"

"What kind of person do you think I am?" Alexandra asked disgustedly. "Do you honestly think I could sit here all evening making polite conversation if I was planning a rotten thing like that?"

"No, you're right. I apologize. But there's something you're keeping from me. It would be a lot easier if you didn't make me drag it out of you."

She could tell by his implacable determination that Chase intended to do just that. Not physically, of course, but that didn't make it any easier to refuse. "All right, if you must know, I told Danny Riker he could come over and spend a little time with Willie."

"That sleazy con artist?" Chase's temper erupted instantly. "Are you out of your mind? The man doesn't have a shred of credibility!"

"You don't know that for sure."

"Come on! Don't tell me you believe his ridiculous story. Nobody could be that credulous."

"You don't have any proof to back up your story, either."

"If I was going to lie, I'd make up a better one than he did," Chase said contemptuously.

"His creativity is not at issue here. Besides, why would he lie? What other reason could he have for wanting custody of Willie?"

"That's a very good question. You should have asked yourself that before agreeing to let him into your house."

Alexandra could have pointed out that the same thing applied to Chase, but it would only have prolonged the argument. "This isn't getting us anywhere," she said impatiently. "That's the reason I didn't want to tell you Danny was coming."

"You knew I'd disapprove." He glared at her accusingly.

"Of course I did. Your interest and his are diametrically opposed."

"My interest is Willie. I have no idea what Riker's is, but I don't trust him—and I don't think you should, either."

"I'm quite capable of making up my own mind," she answered tartly.

"Not when the outcome might affect my nephew."

"What do you expect Danny to do, kidnap Willie?"

Chase moved closer to her. "I wouldn't want to be in your shoes if that happened." His voice was soft, which added to its menace.

Alexandra stood her ground, although she was very aware of the power in his taut body. "At least Danny never threatened me—which is more than I can say for you."

"It wasn't a threat, it was a promise. Willie is my last link to a brother I loved very much. I agreed to your terms because I thought it would save time. But if I think you're endangering the boy's welfare, I won't hesitate to fight for him. And right now I have serious questions about your judgment."

"Don't you think you're overreacting?" Alexandra hated to give Chase the satisfaction of backing down, but it was in her own best interest to placate him. "Danny owns a well-known restaurant in town. He isn't some transient who just popped up out of nowhere. I took all of that into consideration before I agreed to let him come over tomorrow night. Willie's welfare is as important to me as it is to you."

"I doubt it." Chase's eyes were sad for a moment, then his expression hardened. "Just see to it that nothing happens to that child. Do we understand each other?"

"Perfectly," she answered coldly.

"Good. I'll be by to see Willie the following night." Without waiting for an answer, Chase strode out the front door.

Alexandra stared after him, speechless with rage. Nobody had ever ordered her around in such a high-handed manner. Chase hadn't *asked* if he could come over, he'd *told* her! As if she had nothing to say about it.

He had no right to get so furious about Danny, either. Privately, Alexandra shared Chase's jaundiced view of Danny. Nothing about his story was plausible. But that wasn't the point. Chase didn't think she could figure it out for herself. He was a male chauvinist who dismissed her as a mere woman whom any man could fool.

Chase had certainly done his share of trying! Her chin set grimly when she remembered how he'd tried to convince her that he was attracted to her. If she hadn't known better, she might even have believed him. His act had fallen apart, predictably, when he was thwarted over Willie.

How far had Chase been prepared to go, she wondered? Would he have made love to her to advance his cause? Remembering the seductive kisses that trailed down to her cleavage, Alexandra had no doubt that he would have.

That made her even angrier. What kind of man would stoop that low? She was almost as angry at herself for being sympathetic toward him—briefly. But no more! From now on, macho man was going to meet the ice princess.

Chapter Five

Alexandra was still in a bad mood when she went to work
the next morning. After ignoring the fact for a while, Tina
finally made a comment.

"Is there something I should know?" she asked. "Like
I'm fired, but you don't know how to break it to me?"

"Don't be ridiculous. I wouldn't know what to do without you."

"That's a relief! Something has ruffled your feathers,
though. Would you like to tell me about it? Maybe I can
help."

"I doubt it." Alexandra sighed. "It's Chase. I know I
shouldn't let him bother me, but I can't help it."

"He's enough to raise any woman's pulse rate." Tina
grinned.

"That's not what I meant. He's determined to get custody of Willie, one way or another. Chase came over last
night and made a big fuss over Willie. He promised to buy

the boy a red fire engine and suggested he call him Uncle Chase.''

"How did Willie react?"

"Positively, as you might expect. Chase is impressive when he makes an all-out effort."

"Kids are pretty savvy about people. They can usually spot a phony. It sounds like Willie really likes Chase."

"Wouldn't you, if he offered to buy you a red fire engine?" Alexandra asked cynically.

"My affections aren't for sale that cheap. It would take a diamond bracelet, at the very least." Tina laughed.

"I'm sure Chase would be willing to buy him the masculine equivalent. I just hope the police locate some of Willie's *known* relatives soon. I don't want Chase hanging around every night."

"We should all have such troubles! Are you seeing him again tonight?"

"No, I told Danny he could come over. He and Chase don't care for each other, to put it mildly."

"Well, at least you're not lonesome," Tina joked as the telephone rang and they both went back to work.

Danny didn't show up as early as Chase had. Alexandra and Willie had finished dinner and she'd cleaned up the kitchen by the time the doorbell rang.

Danny arrived bearing gifts, a bouquet of flowers for Alexandra and a large box of building blocks for Willie. The little boy immediately spilled them out on the living-room floor and started to play with them.

Danny watched with a gleam of excitement in his eyes. "I can't believe I finally got to talk to him."

"You'll have to compete with the toy you brought." Alexandra smiled at the little boy's absorption.

Danny barely heard her. "You look just like your mother," he told Willie, who paid no attention. "I was a good friend of your mother's. You and I are going to be good friends, too, aren't we?''

"Guess so," Willie answered indifferently, trying to join two mismatched pieces. "These won't stay together, Alex. Can you make them do it?"

"In a few minutes," she promised. "Right now, Mr. Riker wants to talk to you."

"Why?"

"Because I want to know what kind of toy to bring you the next time I come over," Danny answered smoothly.

"Uncle Chase is gonna buy me a red fire engine," Willie said. "Will he be here again tonight, Alex?"

Danny glared at her. "You kept me waiting a couple of days, but you let Mainwaring see the kid?"

"Don't you go ballistic on me, too." Alexandra sighed. "I'm trying to be fair. Until I hear differently, you both have an equal right to see Willie. Chase just happened to ask first."

"Mainwaring is a fast worker. He's already got the kid calling him Uncle."

"Possibly because he spent his time with Willie instead of arguing with *me*," she said coldly. "And will you please stop calling Willie, the kid? He has a name, although you seem to have trouble remembering it."

"I'm sorry, it's just the way I talk." Danny tried to mask his anger as he turned to the child. "I don't know much about little boys. What do you like to do? Where did your mother take you here in San Francisco?"

"One time we walked down a great big hill to a restaurant. I wanted a hamburger, but they said they didn't have any—only stuff I never ate before. It was a real funny place. People were eating their dinner with long sticks."

"It sounds as if she took him to Chinatown," Alexandra remarked. "It's only a couple of blocks from the Nob Hill hotel where they were staying."

"There were lots of stores near the restaurant," Willie

said. "Mommy bought me a toy that has rows of wooden beads. You can push them up and down."

"An abacus," Alexandra murmured.

"Yep! That's what she called it. I want to play with it. Will you get it for me, Alex?"

"I'll talk to the police about giving your things to me," she said. "I don't know why they'd want to keep them any longer. You need your clothes."

Danny broke in impatiently. "Did your mom take you anyplace else—like to the airport or a Greyhound bus station?"

"What's a greyhound?" Willie stared at him with interest. "Is that different from a regular bus?"

Alexandra was puzzled. Was Danny trying to trace Brenda's movements? Surely he knew the police had been over that ground. Besides, Willie hadn't been with his mother when she disappeared, so how would he know where she went?

"Could I have a glass of water?" Danny asked unexpectedly.

"I'm sorry, I should have offered you something. Would you like coffee or perhaps a drink?"

"No, water will be fine. With ice in it, if it isn't too much trouble."

"I want a root beer," Willie announced, trailing after her to the kitchen.

Danny muttered an expletive under his breath. His attempt to get the boy alone had failed. It would be hard enough to make the kid understand what a locker was. With Alex listening in, it would be impossible. If Brenda *had* stashed the diamonds in a locker or something similar, there had to be a key or a claim check. The question was, how could he ask about them without tipping his hand?

When Alexandra returned with his ice water and a plate of cookies, Danny said to her, "I don't want to louse up your evening. If you have something to do in the kitchen or someplace, Willie and I will be fine together.''

"That's quite all right. I finished the dishes before you got here, and he's had his bath." She looked at her watch. "I'm afraid he'll have to go to bed soon."

"I barely got a chance to talk to him," Danny protested.

"I honestly don't think you're going to find out anything from Willie," Alexandra said gently. She didn't have the empathy for Danny that she had for Chase, but he did look upset.

"I wasn't pumping the ki—I mean, Willie. What gave you that idea?" Danny asked with exaggerated innocence.

"It's understandable. We all hoped he could give us some clue to Brenda's disappearance, but he's only four years old. He wouldn't know he knew anything, even if he did."

"You said the cops went through her hotel room. Did they find anything useful?"

"Somebody had ransacked it before they got there."

"You'd think a fancy place like that would have better security."

Alexandra shrugged. "I suppose no system is foolproof, especially for a professional thief."

"Hotel thieves are usually looking for jewelry and money. Maybe they overlooked something just as important—to us, I mean. I'd like a chance to examine her things," Danny said casually.

"You'll have to talk to the police about that."

"You said you were going to ask for them to be released to you."

"Willie's things, not Brenda's."

"Are you talking about Mommy?" Willie looked up from the blocks he'd resumed playing with. "When is she coming to get me?"

"Soon, I hope, honey. It's bedtime now." Lowering her

voice, she said to Danny, "I don't think we should talk about her in front of him."

Danny didn't offer to leave, and Alexandra couldn't very well ask him to, although their business together was over. When she returned to the living room after tucking Willie into bed, Danny looked set for the evening.

"I believe I'll take you up on that offer of a drink," he said. "I didn't like to have one in front of the boy."

"What would you like?" she asked. "I'm afraid my selection is rather limited."

"That's okay, I'm not fussy. Scotch if you have it, and anything else if you don't."

He followed her into the kitchen and stood next to her as she reached up to get a bottle out of the cupboard. Alexandra was reminded of the night before, when Chase had stood in almost the same spot. But the similarity ended there. Chase had radiated masculinity, setting her nerve ends tingling, while Danny was merely irritatingly close.

"It's a small kitchen," she remarked. "Why don't you go into the living room while I make the drinks?"

"That's my profession. I own a bar, remember?" He smiled as he took the bottle out of her hand. "You'll have to be my guest for dinner some night. Have you ever been to the Time Out?"

"No. I know where it is, but I've never been there."

"Let me know when you're coming and I'll run interference for you. A beautiful girl like you must have to fight the guys off with a whip. Don't get me wrong, though," he said hastily. "It's a nice place. I don't allow any hanky-panky."

"That's reassuring," she said ironically. "Did Brenda spend much time there?"

Danny slanted a glance at her and moved away. "She didn't care much for bars."

"It must have been difficult for you to find time to spend

together. Since you work nights, I mean,'' Alexandra commented as they started back to the living room.

"That's the advantage of being the boss. I can take off whenever I want."

"You're very fortunate that your business runs itself while you're away. You did go down south to visit her, didn't you?"

"No, I didn't know that's where she was from. I would certainly have told the police if I had," he said smoothly. "Brenda never actually said so, but I got the impression that she was from a little town in the Central Valley."

"It's hard to believe you knew so little about her." Alexandra stared at him incredulously.

"It didn't seem to matter. You know how it is when a guy's in love." Danny adroitly changed the subject. "A stunner like you must have dozens of lovesick men hanging around. Or are you already engaged?"

"No, my life is complicated enough without being involved with anyone."

"You'll change your mind." He looked her up and down with obvious male appreciation. "A gorgeous gal like you won't be alone long."

Chase had said essentially the same thing, but with a great deal more finesse. Danny's behavior was bizarre. How could he come on to her when he was supposed to be distraught over his fiancée's disappearance? His credibility was lessening by the minute.

"I suppose *you* won't be alone for long, either," she commented sardonically.

He was quick to pick up on her disapproval. "Nobody could ever take Brenda's place. I try to keep up a brave front—you know, joke around and everything. But deep down, I'm really hurting."

"I'm sorry for you," Alexandra said in a perfunctory voice. "I hope she'll be found soon."

"I hope so, too, but until she is, it would comfort me a

lot to have her boy. Even if it's just for a couple of days, to help me get over the shock of losing Brenda. It would be like having a little piece of her back.''

"I'm sorry, but I can't agree to that.''

"How can you be so heartless?'' he demanded. "Do you enjoy seeing me suffer?''

"Of course not! But Willie was placed in my care—by both his mother and the police. I can't just give him away like a piece of merchandise!''

"You could let him stay with me for a couple of days. That's all I'm asking. Call it a visit.''

Alexandra kept trying to make him realize that she wasn't just being arbitrary. But Danny refused to take no for an answer. Finally she agreed to think about letting Willie stay with him for a few days, because it seemed to be the only way to get rid of him.

"You don't know what this means to me!'' He grabbed both of her hands and crushed them between his. "You saved my life.''

She couldn't help smiling. "Isn't that a little extreme?''

"I mean, you've made me very happy. For the first time since Brenda disappeared. When will you let me know?''

"As soon as possible,'' she promised, urging him toward the door.

Alexandra breathed a sigh of relief when he finally left. To make sure he was really gone, she moved to the window to watch him get into his car.

While she waited for Danny to come out of the downstairs entrance, Alexandra noticed someone standing directly across the street. It was a moonless night, so she couldn't tell if it was a man or a woman. The person was bundled up in a long coat and a hat with a wide brim, not unusual attire for a chilly San Francisco night. There was something eerie, though, about the motionless figure. It sent a chill up her spine.

Then Danny came out onto the sidewalk and the figure

melted away. One moment it was there and then there was nothing, just swirling fog that made moving shadows. But Alexandra knew she hadn't imagined the silent stranger.

She turned away from the window, wondering who was out there. Could it be Chase, making sure that Danny didn't take Willie? She couldn't imagine Chase lurking on a street corner. It would be more like him to come barging into the apartment and have a confrontation with Danny. Still, she couldn't rule him out.

But if it wasn't Chase, who else could it be? Danny was here with her all evening, so he was in the clear. Alexandra's breath caught in her throat as she thought of another possibility—Brenda! That would mean she was alive, something Alexandra was reluctantly starting to doubt. But why wouldn't she come for Willie? Especially if she cared enough to hang around where he was staying.

Finally Alexandra gave up trying to find the answer, although her uneasiness didn't lessen. Before going to bed she double-checked the locks on the front and back doors.

Alexandra was still jumpy the next morning when Chase phoned.

"I called to tell Willie I got his fire engine," he said coolly. "May I speak to him?"

"He...uh...he isn't here right now."

She could almost see the scowl on Chase's face. "Where is he?" he asked.

"Tina took him to the bank with her," Alexandra improvised rapidly.

"Well, I suppose that's better than having him sit around an office the entire day. I'll be in meetings all afternoon, so tell him I'll see him tonight."

"Chase, wait!" Alexandra didn't want him to hang up before she found out where he'd been the night before. It was going to be tricky. "I explained to Willie why you couldn't bring his toy last night," she began.

"Really? What did you tell him? That you allowed a con artist to sell you a sob story any normal person would laugh at?"

She controlled her temper and managed to sound regretful. "I can tell you're still angry at me."

"I think I have a right to be! But we've been through all that."

"I'm really sorry. I hoped we could be friends."

"Why? I believe you were the one who said we didn't have anything in common except Willie."

"I suppose you're right. I'm nothing like the women you date."

"You're nothing like anyone I ever *met* before!" He sounded baffled. "Every time I think we're getting along, you throw me a curve."

"That's because you're constantly surrounded by people who agree with everything you say." She couldn't keep a slight edge out of her voice. "When I don't follow the pack, you go off the deep end."

"I'm entitled to, when it concerns Willie. What did you accomplish by letting Riker visit with him? Did he convince you that he's been through an epiphany and he now loves little children?"

"No. I share your skepticism."

"I suppose you told him the same thing about me."

"You really are impossible!" Alexandra exclaimed angrily. "You can find something to complain about even when I agree with you."

"I suppose you're right," he agreed grudgingly. "But just this once."

She couldn't help laughing. "Well, one in a row is a start."

Chase unbent slightly. "What did Willie think of Riker?"

"Not much. Danny didn't make a great effort, beyond

asking him a lot of questions. There were times when I had the feeling Willie wasn't his main priority.''

"That was predictable." Chase's voice was definitely warmer now. "Maybe we've discovered his true agenda. He's partial to honey blondes in plunging necklines.''

"My neckline was not low," she said uncomfortably. "I had on the same blouse and skirt I wore to work.''

He chuckled deeply. "It must have been as sexy as the one you wore when I was there.''

"I *meant* when you were here. Last night I had on something equally businesslike. I wasn't implying that Danny was interested in me.''

"I told you there was something suspect about the man," Chase teased.

"I wouldn't know about that, but he is boring." Alexandra had finally worked the conversation around to where she wanted it. "I hope you had a more stimulating evening," she remarked casually.

"Compared to him, I suppose anything would be.''

"What did you do?" she persisted.

"Nothing exciting. I worked late, had dinner in a restaurant near my office and went home.''

"It's nice to have a quiet, relaxing evening like that once in a while.''

"I was far from relaxed," he said in a clipped tone of voice. "In fact, I went out about ten o'clock for a long walk to relieve my tension.''

After a moment of silence, Alexandra said, "It wasn't a very nice night. I hope you wore a hat and coat.''

"You sound like my mother. I have a meeting in five minutes, so I'd better go. Tell Willie I'll see him tonight.''

Alexandra replaced the receiver slowly. If Chase had something to hide, would he admit he'd gone out for a walk about the time she'd seen the mystery man? It didn't seem plausible. But he *had* brushed aside her question about whether he'd worn a hat and coat. Or was that a normal response? She didn't know any more now than she had before.

While Alexandra was puzzling over her problem, Danny had a more serious one. He was trying to justify himself to his boss. Victor Karpov had called him early in the morning, a time when Danny was never at his best.

"I expected to hear from you by now," Karpov said in measured tones.

Danny sat up straighter in bed and reached for a package of cigarettes on the nightstand, as he always did under stress. "Yeah, well, I was going to call you, but I've been busy working on our problem. And I'm happy to say I'm making progress."

"You've located Brenda?"

"Well, no, not yet. But I saw the kid last night."

"So what? It's his mother we want."

"He's part of my game plan. I took him a toy and got real chummy with Alex, the chick who's got custody of him for now."

"I'm not interested in your love life," Karpov said bitingly. "You're supposed to be doing a job for me."

"That's what I was doing last night, covering all bases. I asked the kid as many questions as I could about where his mother took him here in San Francisco. It occurred to me that maybe Brenda stashed the stones someplace. She's on the run and it's dangerous to carry around stuff worth a couple of mil. What if her purse got snatched?"

"The diamonds will fit into a small pouch. She could easily conceal them on her body, which is undoubtedly where they are. She'd need easy access to them when she decides to leave town—if she hasn't already," Karpov added grimly.

"No, boss, she's still here! I caught sight of her last night, hanging around outside Alex's place. I told you she wouldn't leave without the kid."

"You saw Brenda and you let her slip through your fingers again?" Karpov asked ominously.

"It was foggy out. She just disappeared. Bill must have taught her a thing or two." Danny was practically groveling. "I'll have a man outside of Alex's apartment from now on."

"Why wasn't that done before now?"

"I was afraid Brenda would spot him and take off. Nate said our best bet was to make her come to us." Danny thought it was time to spread the blame around. "That's the only reason I was romancing Alex last night. To convince her to let me have the kid."

"And did she agree?"

"I came this close." Danny held his thumb and forefinger a fraction of an inch apart, despite the fact that the other man couldn't see them. "I've got Alex eating out of my hand. All I need is a little more time."

"Why should I believe you? The only thing I've had from you so far are excuses. I'm starting to wonder if you haven't outlived your usefulness," Karpov said ominously.

"You don't mean that, boss! How about all the money I've laundered through my bar? Not to mention our betting operation. Look how much that brings in. This thing with Brenda is taking a little more time than I anticipated, but I'll deliver for you. You can count on me."

There was a short silence while Danny sweated and Karpov deliberated. Finally the older man said, "All right, you have a week—but that's all. At the end of that time I expect to see those diamonds on my desk. Is that understood?"

"You'll have them," Danny said, hoping he sounded confident.

Alexandra was at the bank the first time Danny phoned that day. He called back several times, but she had instructed Tina to tell him she was unavailable.

"What does he want?" Tina asked curiously. "And why don't you want to talk to him?"

Alexandra explained the situation. "I don't know what I'm going to do if he keeps calling me like this."

"Tell him if it was up to you, you'd let him have Willie for a couple of days, but the police won't let you."

"That's probably true. Connor used his influence so Willie could stay with me temporarily, but I'm sure I don't have the authority to just hand him over to somebody else."

"Well, there you are," Tina said. "Your problem is solved."

Alexandra wished it were that simple, but she knew better. Danny wasn't going to let up and neither would Chase. She was beginning to feel like a bone fought over by two dogs. Although Willie was the prize they were after, not her.

The ruthlessness she sensed in both men made her uneasy. As Alexandra drove over to Mandy's to pick up Willie after work, she noticed a nondescript black car following her. Or at least she thought it was. But after she turned around at a stoplight to get a better look at the driver, the car moved into a different lane.

"You're getting paranoid," she muttered to herself. "You're starting to suspect everybody!"

Her whole life had been turned upside down since Brenda Clark walked into her office that fateful day. Had it been foolish to insist on keeping Willie? He wasn't really her responsibility, and she was finding out that children took a lot of care.

But then Alexandra thought of the compensations. Her mouth curved in a tender smile as she remembered the way he gave her a hug and a kiss after she tucked him into bed. The way he ran to greet her when she went to pick him up at night. She had become very important to Willie, and he had worked his way into her heart.

Alexandra's jaw set grimly. If somebody out there was

threatening him, they'd have to deal with her. She intended to protect him, no matter what it took.

Chase didn't show up at Alexandra's until after she and Willie had finished eating.

When he finally arrived, she said, "I expected you for dinner, but Willie got hungry and I had to feed him. Have you eaten? I can warm up something for you."

"Don't bother," he said. "I had a late lunch. I'm not hungry."

"Did you bring it, Uncle Chase?" Willie raced over and tugged on his arm. "Is that my fire engine?"

"I promised, didn't I?" Chase handed him a large box.

"Oh, boy!" Willie seized the box and sat on the floor to rip off the wrappings.

Chase helped him take the toy and all of its many accessories out of the cardboard box. The little boy eagerly seized the ladders and brass bell, but he had trouble attaching them.

"Why won't they stay on?" he asked. "Is it broken?"

"No, we just have to read the instructions," Chase said reassuringly.

"I don't know how to read."

"Fortunately I do." Chase smiled. "These are the batteries. That's what makes the ladder go up and down. Let's find out where we're supposed to put them."

Alexandra watched silently as Chase assembled the fire engine, with Willie trying ineffectually to help. Chase never got impatient. He explained where the parts went and gently helped the little boy fit them into place.

They were too engrossed to know she was in the room, which caused mixed emotions in Alexandra. There had always been an undercurrent of attraction between herself and Chase, even when they argued. He'd never been indifferent to her. But that was only because he found her challenging. His present absorption with Willie was proof that the child was his only real interest. Alexandra finally admitted to herself that she wanted to believe Chase when he denied it.

She'd never met a man who attracted her this strongly. If they'd met under different circumstances, she could easily have fallen in love with him. But they hadn't, so she'd better not get any silly ideas.

Willie was ecstatic when the fire engine was finally functional. He scrambled after it, mimicking the sound of the siren as the truck careened around the room.

Chase sat cross-legged on the floor, watching him fondly. Eventually he looked up at Alexandra. "Isn't it nice when realization is as good as anticipation?"

"That only happens when you're a child," she answered.

"I wouldn't say that. Hasn't anything ever lived up to your expectations?"

"I suppose so, although I don't think you ever feel that kind of pure joy after you grow up."

His expression changed subtly. "I'd be sorry to think you really meant that. Some of life's greatest pleasures are reserved for adults."

Alexandra knew what he was referring to. Lovemaking was probably Chase's major hobby. "You're more of an authority on the subject than I am," she said tartly.

"I'd be happy to share my expertise." He grinned.

"So you don't deny it?"

"You were the one who decided I'm an expert. I would never make such an immodest claim. But purely to satisfy your curiosity, I'd be willing to let you find out for yourself."

"I'm not the least bit curious," she said coolly.

"Are you sure?" he asked softly. "If I'm as good as you say I am, it would be a night to remember."

Chase's long, relaxed body and her treacherous imagination told Alexandra what a special night it would be. She was quiveringly aware of everything about him, his firm yet sensuous mouth, his masculine hands with their long, tapering fingers. They would glide erotically over her body, pausing tantalizingly to probe her intimate secrets.

The disturbing vision vanished when Willie knelt in front of him. "Something happened, Uncle Chase. It won't go anymore. Can you fix it?"

Chase's attention was immediately diverted to the boy, which brought Alexandra to her senses. When was she going to realize that she was simply a pleasant diversion to Chase, at best?

While he tinkered with the toy fire engine, she went into the kitchen and turned on the dishwasher—for something to do other than look at Chase.

"It's all fixed, Alex," Willie called. "Uncle Chase made it work. He knows how to do everything."

She returned to the living room and remarked, "Yes, Uncle Chase is very clever, all right."

"Why doesn't that sound like a compliment?" he murmured to her as he uncoiled his long legs and stood.

"You're awfully hard to please. I don't know what more you want from me."

"That's a very provocative statement. Unfortunately I'm not in a position to tell you at the moment. Is that what you were counting on?" Without waiting for an answer he turned to Willie. "I have an idea. Why don't the three of us go out for ice cream?"

The small boy's face lit up. "Can I have chocolate on mine?"

"What's ice cream without chocolate sauce?" Chase smiled. "Maybe we'll go for broke and have whipped cream and a cherry on top."

"I have ice cream in the freezer," Alexandra said.

"No, I wanna go out," Willie said. "Uncle Chase said we could."

"He doesn't realize it's almost your bedtime."

"No, it isn't," the little boy protested. "It's still light outside."

"That's because daylight saving time just started."

"We won't be gone that long," Chase said mildly.

"Can we, Alex, can we?" Willie clamored. "Say yes!"

"How can I refuse?" She gave Chase an annoyed look. "Do you always have to get your own way?"

He smiled meltingly. "If I don't, I keep on trying."

Chestnut Street, near Alexandra's apartment, was the heart of the Marina shopping district. It was lined with small stores, coffeehouses, restaurants and other businesses, something to appeal to every segment of the diverse population of the neighborhood.

The ice-cream parlor was crowded with teenagers and families with small children, grouped around little round tables littered with paper napkins. The noise level was high, as raised voices competed with a background of rock music.

The older woman sitting at a table in the corner was an unlikely customer in a place like this. She was perhaps in her late fifties and impeccably groomed. Her expensive gray silk suit was designed to be tastefully unobtrusive, but it stood out among the jeans and sweatshirts of the other occupants.

She didn't seem to notice the people or the noise. Her eyes were trained on the door. When Chase entered, their eyes met. Then her gaze shifted to Willie and her detachment vanished. A hint of tears glistened in her eyes as they wandered over his features.

"It's really crowded, isn't it?" Alexandra commented.

"I see a place!" Willie darted over to an empty table in the middle of the room.

The large menu listed a variety of ice-cream concoctions with fancy names like Choc O' Mint Surprise and Caramel

Nut Whirl. Willie wanted the whole menu read to him before he would make up his mind.

"They have hamburgers, too," Alexandra said to Chase. "Why don't you order one? You haven't had dinner yet."

"I'm not hungry," he answered absently.

She glanced at him with a frown. Chase seemed suddenly tense, and he was acting strangely. When Willie started to scramble into a chair, Chase had suggested a different one, facing the back of the room.

Willie finally made up his mind. He selected a sundae called the Daily Double. It came with two scoops of ice cream, two different toppings, plus whipped cream and chopped nuts.

Alexandra protested vigorously. "He shouldn't eat all that!"

"I'm sure he won't," Chase answered.

"If he does and he gets sick, are you going to come over in the middle of the night and clean up after him?"

It was the kind of question that usually brought a mischievous reply. But Chase merely said, "Don't worry about it."

After a moment's hesitation, she asked, "Is anything wrong?"

His gaze finally focused on her. "I hope you won't think so."

"I don't understand."

"You might be angry at me for this, but it's something I had to do." Chase stood and walked over to the table where the older woman was sitting. He returned with her and said, "I'd like you to meet my mother, Estelle Mainwaring. This is Alexandra Reynolds—and Willie," he told the woman.

"I can tell," she said softly, gazing at the little boy with a mixture of love and sorrow. "I'd know him anywhere."

Willie looked at her curiously. "Are you really Uncle Chase's mommy?"

"Yes." She smiled, warding off tears.

"My mommy went away someplace."

As Estelle answered him, Alexandra whispered fiercely to Chase, "How could you do such a thing?"

"You left me no choice. I asked you to let her see him, and you kept putting me off."

"For *her* sake! We've been through all this. You're strong, you can take it if Willie isn't who you think he is. Imagine what heartbreak you might be setting her up for."

"I'm not wrong, but Mother is strong, too. You'll find out."

Estelle Mainwaring's patrician face showed no signs of the trouble Alexandra knew she'd had with her younger son. Perhaps he was responsible for the dusting of silver in her dark hair, but she was the kind of woman who didn't look for sympathy. Her calm air of invincibility reminded Alexandra of Chase. He looked like his mother. They had the same high cheekbones and direct gaze, the same elegance.

"Forgive my manners." Estelle finally turned away from Willie and extended her hand to Alexandra. "It's so good to meet you, my dear. Chase has told me so much about you."

"Most of it bad, I'll bet." Alexandra laughed.

"Not at all. He told me what a caring person you are. I can't tell you how grateful I am to you for taking such good care of my...of Willie."

"Mrs. Mainwaring," Alexandra began hesitantly.

"Please, call me Estelle."

"I'd be happy to, but I wish we'd met under different circumstances. Chase must have told you why I didn't want to bring Willie to see you, why I thought it would be better to wait."

"Uncle Chase said you have stairs in your house and I can go up and down them," Willie said. "But I can't slide down the banister. Does Uncle Chase live in your house, too?''

''Not anymore, but he used to. His tin soldiers are still on a shelf, and there's a basketball hoop attached to a wall in the garden. Maybe you could come over and play someday.''

''Yes, I wanna do that. Can I, Alex?''

''I don't see why not,'' she answered. She'd done all she could to shield Chase and his mother, but Estelle had the same tunnel vision as her son. Neither believed there was a possibility they could be wrong.

The waitress brought their order and Chase ordered coffee for his mother, which was all she wanted.

After the waitress had left, Chase said to Alexandra, ''How about taking Willie for a visit tomorrow? It's Saturday and you don't have to work.''

''I suppose that would be all right,'' she answered.

''I'd love to have you, but don't let my son pressure you, my dear,'' Estelle said. ''He can be quite insistent about getting his own way.''

''You don't have to worry about Alex.'' Chase grinned. ''Nobody can talk her into anything she doesn't want to do.''

''I used to believe that,'' Alexandra said wryly. ''But that was before I locked horns with you.''

''If I was really that persuasive, both our lives would have been more eventful,'' he answered mischievously.

She slanted a glance at his mother before saying tartly, ''I don't think I could take any more excitement in my life.''

''Have you heard anything at all from his mother?'' Estelle asked, nodding toward Willie.

''Not a word, which really disturbs me. I'm sure she'd contact me if she could.''

''Was she a nice person?'' Estelle asked wistfully.

"I didn't really get to know her, but I can tell you she was a good mother."

Chase gripped his mother's hand. "And she loved Bill."

Willie looked up from his ice cream. "My daddy's name is Bill. I wish he and Mommy would come home. When will they, Alex?"

As she hesitated, looking for an answer that wouldn't raise his hopes, Chase said, "I heard the circus is in town. Would you like to go?"

Willie's eyes shone. "Yes! I've never been to a circus. When can we go?"

"We have to clear it with Alex. Would Sunday afternoon be all right?" he asked her.

"If we go to your mother's tomorrow and the circus on Sunday, when will I manage to get to the dry cleaner and the market and a dozen other places?" she asked helplessly. "Weekends are the only chance I have."

"I'll run errands for you tomorrow morning," Chase promised.

"I bet you've never done any of those things for *yourself*," she scoffed.

"Then it's time I learned. I'm sure I can find my way to the dry cleaner and back."

"No doubt, but you can't get a manicure for me."

"That's true." He paused before saying in a casual voice, "You don't have to come with us if you don't want to. You'll probably get a lot more done by yourself."

"I couldn't let Willie go anywhere without me," she answered promptly.

Chase frowned. "We might not agree on everything, but do you honestly think I'd do anything to hurt him?"

"I'm sure you wouldn't," she said quickly.

"Well, then?"

Alexandra knew she could trust Chase with Willie, so why was she so reluctant to let him take the boy without her? The answer was something she didn't like to admit. That she looked forward to being with Chase.

After noticing her troubled expression, Estelle said gently, "You don't have to come over tomorrow. We can make it another time."

"No, it's all right." Alexandra made up her mind.

Chase was stimulating company. What woman wouldn't want to be with him? It didn't mean anything, so why not indulge herself? The weekend promised to be a lot more interesting than having her nails done.

"Does that mean you'll come with us to Mother's house tomorrow?" Chase asked.

"If you're serious about doing my errands." She grinned. "I'm giving the women at the Laundromat a gift."

"That's the first flattering thing you've ever said to me." He chuckled.

As Estelle watched them banter back and forth, the fine lines of strain in her face relaxed.

"Will you give us lunch tomorrow, Mother?" Chase asked.

"I'll be happy to." Estelle included Alexandra in her smile. "I hope this will be the beginning of many of them."

Chapter Six

The Mainwaring house was in Pacific Heights, a prestigious section of San Francisco where most of the homes were surrounded by brick walls or high wrought-iron fences. Estelle's house looked like a palace. Broad steps led to a massive front door that was in scale with the rest of the building.

As they got out of the car that Saturday, Willie clutched Chase's hand. "Is this where your mommy lives?" he asked in a subdued voice, staring at the Italianate mansion.

Alexandra shared his awe as Chase opened the iron gate and led them inside. She'd known he was wealthy, but this was serious money. It became even more apparent, when a butler in a dark suit opened the front door.

"Good afternoon, sir," the man greeted Chase, flicking the barest glance at Alexandra and Willie. "Your mother is waiting for you in the morning room."

"Is he your daddy?" Willie asked Chase.

"No, this is Joseph." He smiled. "Joseph has lived with

us since I was a boy. This is Miss Reynolds and Willie," Chase said to the older man.

The butler nodded gravely to Alexandra, but his formal manner softened as he looked at the child. "He's the picture of his father, sir."

Chase squeezed the man's shoulder in a silent moment of shared emotion before saying, "You don't have to announce us."

Alexandra stared avidly at all the beautiful rooms opening off a central hall, as she and Willie accompanied Chase to the back of the house. The rooms were furnished elegantly, which she had expected, but they were also filled with light. This house was no museum where the drapes were kept drawn to keep delicate fabrics from fading.

The morning room was the sunniest of all. The octagonal-shaped area was filled with greenery and the sparkling glass windows looked out on a large walled yard. Estelle was sitting at a round marble table, reading the morning newspaper. She looked up with a smile that included all of them, as Chase kissed her cheek.

"Here we are, Mother, right on time," he said. "I know Margaret has a fit when guests are late for meals."

"You aren't a guest, darling, and she's always too delighted to see you to make a fuss. Margaret is our cook," Estelle explained to Alexandra. "She's been with us for years."

"Your house is lovely," Alexandra said. "And what a luxury to have such a big backyard in the heart of the city."

"I think that's part of the reason I never wanted to move. Even though the house is much too big for me now," Estelle acknowledged.

"Don't let her fool you. Mother isn't some lonely recluse rattling around here alone. She entertains constantly, and not just stuffy affairs for the geriatric set," Chase teased. "Some of her friends are my contemporaries, friends of mine actually."

"They're married and have children," Estelle replied. "If you won't provide me with grandchildren, I have to settle for being a surrogate grandmother."

"I should have quit while I was ahead." He laughed.

His mother was wise not to wait for Chase to provide her with grandchildren, Alexandra thought cynically. He liked playing the role of father—but not husband.

Willie was bored by the adult conversation. "Can I see Uncle Chase's soldiers?" he asked.

"Of course you may, darling." Estelle rose and extended her hand to the little boy.

"I'd like to come, too, if I may," Alexandra said. She didn't care about the soldiers, but it was a way to see the upstairs without asking.

"By all means," Estelle answered. "I haven't used that wing since the boys left, but I think it's reasonably presentable."

"Alex won't look under the bed for dust bunnies," Chase said as he trailed along after them.

She was sure there weren't any. The upstairs was as sparkling clean as the rest of the house. Chase's former bedroom was actually a corner suite. The furnishings had evidently been changed. It looked more like a guest room than a boy's room now, but his toy soldiers were still arranged on the upper shelves of a bookcase, and there were other reminders of Chase as a youngster.

He picked up a trophy that sat on a desk. A gold figure of a man with a tennis racket was attached to a wooden base. "Don't you think it's time this got tossed out, Mother? I won it back in high school."

Willie's attention was attracted to the statue. "My daddy's got one of those," he said excitedly. "He lets me play with it whenever I want."

Chase's gaze met his mother's over the little boy's head. He cleared his throat before saying to the child, "You can have this one if you like."

Willie was ecstatic. "Then me and Daddy will both have one. I'll show it to him as soon as he comes home."

Alexandra knew how painful this must be for Chase and his mother. If Brenda's story was true, Willie would never get that chance. Before Willie could ask again when his father was coming home, she said quickly, "Look at those toy soldiers, Willie, aren't they neat?"

His attention was instantly distracted. While Chase and Estelle lifted them down for him, Alexandra drifted over to the door. She was looking down the hallway when Chase came over to join her.

"This can't be very interesting for you," he said. "Would you like to go downstairs?"

"Are you trying to get rid of me?"

"Never. I used to dream about having a girl like you in my bedroom."

"Now you're grown-up and it's a reality," she said lightly.

"I didn't picture having my mother and my nephew here at the same time," he joked. When Alexandra's smile faded, he said, "How can you still have any doubts about Willie?"

She evaded the question with one of her own. "Was your brother's room up here, also?"

"He had the other corner suite. Come on, I'll show you."

The doors opening off the hall led to guest rooms, an upstairs den and various utility closets. Bill's former room was a duplicate of Chase's, except that it hadn't been converted to a guest suite.

It was exactly as Alexandra imagined it had been when Bill left home. There were vestiges of his college days, pennants and posters, as well as the more contemporary books and paintings he would have acquired as a young adult. On one wall was a bulletin board filled with tacked up photos from years past, judging by the clothes and hair-dos.

"Mother never wanted to change anything in here," Chase said soberly. "She always hoped..." his voice trailed off.

Alexandra moved over to look at the snapshots. "Which one is your brother?"

Chase pointed silently to several photos of a young man who was either laughing or had a smile on his face. Bill Mainwaring was handsome and obviously personable. There was a slight family resemblance to Chase, but Bill's hair was lighter and he wasn't as tall. Alexandra looked for some resemblance to Willie, but she couldn't see it in the small, not always in focus snaps.

"These are pictures of Bill when he was little," Chase said. Next to the bulletin board was a long frame containing a montage of studio shots of a small boy at various ages. "Mother hung it in here after I persuaded her to take it out of her own room."

Alexandra now understood why Chase was so convinced that Willie was his nephew. The little boy in the photographs looked strikingly like Willie, the same laughing eyes, the same curly hair.

"Bill's hair was the color of Willie's when he was that age," Chase said gruffly. "It darkened as he grew older."

"He was a beautiful child," Alexandra remarked non-committally.

"Can't you see the resemblance?" Chase exclaimed.

"Children tend to look alike when they're little. They're all sweet and cuddly—like Willie," she added deliberately.

"I give up!" Chase's strong face was filled with frustration. "You refuse to believe your own eyes."

"And you find it impossible to be objective," she said quietly. "I agree that Brenda contacted you in good faith. But has it occurred to you that if she was mistaken about her relationship to you, your brother might still be alive somewhere?"

"Don't you think I want to believe that? I'd give anything if it were true! But there are too many indications that Brenda was telling the truth. Why would she have called me, if she didn't have good reason to think Bill was my brother?"

"I wish I had the answer." Alexandra sighed.

"Lunch is ready, children," Estelle called.

"They aren't children," Willie giggled. "They're big grown-up people."

"That's true," Estelle said as they all walked down the stairs. "But your Uncle Chase will always be my little boy. Even though I can't tell him what to do anymore," she added with a smile at her son.

"What do you want him to do?" Willie asked.

"Nothing much." Chase chuckled. "Just get married and produce lots of grandchildren."

"One would be a nice beginning," his mother said dryly. "Preferably before you have to bring him to see me in a nursing home." When they reached the ground floor, she said to Willie, "Come into the kitchen with me. I want you to meet Margaret."

"I'll say hello, too," Chase said, taking Alexandra's hand to bring her along.

The large kitchen was as well equipped as the ones in top restaurants. The six-burner stove had a copper hood and long counters held every kind of small appliance.

Margaret was a short, plump woman with graying hair. She was about Estelle's age and had her employer's assurance, if not her elegance. This was clearly Margaret's domain, but she unbent for Willie.

Touching his hair lightly, she said in a softened voice, "It's like seeing Master William all over again."

After giving Alexandra a triumphant look, Chase introduced her to the cook. "What are you giving us for lunch,

Margaret?" he asked. "Your mushroom crepes with mornay sauce? Or did you make my favorite, lobster soufflé?"

"Those aren't suitable for a child," she scolded.

"What's wrong with teaching him to be a junior gourmet?"

"Whatever Margaret made will be delicious," Estelle said. "Let's go sit down and get out of her way."

Lunch was served in the morning room rather than the large, formal dining room. The table was set with colorful place mats and a centerpiece of fragrant sweet peas in a ceramic pot.

Joseph served the first course, a delicious cream of tomato soup in thin china bowls. But Chase raised his eyebrows at the main course. The plate Joseph set in front of him held small triangular sandwiches with trimmed crusts, surrounding a molded fruit salad on a lettuce leaf.

"This is a ladies' lunch, not a meal for two he-men," he complained.

"I like it," Willie said. "Will you cut my sandwiches like this, Alex? They don't lose their insides like the big ones."

"It won't hurt you to eat lightly for one day," Chase's mother told him. "You look as if you've gained a bit of weight."

Alexandra couldn't imagine where. Chase's tight jeans clung smoothly to his flat stomach and lean hips. The Harvard sweatshirt he wore over them was baggy, but there was no bulge underneath it. He looked fit and trim.

Staring at the finger sandwiches disdainfully, he said, "I didn't have to play handball all morning for this."

"Is that how you stay in shape?" Alexandra asked. "I keep promising myself I'll join a gym, but I never seem to find the time. And that was *before* Willie came into my life."

"It must be difficult to work and take care of a child,"

Estelle remarked. "I don't know how you young women do it."

"I guess you become more organized," Alexandra said. "And of course most women have time to plan for a child. I'm still just sort of playing it by ear."

"That's something we need to talk about," Chase said. "Things can't go on this way much longer."

She cast a covert glance at Willie, who was happily digging into his fruit salad. "I don't think this is the time to discuss it."

"You always have some excuse," he said sharply.

"They aren't excuses, they're reasoned judgments," she answered, just as sharply.

Estelle also glanced at Willie, who had looked up at their raised voices. "Alexandra is right," she said. "This is not the time."

"I've tried being reasonable and it doesn't work." Chase's jaw set grimly. "You might be willing to wait indefinitely, I'm not."

"That will do, Chase," his mother stated firmly.

Willie looked at him doubtfully. "Is Uncle Chase mad about something?" he whispered to Alexandra.

"No, honey," she said reassuringly. "Grown-ups sometimes talk loud, but it doesn't mean anything."

When Willie still seemed uncertain, Chase smiled at him. "How would you like to throw a ball around in the yard after lunch?"

Before he could answer, Estelle said, "One of my friends has her daughter and grandson visiting from New York. He's about Willie's age and I thought it might be nice if the two boys played together for a bit. Charlotte only lives a block away, and David, her grandson, is rather lonely here. Would you mind if I took Willie over there for a short time?" she asked Alexandra.

"Not at all, if he wants to go," Alexandra answered.

"Would you like to play with a little boy down the street?" she asked him.

His face lit up. "Yeah, I wanna do that! I used to play with my friend, Sean, but I haven't seen him in a long time. Can we go right now?"

"As soon as we have dessert," Estelle promised.

"I don't want any. I want to go now."

Willie was such a good child that Alexandra hadn't realized how much he missed his friends, as well as his parents. This situation was hardest on him, although he rarely complained.

The little boy was persuaded to have dessert, after Estelle explained that David was still having his own lunch.

When Willie was finished and impatient to leave, Estelle said to Alexandra, "You're welcome to come, of course, but it isn't necessary. I promise to take good care of him."

"I don't have any doubts about that." Alexandra smiled at the older woman.

"Splendid, then why don't you and Chase relax in the garden until we return?"

Alexandra didn't expect to relax with Chase after his outburst at lunch. She was prepared for a battle when they went out onto the terrace after Estelle and Willie had left. But Chase confounded her, as usual.

"It was very nice of you to let Mother spend a little time alone with Willie," he said. "I know she appreciates it."

"I'm not *trying* to be difficult, Chase."

"You mean it just comes naturally?" he teased.

"That's better," she said dryly. "For a minute I thought you were beginning to like me."

"I don't know *how* I feel about you." He gave her a puzzled look. "One minute I want to knock some sense into your stubborn head and the next minute I want to kiss you silly."

"Do I get a choice?"

"That depends." He moved closer. "Which would you choose?"

"It's a tough call." She grinned.

He cupped her cheek in his palm. "Would a sample help?"

She was mesmerized by the glow in his eyes, seduced by the sun-warmed scent of his skin, the hand curving around her cheek. As his head descended slowly, she could see each spiky black lash that fringed his blue eyes. It wasn't until his arm curled around her waist that she summoned the willpower to move away.

Attempting a light tone, she turned toward the garden saying, "What would the neighbors think?"

"They can't see over the wall." He snaked an arm around her waist and drew her back against him. Lifting her long hair, he strung a line of kisses across the nape of her neck.

The intimate contact with his hard body made her legs tremble. How long could she keep on resisting him? But then Chase said something that brought her to her senses.

"I just decided I'd rather kiss you silly than try to reason with you," he murmured.

Alexandra removed his arm and turned to face him. "It doesn't pay to get overconfident," she said acidly.

He looked at her blankly. "What are you talking about?"

"Don't pretend innocence," she snapped. "We both know why you're being so seductive all of a sudden. It's quite a change from the temper tantrum you threw at lunch. But you can knock it off, because it won't work. I'm keeping Willie until I have a good reason to turn him over to somebody else."

"Who appointed you judge and jury?" Chase asked furiously. "You won't believe the evidence when it stares you in the face."

"You have no hard evidence," she answered, just as

angrily. "Only a few photographs, a tennis trophy and an alleged phone call."

"Are you doubting my word?"

"Let's just say, I'd have a lot more respect for you if you didn't try to use dirty tricks to get what you want."

His eyes shot sparks of blue fire. "When I tried to kiss you just now it was because I wanted to—although at this moment I can't imagine why."

"Forgive me if I don't believe you."

"Why doesn't that surprise me?" he asked witheringly. "You wouldn't believe today is Saturday if *I* told you."

"You'll have to admit you did try to influence me."

"Not the way you're accusing me of."

"Oh, no? When we first met, you found it difficult to say a civil word to me."

"You weren't exactly gracious, yourself."

"Maybe not, but I didn't do an about-face overnight. You expect me to believe you changed your mind about me that fast?" Alexandra demanded.

Chase looked uncomfortable. "I will admit my attorney advised me to...be pleasant."

"And you decided that making love to me would be even faster," she said scornfully.

A muscle bunched at the point of his square jaw. He forced down his anger and looked her over insolently. "It's been known to work," he drawled.

Alexandra had been aware of his motivation from the beginning, but it hurt to hear him admit it. "At least you're finally being honest. I appreciate that," she said stiffly.

Her mobile face expressed more than she realized. Chase stared at her moodily for a moment, before jamming his hands into his pockets. "I don't know why we always end up in a shouting match. We both want what's best for Willie. We just have different opinions on what that is."

"I'm glad you realize it's nothing personal."

After a moment's hesitation he replied, "On my side,

either. But we can't go on like this. Willie's future has to be decided.''

"I keep hoping Brenda will come back or the police will find her.''

"That's beginning to seem unlikely. So where do we go from here?''

"After meeting your mother and seeing your home, I have to agree that Willie will be better off with you,'' Alexandra said reluctantly. It was one of the most difficult decisions she'd ever made. Willie had become very dear to her, but she had to think of him rather than herself.

Triumph blazed on Chase's face. "We can have him?''

"I don't have the authority to decide that. Your attorney can advise you, but I'm sure you'll have to go to court. It won't be a slam dunk, either. Danny is almost certain to make an opposing claim. He's been pressuring me to let Willie stay with him for a few days.''

"You don't honestly believe his story?''

"No, I never did. It's too bizarre. I can't imagine why he wants Willie, but it makes me uneasy.''

"Don't worry about it. My lawyers will have him laughed out of court—if it goes that far, which I doubt.''

Alexandra smiled wryly. "I know it's silly, but I feel like a mother who's giving her child up for adoption.''

Chase looked at her curiously. "Did you really plan on keeping Willie? I know there are a lot of loving single mothers, but children require a big commitment.''

"I guess I didn't think that far ahead. I simply got attached to him very quickly. He's a dear little boy.''

"Willie is a charmer, all right, just like his dad.''

"There's one thing that bothers me,'' she said slowly. "If for some reason Willie isn't who you think he is, what will you do then? I won't allow him to be put into foster care, where he might be bounced from family to family like a tennis ball.''

"I don't share your doubts about his identity, but if I

should happen to be wrong, it won't make any difference. You aren't the only one who's become attached to him. Willie will have all the love he deserves."

"That makes me feel better."

Chase gave her a dazzling smile. "Then we can call a halt to the hostilities?"

"I'd like that. Contrary to what you think, I always wanted to be friends."

"From the very beginning?" he teased.

"Well, maybe not." She smiled. "We got off to a bad start, and everything went downhill from then on."

"It wasn't all bad. We had a lot of fun together when we weren't fighting—at least I did."

"Winning has made you charitable," Alexandra observed dryly.

"I don't think of it as winning or losing," he protested. "My personal feelings never entered into it."

"I know." She turned away and walked onto the lawn. "I suppose you'll want to speak to your attorney first thing in the morning. I know how impatient you are, but he'll probably tell you that Willie has to remain with me until the court approves custody of him. I hope that won't cause problems between us again. I'm sure with your connections it won't take long, and then this whole thing will be over."

He gave her a dissatisfied look. "You're making me feel as if I'm taking advantage of you. I thought we were in agreement."

"We are. I just meant our lives would return to normal."

"We'll still keep in touch." He glanced at her obliquely. "I know you'll want to see Willie."

"I'd like to, but you never know what will happen," she said vaguely.

"Is it because of me? Have I made your life so miserable that you don't want to see me again after this is all settled and you're not obliged to?"

"Certainly not. But there won't be any reason for us to see each other."

"I thought we agreed to be friends. We've been through a lot together. You don't just drop a friend for no good reason."

Why did Chase want to be friends? Maybe because he'd never had a female friend and it was a novelty, Alexandra thought cynically. Or perhaps he could only be friendly with a woman he wasn't romantically interested in. Neither reason was very palatable.

"We could go out to dinner once in a while," he said persuasively.

"Sure, why not?" It was easier than arguing, and if Chase did call it wouldn't be for long.

Estelle brought Willie home a short time later. The little boy couldn't wait to tell Alex what a good time he'd had.

"David and me played hide-and-seek and I won! I found him three times and he only found me twice. Then we played some more games and after that Mrs. Van Ailen gave us ice cream."

"I hope it didn't spoil your appetite," Chase commented. "I'm looking forward to an early dinner."

Willie barely heard him. "And tomorrow Auntie Estelle is gonna take me to a birthday party. She says it has to be all right with you, Alex. It is, isn't it?"

"I thought we were going to the circus tomorrow," Chase reminded him.

The little boy was torn by indecision. "Could we go the next day? I wanna go both places."

"I suppose that could be arranged," Chase said indulgently. "We can't go on Monday, but we can postpone the circus until next weekend."

"Oh, boy. Super!"

"Willie had such a good time today, that I thought he'd enjoy being with a group of children," Estelle said.

"Yes, it's something he's obviously missed," Alexandra agreed. "I think it will be good for him."

"I'm glad you agree. You're welcome to come, too, Chase. The party is being given by your friends, Patty and Doug. A lot of the fathers attend."

"I'm not a father. Or is that the point you're making?" he teased.

"Not at all. I simply thought that since…" Her voice trailed off as she glanced at Willie, reminding Chase that the boy didn't have a father.

"I'll be happy to come," he said soberly. "How about you, Alex?"

"I lack the same credentials you do. But I'm a pushover for birthday parties—as long as I'm not the one who's getting a year older." She laughed.

"You're just a youngster," Estelle assured her. "Have you ever seen such beautiful skin?" she asked her son.

"Never. It's positively pearly. I believe I mentioned that to her once." Chase grinned.

"That's nice," Estelle said approvingly. "It's always pleasant to get compliments."

"He's quite good at them. He must get a lot of practice," Alexandra remarked with an innocent expression.

"Can I go inside and play with the soldiers?" Willie asked.

Chase looked at his watch. "For about half an hour, and then we'll go out for an early dinner."

"I'm not hungry," Willie said.

"He had a big dish of ice cream and several cookies at Charlotte's," Estelle said. "I'm not surprised that he isn't hungry."

"Oh, great!" Chase groaned. "That minuscule lunch you gave me wore off long ago."

"Can I go?" Willie asked impatiently.

"Yes, run along, dear." When the little boy had gone inside, Estelle said to Chase, "Why don't you take Alex-

andra out to dinner? I'm not hungry, either, so Willie and
I can have something to eat later on. He can even stay the
night," she added casually.

Alexandra looked doubtful. "It might be a little too
much excitement for him. He's going to have another big
day tomorrow."

"Alex is right. Maybe tomorrow night would be better,"
Chase said.

"I hate to keep saying no, but that would be a problem
for me," she said. "A friend of mine takes care of Willie
during the week. I won't have time to pick him up here
and take him to Mandy's before going to work."

"I didn't know he spent the day somewhere else," Chase
exclaimed.

"You were the one who told me an office was no place
for a child," she answered evasively, not wanting him to
know she'd concealed the fact deliberately.

Estelle looked disappointed, but she said, "You two can
still go out to dinner. It would really be a favor to me,"
she told Alexandra. "I don't want to hear Chase complain
about his lunch anymore."

"Okay, I've said my last word on the subject." He
chuckled. "I'll go home and change clothes, as long as we
aren't going to a pizza parlor or the equivalent."

"I have to change, too," Alexandra said.

"I'll drop you at home first, and come back for you."

As she thanked Estelle for lunch, Alexandra wondered
how she'd let herself be maneuvered into dinner with
Chase. She knew the older woman's motive; Estelle wanted
Willie all to herself. But why had Chase gone along with
her plan? Because he wanted to make his mother happy?
Probably it was because he decided it was expedient to
maintain friendly relations until the court appointed him
Willie's guardian, Alexandra thought sardonically.

Alexandra took a quick shower when she got home. The
telephone rang while she was rushing to apply her makeup

and get dressed. She only answered it because she thought Chase might be calling with a change of plans—hopefully to say he'd be a little late. She could use the extra time. When Alexandra heard Danny's voice, she was sorry she hadn't let the phone ring.

"I've been trying to get in touch with you," he said in a flinty voice.

"I know. I've been terribly busy. In fact I'm getting ready to go out right now."

"How long do you think you can get away with brushing me off?"

"I'm sorry I haven't had time to talk to you, but you don't have to be unpleasant about it," she said coolly.

"You don't know just how unpleasant I can get, lady!"

"Are you threatening me?"

Danny tried to control his temper. "Maybe that was a little out of line. But wouldn't you be steamed? First you tell me I can have Willie for a few days, and then I find out it's all a con. I can't even get you on the phone."

"Perhaps I should have talked to you," she admitted grudgingly. "But I never promised to let you have Willie. I merely said I'd think about it."

"That's not the way I heard it. I'm through dancing around with you. I want that kid!"

"You have no right to him. You haven't provided me with a shred of evidence to back up your highly unbelievable story—and that's putting it charitably." Alexandra was having trouble with her own temper.

"I suppose you believe every word Mainwaring tells you," Danny sneered. "Money sure talks, doesn't it?"

"Not to me. Chase's money or lack of it doesn't concern me."

"Give me a break! Is that why you and the kid went out with him last night and again today?"

"How did you know that?" she demanded.

"It doesn't matter. If you're not playing house with him, you'll give me the same consideration you're giving him."

"Your crude insinuation is both insulting and untrue," Alexandra said icily. "It also reinforces my opinion of you. I wouldn't trust you to lead Willie out of a burning building!"

"You better reconsider or you're going to be one sorry chick," he said furiously. "I'll give you until tomorrow to change your mind." He hung up before she could answer.

Alexandra replaced the receiver slowly. The change in Danny was chilling. She'd never cared for him, but it hadn't occurred to her that he was potentially dangerous. He must have been the one who searched her apartment and had her followed. She hadn't imagined those things. How else would he know where she went and who she was with?

The problem was, she had no proof. She hadn't told anyone but Mandy about the break-in, and she hadn't even told *her* about being tailed. The police might think she was being dramatic. Even if they believed her, there was nothing they could do without some evidence besides her say-so.

She could tell Chase, but his reaction would be predictable and immediate. He'd beat Danny to a pulp. Not only would he get into trouble, it would ruin his chances of convincing the court that he was a responsible guardian for Willie.

There didn't seem to be a solution, at least not one she could think of at that moment. It was an unpleasant situation, but what could Danny actually do? The courts had given her temporary custody of Willie, and even had she wanted to, she couldn't just hand the boy over to Danny. He must understand that. She intended to be on her guard—that was only sensible—but there was no need to panic.

Alexandra would have changed her mind, if she'd heard Danny's conversation with his boss.

Danny's phone rang only moments after he'd hung up on her. He answered it with a snarl, ready to vent his anger on the first person he encountered. "Yeah? This better be important, because I got other things on my mind."

"I hope one of them is concern for your health," Victor Karpov answered ominously. "I'd say it was in a very precarious state."

"Oh...hi, boss. I didn't know it was you. Some guys have been calling me to whine about their gambling losses. I was just giving them the brush. We're taking in a bundle at the club," Danny said eagerly.

"Two million dollars?"

"Well, no. But give us time." He forced a laugh.

"I've given you more than enough time and gotten nothing back to show for it. You've run out of time," Karpov stated.

"We agreed on a week!" Danny said in alarm.

"That was your idea, not mine."

"But you said it was okay. You went along with me. It's only been a couple of days," Danny babbled. "I just need a few more."

"How long do you think you can string me along? If you'd made any progress, you would have reported it to me. Instead of that, I have to track you down. You don't even give me the courtesy of returning my phone calls."

"You mean the one you made to me at the club last night?" Danny pretended innocence, although he'd been ducking the other man's calls. "I was just about to call you when the phone rang, honest to God! It must be mental telepathy or something."

"That would involve two fully functional minds," Karpov said bitingly. "How about the other messages I left for you?"

"Did you leave more? I didn't get them, I swear! I'll have somebody's head for this. It's just goddamned incompetence and I won't put up with it!"

"Spare me the histrionics. We both know you've been avoiding me, which means your bumbling attempts to get the boy have failed. I approve of using him as bait—it's the one good idea you've had."

"It'll work, boss!"

"I know it will, but not by sweet-talking some broad. From now on we'll do this thing my way. Is that understood?" Karpov asked in a steely voice.

"Sure, boss, anything you say," Danny agreed hurriedly.

"It's very simple—just snatch the boy."

"We talked about that as an alternative—" Danny began.

Karpov cut him off. "I said do it—now!"

"If you say so, but that might take a couple of days, too. The only time Alex took the kid out at night, she had that Mainwaring jerk along with her. He's a big guy, looks like he used to play football."

"Why do you have to wait for her to go out with the child? Simply take him from her apartment at gunpoint. Do I have to tell you how to do your job?"

Danny was fairly certain that Alexandra would refuse to let him in after his recent tirade. Why had he allowed himself to blow his top? Besides that, Karpov's plan had one big flaw. Danny couldn't do the job personally, because Alexandra might recognize him—even in a disguise. He didn't intend to jeopardize his own sweet operation, but of course he couldn't tell Karpov that.

"Okay, boss, I'll handle it your way," Danny said.

"And soon," Karpov said in measured tones.

Alexandra's nasty confrontation with Danny made her late. When Chase rang the bell, she ran to answer the door in her bathrobe. He raised an eyebrow at her bare feet and the long honey-colored hair pinned haphazardly on top of her head.

"Weren't we supposed to be going out to dinner?" he asked.

"I got a phone call that held me up, but I'll be ready in a couple of minutes," she promised.

"I thought maybe you had more interesting plans for the evening." He grinned. "I'll be glad to swap my plans for yours."

"You've been complaining about how hungry you are, so there's no danger of that." She took the pins out of her hair and it fell in a shining curtain around her shoulders.

"A man has other appetites," he murmured, moving toward her.

"If you don't stop clowning around I'll never get ready." She turned and went into the bedroom. "Where are we going for dinner?" she called.

"I made a reservation at the Topaz Room. Is that all right?"

"It's fabulous!" The restaurant he'd chosen was one of the most expensive in the city. "I just wish you'd told me sooner. I don't know what to wear."

"Whatever will take the least time. It's only dinner. You don't have to get all gussied up."

"Are you always this cranky when you're hungry?" she teased.

"No, mainly when I can't get anywhere with a beautiful woman." He chuckled.

Chase was watching the news on television when Alexandra joined him. His expression changed when he turned and saw her. She was wearing a short red dress draped to one side, sheer red panty hose and spike-heeled sandals.

"Wow!" he exclaimed. "You look positively incendiary."

"Is that good or bad?"

"It's fantastic." His eyes traveled over her admiringly. She handed him a strand of pearls and turned her back to him, lifting her long hair. "Will you fasten these for me? They have a tricky clasp. I always have trouble with it."

Chase had difficulty, too. As he fumbled with the clasp, Alexandra began to have second thoughts about asking for assistance. His breath warmed her skin as he lowered his head for a closer look, and his long fingers felt seductive on her neck. She was uncomfortably aware of how close their bodies were.

"Stop fidgeting," he commanded. "This thing really is tricky."

She forced herself to stand still, but when he finally got the necklace clasped, Chase leaned down and kissed the nape of her neck. A ripple ran down her spine and Alexandra skittered away as if he'd branded her.

He looked at her with amusement. "Is that a ticklish spot?"

She nodded, grateful to him for providing her with an excuse. "I don't like my ears nibbled, either."

"It's nice to have all this information. I only hope I get to use it someday," he remarked dryly. Before she could reply, Chase put an arm around her shoulders and led her toward the door. "If you're finally ready, let's go eat. I'm starving."

Chapter Seven

By the time they arrived at the Topaz Room, Alexandra had put Danny and his vague threats out of her mind. Chase looked especially handsome in a dark gray suit and a blue shirt that matched his eyes. More than one woman stared at him as he led Alexandra to a window table in the elegant restaurant with a view of the city.

After the waiter had brought them each a drink, Chase raised his glass in a toast. "Here's to the end of all our problems."

Alexandra dutifully raised her own glass, but she was abruptly reminded that their problems weren't over. Danny was a menacing shadow hanging over them.

Chase caught the troubled expression that crossed her expressive face. "Is anything wrong, Alex?"

"No, nothing." She turned her head to look out the window. "Isn't that a beautiful view?"

"Don't change the subject." He reached over and took her hand. "Are you feeling badly about giving up Willie?"

"I'll miss him," she admitted. "He changed my life drastically."

"Look on the bright side. It should be a lot easier now. You've had to put your personal life on hold. There must be some very frustrated men out there," Chase remarked casually.

"Dozens of them, all threatening suicide if I don't go out with them." She smiled.

"I'm serious."

"You don't think I am?"

"I think you could fill a man's head so completely there wouldn't be room for anyone else," Chase said in a deepened voice.

"You're a man, and I wasn't enough to drive Willie out of your mind." She was careful to keep her voice light.

"What can I say to convince you that my feelings for the two of you are quite different?"

"I believe *that*," she said dryly.

"You know very well what I mean. I'm not here tonight because of Willie."

That was debatable, but it would be futile to pursue it. "Then let's not talk about him. You had a life, too, before you found out about him. Tell me about all the women who are waiting impatiently to get you back."

"Why would I talk about other women, when I'm with the loveliest one of all?"

"I'll tell you about mine, if you tell me about yours," Alexandra said mischievously.

Chase laughed. "It's a deal, if you go first. Who was your first date?"

"You're really going back in time. Okay, his name was Arnold Watkins and he was the handsomest boy in the seventh grade."

"Come on! How could he be, with a name like Arnold Watkins?"

"Names are simply something wished on you by your

parents. They don't have anything to do with who you are. Cary Grant was just as handsome when his name was Archibald Leach.''

"Then why did he change it?"

"Maybe because it wouldn't fit on a theater marquee.''

"Okay, I'll buy that, if only because I want to hear the rest of the story.''

"It has a sad ending. My best friend, Tiffany Rogers, made a play for Arnold and he dumped me.''

"What a jerk! He probably grew up to be an auditor for the Internal Revenue Service. You were well rid of him.''

"Now it's your turn," Alexandra said. "But I want to hear about your more recent conquests.''

"A gentleman doesn't kiss and tell.''

"I wasn't asking for the intimate details," she protested.

"But you're positive that all of my dates are filled with them. I don't know where you got the idea that I spend all my time making love.''

"You talk about it a lot," she said defensively.

"Some people say talking is a substitute for doing." He laughed.

"I don't think you practice celibacy.''

"I'm an adult male, Alex, not a schoolboy. Are *you* a virgin?''

Her cheeks bloomed like roses. "That's a very personal question!''

"I didn't object when you commented on *my* sex life," he said calmly.

"You're right, I shouldn't have." Alexandra wondered how conversations with Chase got around to sex so often. "Let's change the subject.''

"Why does it bother you so much to talk about making love? It's the ultimate bonding between a man and a woman.''

"If they care about each other," she corrected him.

"I thought that was understood. There is no experience

quite like holding that special person in your arms and hearing her call out your name as you bring her pleasure.''

Chase's eyes held hers, urging her to fantasize along with him. It was almost impossible not to. She knew instinctively how it would be. His seductive hands would caress her nude body and encourage her to do the same to him. His skin would be smooth over hard muscles that would grow taut as his passion climbed.

With an effort, Alexandra forced herself to sit back in her chair and take a deep breath. ''I'm tempted to go to bed with you just so you'll stop trying to convince me,'' she said with a shaky laugh.

''I don't want to take you to bed. I want to make love to you. I hope one day you'll want me as much as I want you. That's the only way it would be any good.''

Before she had to answer, the waiter came over to take their order. After he left, Chase didn't return to the subject.

For the rest of the evening he was utterly charming. Alexandra was wary at first, but Chase was the perfect date. He told her funny stories and kept her so amused that the evening flew by.

When she realized what time it was, Alexandra gasped. ''I had no idea it was so late! We've been talking for hours.''

''And we didn't have a single argument,'' he teased. ''We're making progress.''

''I feel guilty for enjoying myself so much that I forgot about Willie. He should have been in bed hours ago.''

''It's too bad you didn't let Mother keep him overnight. You still can. We could call her. She'd be delighted.''

''He doesn't have his pajamas, and I told him I'd be back for him. Besides, you were the one who said he should have a routine he can count on.''

''I guess you're right,'' Chase answered reluctantly. ''I'll get the check.''

* * *

When they reached the Mainwaring house, Estelle was reading in the den, a wood-paneled room with a Persian rug and impressive oil paintings on the walls. A cheery fire in the fireplace made the room seem homey in spite of its elegance.

"I'm sorry we're so late," Alexandra apologized.

"It was my fault," Chase said. "Alex was such a good audience that I lost track of time."

"We both did," she said.

"That's quite all right," Estelle assured them. "Willie and I had a lovely time together. He ate all of his dinner and he taught me to play Go Fish."

"Where is he?" Alexandra asked, glancing around.

"He was falling asleep, so I took him upstairs and put him down on Bill's bed. Are you sure you don't want to leave him here?" Estelle asked wistfully.

As Alexandra hesitated, not knowing how to refuse the older woman, Chase said, "There will be lots of other nights, Mother. We don't want to make it harder on Alex. She's been more than generous already."

"You're right, of course," Estelle said. "His shoes are at the foot of the bed, and be sure you don't forget his teddy bear."

"We'd have to come back for it." Alexandra laughed. "He and that bear are inseparable."

"You'd better give me a blanket to wrap Willie in," Chase said. "The fog has rolled in and it's wet and chilly out."

Willie awakened when Chase lifted him, but he went back to sleep immediately, hooking an arm trustingly around Chase's neck. Alexandra followed them downstairs, carrying the little boy's shoes and teddy bear.

They could be any young couple picking up their son at Grandma's house after a night on the town, she thought poignantly. Which showed how deceiving appearances could be.

Alexandra held the sleeping child on her lap during the ride home, then Chase carried him into her apartment.

After Willie was tucked into bed they returned to the living room where Chase relaxed in an armchair, resting his head on the back and stretching out his long legs.

"This is beginning to feel like home," he commented.

"I imagine it's a lot smaller than your apartment," she said.

"The size isn't important." He smiled warmly at her. "It's whom you share your space with."

Alexandra knew Chase was just feeling mellow. He didn't want to share his space with anyone on a permanent basis.

"It must have been difficult to move into an apartment after living in your parents' big house," she remarked.

"Not really. I can leave my socks and shorts on the floor in my own place." He grinned.

"I can't imagine you doing that."

Chase was always so fastidious and well-groomed. Even this afternoon, in jeans and a sweatshirt, he'd looked like an ad for casual chic in some upscale men's magazine. His public image couldn't be that different from his private one.

"People who live alone don't have to be neat," he said. "Some of the bonuses are being able to toss your bath towel over the rod without folding it neatly and walking around the apartment in the nude. Don't tell me you never do things like that."

"My apartment might not always be as neat as I'd like it, but I certainly don't walk around naked."

"Why not?"

"I don't know why anybody would want to."

"Because it's a wonderfully free feeling. You're welcome to come over and be my roommate for a few days," he said mischievously. "I guarantee it would get rid of all your inhibitions."

"I couldn't be roomies with a man who didn't fold his towel neatly." She kept her voice light.

"I'd be willing to change my ways."

"I wouldn't want to bet on it," she answered dryly.

"Have I ever lied to you?"

"Not that I know of, but you could be so adept at it that I can't tell," she joked, rising from the couch. "I think I'll make coffee."

As she walked by his chair, Chase caught her wrist and toppled her onto his lap. "Forget the coffee," he said. "I want to talk seriously for a minute." When Alexandra tried to get up, he restrained her with an arm around her waist. "We joke around a lot, but I hope you know that when it comes to the important things, I'm dead serious."

If he was trying to get her attention, he'd succeeded! She always reacted physically to Chase—his arm around her shoulders, his hand squeezing hers. Those things didn't mean any more than this did, but the close contact with his disturbingly masculine body was making her pulse race.

"Let me up, Chase!" She struggled against his restraining arm.

"After I'm sure we understand each other." He captured her chin with his fingers, immobilizing her even more. "My family owes a great deal to you. Do you really think I'd pay you back by trying to take advantage of you?"

"I guess not," She tried to avoid looking at him, which was difficult since their faces were so close.

"That's not exactly a vote of confidence," he said wryly.

"Well, you must admit you do make a lot of suggestive remarks."

"I suppose I do, but it's difficult not to. You're very lovely." His grip on her chin loosened, but he didn't remove his hand. "I'm just sorry that I've made you uncomfortable. That was never my intention."

"I knew you were joking," she said carefully. "But I'm not good at sexual games."

"I think you'd be very good," he teased. "In fact, I think you'd be terrific."

Chase had removed both his hand and his arm. Alexandra was free to get up, but she couldn't seem to move—because she didn't want to. It was foolish and foolhardy, but this was where she wanted to be, in Chase's arms.

His teasing expression changed as he gazed down at her lambent face. Alexandra's head was pillowed on his shoulder, long lashes veiling her eyes, her lips parted invitingly.

Chase drew in his breath sharply. "Alex, darling," he said in a husky voice. "I hope I'm not getting my signals mixed."

He lowered his head slowly, almost tentatively, tantalizing her with his indecision. Alexandra flung an arm around his neck impatiently and pulled his head down. When their lips touched, she uttered a small sound of satisfaction.

Chase's eyes blazed triumphantly as he tightened the embrace, crushing her breasts against the hard wall of his chest. His mouth captured hers possessively and his tongue entered her parted lips for a probing exploration that made her entire body throb.

Alexandra clung to him with mindless desire, lost in the male magnetism of him. She'd never wanted any man with this intensity.

Chase finally dragged his mouth away and buried his face in her fragrant hair. "Sweet, adorable, little Alex. I've wanted to do this for such a long time."

"I have, too," she whispered, but too softly for him to hear.

He kissed her eyelids, then his lips slid down her cheek to the corner of her mouth. His kiss was less urgent this time, but more seductive—a promise of what was to come. Alexandra drew in her breath sharply as his hand cupped her breast and he slowly rotated his thumb over the sensitive tip.

The rest of the world ceased to exist for both of them;

nothing mattered except each other. The rising excitement was mounting like a rocket about to explode. At first they barely heard Willie call. It was a distant sound intruding on their private paradise.

Then he called again. "Alex! Where are you? I can't find Teddy!"

Chase and Alexandra stared at each other in bewilderment for a moment, as they were wrenched back to earth. Then reality set in and they both jumped up and hurried into the bedroom.

"It's all right, honey, we're here." Alexandra sat on the edge of the bed and put her arms around the little boy, while Chase smoothed his hair reassuringly.

"I want Teddy," Willie wailed. "Where is he?"

"We must have left him at Mother's house," Chase said to Alexandra.

"No, I gathered him up, along with Willie's shoes," she said. "I simply forgot to bring him upstairs."

"Teddy's losted again." Tears ran down the child's face.

"He isn't lost, he's just downstairs in the car," Chase said reassuringly. "I'll go down and get him and be right back."

Willie's tears stopped, but he continued to look anxious until Chase returned with the stuffed toy. A smile lit up his face when the bear was placed in his outstretched arms.

"See? You got all upset over nothing," Alexandra said, tucking the covers around the little boy. "Go back to sleep now."

"I want a drink of water first."

While Chase went to get it, Willie crooned happily to his bear. He was wide-awake now and reluctant to go back to sleep. It took a good fifteen minutes before the adults could convince him that Teddy was sleepy even if he wasn't, so he'd have to stay in bed.

When Chase and Alexandra finally returned to the living room, Chase said wryly, "Talk about your bad timing!"

She avoided looking at him. Willie's timing was just right. Alexandra didn't want to think about what would have happened in another couple of minutes.

"I suppose he'll go back to sleep," she remarked.

"I don't think we should count on it."

She darted a quick look at him. Did Chase think she wanted to take up where they left off? "Well…it's getting late," she remarked.

"Yes, I should leave—unfortunately."

As Chase moved toward her, Alexandra sidled around him and went to the front door. "It's been a lovely day," she said formally. "Thanks for everything."

"I wish it could have ended differently."

He reached for her, but she took a step back. "It might have been worse," she answered in an attempt at lightness. "You could have had to drive back to your mother's to get Teddy."

Chase looked at her with a puzzled frown. "What's wrong, Alex?"

"Not a thing, now that Willie has his bear. I wonder if he's *too* attached to it. Maybe it's a substitute for the real-life friends he actually wants."

"Forget the damn bear! What happened between us, Alex? A short time ago we were on the verge of making love. Now you're treating me like a guest who's overstayed his welcome. Why?"

"You're imagining things," she said dismissively.

"Am I? Then why won't you let me kiss you goodnight?"

"It's late and I'm tired, Chase. Can't we discuss this some other time?"

"No. I want to find out what I did wrong."

"Nothing!" When he simply waited in silence, she said reluctantly, "I just realized that what almost happened between us would have been a mistake."

"You didn't feel that way when you were in my arms. You were a willing participant. I didn't seduce you, Alex."

"I didn't say you did." Her cheeks flushed as she remembered just how eager she'd been.

Chase put his hands on her shoulders and kept them there, even though she stiffened warily. "You've obviously changed your mind. I don't know why, and I can see you're not going to tell me. It's too bad. I think we would have been quite wonderful together, but it's your decision. As I told you before, I always take no for an answer."

"I appreciate that," she said in a low voice.

"I hope this won't affect our friendship. I made a mistake, but I promise it won't happen again."

"It wasn't anyone's fault," Alexandra murmured. "But maybe it would be better if we didn't see each other anymore. Like on a date, I mean. You can see Willie, of course."

"You don't trust me to keep my word?"

"I'm sure you always do. That has nothing to do with it. I just think it would be…less awkward."

"I'm sorry if I've made you uncomfortable. I'll try to remedy that in the future."

Which meant he intended to revert to their former casual relationship. Alexandra didn't think she could manage it, but there was no need to tell him that now. She could always make up an excuse the next time he asked her for a date.

"I'll pick you up tomorrow around eleven-thirty." When she gave him a startled look, Chase said, "We're taking Willie to a birthday party, remember?"

"I guess I forgot for a minute."

He smiled sardonically. "It's understandable after everything else that's happened here tonight. Stop worrying about it, Alex," he said more gently. "I'd like to have been your lover, but I'll settle for being your friend."

Alexandra breathed a sigh of relief after Chase left. He

was usually as tenacious as a bulldog when he wanted answers, and she couldn't have held out much longer. But Chase must never know the real reason she didn't want to see him anymore—that she'd fallen in love with him.

There was no use denying it any longer. She'd told herself it was merely sexual attraction, that Chase was an outstandingly handsome man with great animal magnetism. That was true, but she wanted more from him than sex. She wanted to spend the rest of her life with him and have his children.

Unfortunately Chase didn't want to be tied down to one woman. He was more than willing to have an affair with her, but that's all it would be to him. When the novelty wore off there would be another woman, and another one after that.

Alexandra knew she'd be devastated if—or rather, when—Chase left her. She'd had a small taste tonight of the ecstasy he could bring. How could she give him up after knowing the full power of him?

It was late by the time Alexandra dragged herself off the couch and went to bed. Her entire body ached for Chase, but that wasn't to be, so she'd better get used to it, she told herself.

Willie was up early, bright and chipper in spite of his disturbed night. "Get up, Alex. We have to go to a birthday party."

She looked at the clock, groaned and put a pillow over her head. "Go back to sleep. It's practically the middle of the night."

"No, it isn't. It's morning, and Uncle Chase said he'd be here early. We have to get dressed."

That was enough to wake her completely. As memories of the night before washed over her, Alexandra didn't want to get out of bed. How was she going to get through another day with Chase?

"Alex, come *on*." Willie pulled the covers back.

Luckily there wasn't time to dwell on her problems after that. She had to fix breakfast for Willie and help him get dressed. Then she had to clean up the kitchen and get herself dressed.

Alexandra didn't know what one wore to a children's birthday party. She didn't want to get too dressed up, but she couldn't wear the usual jeans that were her uniform on weekends. Finally she settled on a pleated pink silk skirt, a matching sweater and high-heeled pumps. The outfit was casual, but not too much so—she hoped.

Chase arrived early, as he'd promised, which was a blessing in one way. Willie had been driving her crazy all morning, asking how soon Uncle Chase would get there.

Alexandra was tense about meeting Chase again. They'd parted on good terms, but the atmosphere between them was bound to be strained. Surprisingly, she was wrong.

Chase acted the same way toward her as he had prior to the incident the night before. Nothing in his manner suggested the man who'd kissed her so passionately while caressing her body until it throbbed with desire. It didn't seem possible they'd almost made love.

Chase wasn't just pleasant that morning. He was completely natural, complimenting her appearance in his usual teasing way, casually discussing their plans for the day. Obviously their romantic encounter hadn't made much of an impression, Alexandra thought bitterly. On him, anyway.

Okay, fine, she could match his cool. "Shall I make some coffee to keep us awake?" she asked jokingly.

Willie objected before Chase could answer. "No, we have to go! We'll be late for the party."

"There's plenty of time," Alexandra assured him. "It doesn't start for an hour yet."

"That's too long. I wanna go now!"

"We could go over to Mother's," Chase remarked. "She won't mind if we're early. In fact, she'll be delighted."

"I guess we might as well." Alexandra sighed. "Willie has been champing at the bit since it got light out."

"I know this isn't the way you'd prefer to spend your Sunday," Chase said. "I don't suppose you have to be there. Would you rather I took him without you?"

Is that what *he* would prefer? The thought was painful, but no more so than the whole situation. Maybe it was the best solution.

"If that's what you'd like," she said carelessly.

"I'd like to be with you." He smiled. "I haven't made any secret of it."

"Teddy and I are ready." Willie looked hopefully at the two adults.

"Okay, pal, we're leaving." Chase gave Alexandra a laughing glance. "You had your choice," he told her. "Now you're stuck with it. We're all going to a birthday party."

The party was at another of the large homes near Estelle's in Pacific Heights. It was as expensive as hers, but not as serenely uncluttered. Patty and her husband, Doug, had two children.

The house was filled with noise and laughter, although most of the children were outside in the spacious backyard. Their parents were milling around inside, at what looked like a big cocktail party.

"Chase! How good to see you again." Patty detached herself from a group and came over to give him a kiss on the cheek.

After all the introductions and greetings had been exchanged, Patty turned her attention to Willie. "He looks like his father," she commented softly.

Willie was a little daunted by all the people and the attention being directed at him. He clung silently to Estelle's hand.

"I'm so glad you could come today, Willie," Patty told

him. "The children are outside playing games. Would you like to go out and play with them?"

When the little boy nodded, Estelle said, "I'll take him. You and Chase stay here and catch up on all the news."

"Patty and Doug and I grew up together," Chase explained to Alexandra, as Doug joined their group.

"And now we see more of his mother than we do of him," Patty commented, after introducing Alexandra to her husband.

"Why would Chase want to hang around with old married people? He has better things to do with his time," Doug said, giving Alexandra an admiring glance.

"You haven't been wasting *your* time." Chase grinned. "You have two beautiful children."

"We're way ahead of you," Patty said. "Stacey, the birthday girl, is five, and Brad is three. They're great kids. I can highly recommend parenthood."

"You're rushing things a bit," Chase said. "I'm the old-fashioned type. I want a wife first."

"That sounds like his intentions are honorable," Doug said to Alexandra.

"He's changed since you knew him," she answered lightly. "Chase is a confirmed bachelor."

"There's no such thing," Patty said. "Men only think they don't want to get married. It's up to women to show them what sad, lonely lives they're leading."

"You're right," Doug chuckled. "My heart breaks when I think of Chase going out every night with a beautiful woman, dancing and drinking champagne. What did he ever do to deserve such a fate?"

"And you wonder why I don't come around more often?" Chase asked dryly.

"I was only teasing and Doug is just jealous," Patty said. "We love you, even if you are a carefree bachelor."

"Not as carefree as I used to be."

Patty's face sobered. "Estelle told us that Willie is Bill's son. It must have been a shock to find out that way. Do the police have any leads on his mother?''

"Nothing so far. At least, nothing they've told us.''

Patty hesitated. "The newspaper didn't mention anything about Bill.''

After a glance at Chase's set face, Doug deftly steered the conversation in a different direction. "How did it feel to become an instant mother?'' he asked Alexandra. "Or do you have children of your own?''

"No, but if they're all like Willie, I wouldn't mind having several,'' she answered.

"You might have second thoughts if you'd started with an infant. You skipped over the wet diapers and the middle-of-the-night feedings.''

"He's putting you on,'' Patty said. "Doug is a doting father. He adores children.''

"With a few notable exceptions,'' he said. "Look who's here, the Applegates and their little terror.''

Patty glanced over her shoulder. "I was beginning to think they weren't coming.''

"I always admired that optimistic streak in you,'' her husband grinned.

"Oh well, if I'm lucky I can steer him outside before he breaks something. Get Alexandra a drink, Chase. The bar is set up in the den.'' With a resigned look, Patty went to greet the newcomers.

"What are all the adults doing here?'' Chase asked Doug. "Birthday parties used to be for kids. We had cake and ice cream and played Pin the Tail on the Donkey. No big deal. Our parents dropped us off and picked us up when the party was over.''

"You're living in the past,'' Doug told him. "Now everything is supposed to be a shared family experience.'' When Chase stared at him with a raised eyebrow, Doug laughed. "Hey, I don't make the rules. I just supply the food and drinks." One of the guests called to him, and he excused himself.

"I guess we might as well get a drink," Chase remarked to Alexandra. As they walked toward the den, he said, "I suppose you're wondering why I didn't tell them about Bill."

"It's a difficult thing to talk about."

"They'll find out soon enough," he said moodily. "I just didn't think this was the time or the place."

"I can understand that. You don't have anything to tell them yet, anyway. I mean, you don't really know what happened to Brenda or your brother."

"I hope Brenda is still alive. I wish I could believe Bill is, but I'm sure she told me the truth about him."

Alexandra wished she could say something to ease his pain, but platitudes wouldn't help. The picture was bleak for both of Willie's parents. Chase was too intelligent not to know that. Fortunately his friends provided a diversion.

The den was even noisier and more crowded than the living room. Couples were clustered around the bar and a group of men were watching a baseball game on a large-screen television set in a corner.

As soon as Chase entered the room, people came over to say hello. There were the usual remarks about his elusiveness, while the women gave Alexandra a covert examination and the men eyed her with open approval.

"It's good to see you again, Chase," a man named Jeff Warren said. "I ran into Tommy Brookings the other day and he asked about you."

"How is old Tommy?" Chase smiled. "Still working on his golf game and pushing junk bonds?"

"In that order," another man, named Gordon, chuckled.

"When he runs out of friends, he'll have to get a real job," Jeff's wife, Pamela, remarked.

They talked about mutual acquaintances, unconsciously leaving Alexandra out. It didn't bother her, since they'd taken Chase's mind off his brother. She was happy to see him so much more relaxed.

Chase realized belatedly that they were excluding her. "I'm sorry, honey. Forgive me for being rude. You're not interested in a lot of people you don't know. Some of them don't even interest *me*."

"It's quite all right," she answered. "You haven't seen each other in a while. Why don't you stay here and visit with your friends while I go outside and see how Willie is getting along."

"I'll go with you," he said.

"It isn't necessary," she insisted.

"I know that, but I want to." Taking her hand, Chase said to his friends, "I'll catch up with you later."

Pamela gave them a speculative look. "Give us a call. Maybe the four of us can go out to dinner one night."

She clearly thought they were having a heavy romance. Alexandra could have told her appearances were deceiving.

The backyard was very festive. Long tables, gaily decorated with paper tablecloths and clusters of balloons, were set up in one corner of the spacious property. Dozens of excited children were watching a magician perform in the center of the lawn, while a couple of clowns with red noses and orange hair were wandering through the crowd, making the youngsters laugh.

A group of chairs were clustered under a large shade tree. They were occupied by older women, grandmothers and aunts, who watched the festivities indulgently. Estelle was among the group.

Chase and Alexandra strolled over to her. "Is Willie doing okay?" he asked his mother.

"He's having such a good time," she answered. "It's a pleasure to watch him."

"Where is he?" Alexandra asked. "They move around so much I can't locate him."

"That's what makes birthday parties fun." Chase put an

rm around her and pointed. "See? There he is. The one vith chocolate all over his shirt."

"Another trip to the Laundromat," she groaned. "I hould make you do the wash this time."

An elderly woman was watching them with interest. "I iaven't seen your son in years, Estelle," she said. "He :ertainly turned out to be a handsome young man."

"I like to think so." Estelle smiled.

"I'll bet you don't remember me, do you?" the woman isked Chase archly.

He looked to his mother for help and she came to the escue. "Of course he does," Estelle said smoothly. "You emember Mrs. Worthington, Chase, Doug's grandmothr?"

"It's been a long time, Mrs. Worthington, and you're ooking as beautiful as ever," he said.

"That kind of flattery only works with pretty girls like your wife," she answered, looking pleased.

"We're not married," Alexandra said swiftly.

"Oh, I didn't realize." The elderly woman gazed at them with a slight frown, noticing Chase's arm around Alexandra and her flushed cheeks. Then the woman's face cleared. "You haven't told anyone yet, is that it? Oh dear, I hope I haven't let the cat out of the bag. You knew about their engagement, didn't you, Estelle?"

"No, we hadn't gotten around to telling her yet." Chase's eyes sparkled mischievously.

"I can't tell you how terrible I feel!" Mrs. Worthington exclaimed.

"It's quite all right," Estelle soothed, giving her son a reproving look. "I would appreciate it, though, if you didn't tell anyone just yet."

"I won't tell a soul," the other woman promised.

Estelle rose and beckoned to Chase. He and Alexandra followed her to another part of the garden.

"It was very unkind of you to make fun of an old lady,'' Estelle told him.

"I'm sorry. That wasn't my intention. It just struck me funny.''

"You have a weird sense of humor,'' Alexandra said stiffly.

"Now I've really done it,'' Chase muttered. "What I meant was, her reason for thinking we were married amused me. I assume it was the fact that I had my arm around you.''

"Jeanette Worthington is an elderly woman,'' Estelle said. "In her day, public displays of affection were only indulged in by married or engaged couples. So if you and Alexandra weren't married, then you must be engaged. I suppose it is rather amusing in light of today's excesses.'' Estelle smiled.

"See, Mother forgives me.'' Chase took Alexandra's hands. "Do you?''

"I've forgiven you for everything else,'' she said wryly. "What's one more thing?''

"Have you been harassing this dear girl?'' Estelle demanded.

"Not lately—at least not that I can remember.'' Chase sighed. "This just isn't my day.''

"At least Willie is having a good time,'' Alexandra said. "That's why we're here.''

"How long do these things last?'' Chase asked his mother.

"Quite a while,'' she answered. "They haven't had ice cream and cake yet, or opened the presents.'' When Chase groaned, she said, "You and Alexandra don't have to stay.''

"You said we should be here so Willie wouldn't be the only one without any parent figures.''

"I thought he might feel a little strange,'' Estelle said. "But he's having such a good time that I don't think he cares whether you're here or not. You can go over and say hello, but after that there's no reason for you to stay. Why don't you and Alexandra go somewhere for an hour or two?"

"That sounds like a winner. How about it, Alex?"

"I guess it would be all right, if Willie doesn't really need us," she answered slowly. Alexandra wasn't anxious to be alone with Chase, but she wasn't happy that his friends thought they were having an affair. Only old Mrs. Worthington believed his intentions were honorable.

"Mother will be here to keep an eye on Willie," Chase said. "Come on, let's try to separate him from the herd."

Willie barely had time to say hello. "You know what? A man pulled a real live rabbit out of a hat!" he said excitedly. "And now we're gonna play some more games, and then we're gonna have ice cream and cake."

Alexandra smiled at his animated face. "I'm glad you're having such a good time."

"We're going to leave for a little while," Chase said. "But Auntie Estelle will be here if you need anything."

"Yeah, okay. I gotta go now or I'll miss my turn. Bye."

"Our little boy doesn't need us anymore." Chase chuckled as Willie ran to join his new friends.

"That just goes to prove that nobody's indispensable," she said ruefully.

"I wouldn't say that." He turned his head to look at her as they went out a side gate. "A person can get attached to someone in a remarkably short time."

Alexandra was looking down at the uneven flagstone path so her high heels wouldn't get caught in the cracks. "Willie is dependent on me now, but that doesn't mean he's formed an attachment—which is fortunate. He won't mind leaving me when the time comes."

"I think you underestimate yourself," Chase murmured.

"No, the transition will be smooth. You'll see."

He didn't comment, because they'd reached the car.

When they were inside, Chase said, "Where do you want to go?"

"Wherever you like."

"That's no answer. What do you feel like doing?"

"Nothing special. Whatever you want," she said.

"One of us has to make a decision or we'll just sit here for an hour. I always choose where we're going, now it's your turn."

"I really don't care, so let me put it this way... What would you be doing today if you didn't have to take Willie to this party?"

"It's been a rough week. I'd probably be flaked out watching the finals of the golf match on television."

"That's fine with me," Alexandra said. "Let's go to my apartment and turn on the TV."

"That's not very exciting for you," he protested.

"I've had all the excitement I can take lately," she said dryly. "I'd welcome a chance to lie down and do nothing. I might even take a short nap."

"Well, okay, if you're sure." Chase turned the ignition key. "But why don't we go to my place instead of yours? It's closer."

"Sure, why not? I know you don't have an ulterior motive. I can't compete against a championship golf match," Alexandra joked.

"Don't be too sure." He smiled. "I might be a sports nut, but I'm not a fanatic."

Chapter Eight

Chase's penthouse apartment was in a tall building on Nob Hill, overlooking both the city and the waterfront. Floor-to-ceiling picture windows provided a stunning view. The living room and dining room were furnished elegantly, yet had a lived-in look. Books and magazines were piled on a heavy glass coffee table, and there were lamps next to comfortable chairs.

"It's lovely, Chase," Alexandra exclaimed. "This is as beautiful in its own way as your mother's house."

"I was the despair of my decorator," he said. "I told her I wanted a contemporary look, and then I kept sneaking in antiques."

He gestured at an inlaid rosewood end table and a Victorian china lamp. Chase's taste was eclectic. A jade elephant sat on a shelf between an old silver goblet and a modern crystal vase. The interesting objects made the elegant rooms warmer and more welcoming.

"I like everything you've done," Alexandra assured

him. "Decorators don't live in the real world. Have you ever noticed their rooms never have reading lamps or television sets?"

"Mine went into shock when I insisted on the lamps," he agreed.

"I see you lost the argument over the television set," Alexandra said, glancing around. "Or do you have a den?"

Chase nodded. "Would you like to see the rest of the place?"

"I'd love to! I was too polite to ask."

"Friends don't have to stand on ceremony with each other." He took her hand. "Come on, I'll give you the grand tour."

He led her through a large, modern kitchen and breakfast room, before showing her the den. It was furnished with leather couches and chairs, bookshelves lined the paneled walls and hand-hooked rugs covered the hardwood floor.

After making admiring comments, Alexandra said, "I don't see a TV set in here, either. Is it built in?"

"No, I don't watch in here. I use this room for working at my computer or reading. Actually I don't watch much TV."

"But you must have a television set. Where is it?"

"In my bedroom. I turn on the news when I'm getting dressed to go out at night or else I watch the late news when I come home."

She looked at him warily. "That's the only set you have?"

"Don't worry, it has a big screen. Come on, I'll show you." When she didn't move, he said, "Is something wrong?"

Alexandra decided she was being foolish. Chase hadn't asked her here to seduce her. He'd accepted the fact that she didn't want to have a relationship with him. His casual behavior today proved that. She'd look like a fool if she made a fuss about a simple thing like watching television in his bedroom.

She had second thoughts a few moments later. Chase's bedroom was very spare and masculine. A king-size bed was flanked by heavy bedside tables. The only other furniture in the room was a round table and two straight chairs. Chests and a large-screen TV were built into the wall facing the bed.

Chase had opened the double doors that hid the set when it wasn't in use. "We missed most of the match, but at least we'll get to see the finish." He turned around and saw Alexandra standing stiffly in the middle of the floor. "Make yourself comfortable," he said, loosening his tie and unfastening the top button of his shirt.

"Where?" she asked bluntly.

"Where what?"

"Where would you like me to watch television? On the bed, I suppose."

"Sure, I can highly recommend it. Pile a couple of pillows behind your head."

"Are there enough for both of us, or do you expect to share mine?" she asked acidly.

His puzzled look turned to amused comprehension. "If that's an invitation, I'll be glad to accept. I expected to take one of the chairs by the table and give you the bed, but I like your idea better."

"Those chairs don't look very comfortable," she said uncertainly, wondering if she'd overreacted.

"They're fine for watching television—unless you had something else in mind," he teased.

"Are you going to talk all through the golf match?" she demanded, to hide her discomfiture.

As he chuckled and went to sit at the table, Alexandra kicked off her shoes and climbed onto the bed. She felt exceedingly foolish, but Chase had had his fun. He was absorbed in the golf match.

She tried to get interested, too, but Chase was a distraction. She found herself stealing glances at him, instead of the screen. It was rather insulting to be ignored so completely. His attention was focused on the set, but he was clearly uncomfortable. Every few minutes he shifted in the straight-backed chair, alternately crossing and uncrossing his legs, then stretching them out in front of him.

"You can't be enjoying yourself very much," she commented. "That chair must be uncomfortable."

"It's fine," he said without taking his eyes off the screen. "Fantastic! Did you see him sink that forty-foot putt?" Chase leaned back and rested his left ankle on his right knee. After a few moments he reversed the position.

"It's silly for you to squirm around on that hard chair," Alexandra said impatiently. "Come over here and lie on the bed. It's big enough for both of us."

That got his attention. He turned his head and looked at her questioningly. "Are you sure?"

"We're two adults, for heaven's sake, not a couple of hormonally challenged teenagers!"

"Grown men have their share of hormones, too." He laughed. "But I'll try to restrain them, because I'm getting leg cramps." He settled onto the bed with a sigh of pleasure.

Alexandra didn't find it as easy to relax. Although Chase was a respectable distance away, she was achingly aware of him.

The golf match was evidently exciting. He groaned when one of the players wound up in a sand trap, and cheered all the shots that landed on the green. Alexandra didn't respond, because it wasn't necessary. She stole glances at Chase's strong profile instead, noticing the clean line of his jaw and the little laughter lines that softened his patrician face.

It took a while, but he finally became aware of her inattention. "You're not enjoying this. I'll turn on something else."

"Don't do that. I'm watching it."

"No, you're not. What would you rather see?"

"This is fine," she insisted.

"You're just being polite. The remote control is on the nightstand next to you. Surf through the channels until you find something you like."

"You're enjoying the golf match and there's nothing I'd rather watch, so leave it on."

"It's ridiculous for you to lie here and be bored. If you're too stubborn to change the channel, I'll do it."

He moved over next to her and reached across her for the remote control, which was on the far end of the nightstand. When he finally grasped it, Chase's body was partially covering hers and their faces were only inches apart.

His weight pinned her to the bed, but Alexandra couldn't have moved anyway. Every nerve in her body was screaming out for him. If her arms had been free, she would have anchored her fingers in his thick hair and forced his mouth down to hers.

After Chase finally grasped the elusive remote, he said, "Okay, no more arguments. You're going to—" The words died as he stared into her luminous eyes and read the desire in them. "Sweet Alex, I hope I'm not getting the wrong signal again," he muttered.

As his lips grazed hers tentatively, she freed one arm and hooked it around his neck. How long could she deny what she wanted so desperately? It didn't matter that their relationship wouldn't be permanent. If all she had was this afternoon, it would be more than nothing.

Chase gathered her in his arms and kissed her with incredulous joy. "Darling Alex, I'd almost given up hope. Do you have any idea how much I want you?"

"Show me," she whispered, gazing at him through lowered lashes.

"I intend to, again and again."

His mouth closed over hers once more, for a torrid kiss that left Alexandra clinging to him. While his tongue probed deeply, his hands worked a different kind of magic. She quivered as he stroked her breasts lingeringly, then slipped his hand under her sweater for a more intimate caress. When his fingers reached inside her bra, she cried out with pleasure.

"Ah, darling, do you like that?" he asked huskily. "I want to make you so happy."

"You do," she murmured, raising her arms so Chase could remove her sweater.

He unclasped her bra and lowered his head to kiss each rosy nipple. Alexandra drew in her breath sharply, as his lips closed around one tightly furled little bud and his teeth nipped gently.

"Oh, Chase, I want you so," she breathed, unbuttoning his shirt with shaking fingers.

"We're going to be so good together, angel."

He shrugged off his shirt before hooking his fingers in the elastic waistband of her skirt and sliding it down her hips. Straddling her legs, he gazed down at her with glowing eyes.

"I knew you'd be this beautiful. Every inch of you is perfect."

Her passion rose as he began to roll down her panty hose. The fleeting touch of his hands was sweet torture, almost making her lose the remnants of her control.

"Please, Chase." She begged for the release that only he could give her.

"Yes, my little love, I want to please you in every way."

He lowered his head and trailed a path of burning kisses down her body while he stroked her thighs seductively. Tiny flames flickered in her midsection, when he raised her leg and kissed the soft skin of her inner thigh. And when he kissed her intimately, the flames threatened to turn into a bonfire.

"I want you now!" she said urgently, reaching for his belt buckle and tearing at it in her frantic haste.

"Not half as much as I want you." He kissed her hard but briefly, before sliding off the bed.

Alexandra followed him. While Chase unzipped his slacks, she tugged impatiently at his briefs. When he was completely nude, her impatience turned to wonder at the perfection of his body. He had the smooth, muscled torso of an ancient Greek athlete. She smoothed her palms over his chest and the flat plane of his stomach, then gently embraced his rampant manhood.

Chase gave a hoarse cry and jerked her against him. The contact of their naked bodies sent a jolt of electricity through both of them. Alexandra wound her arms around his neck and for a few frantic moments they kissed and moved against each other, heightening the tension.

When it demanded release, Chase lifted her and plunged deeply. She wound her legs around him so they were joined tightly in the ultimate embrace. His driving force was like nothing she'd ever experienced before. He filled her with ecstasy that seemed to build endlessly.

The throbbing conclusion thundered through both at the same time. A burst of sensation that grew in power, radiating throughout their bodies until it culminated in a euphoric feeling of satisfaction.

Chase lowered Alexandra's feet gently to the floor without releasing her from his arms. They clung together, as close in spirit as when they were joined physically.

He kissed her closed eyelids. "I told you we'd be good together, but I didn't realize just how terrific."

"I did." She smiled and kissed the hollow in his throat. "I knew you'd be a great lover."

"I'm happy that you think so, but it's all due to you. You're utterly irresistible." He swung her into his arms and carried her to the bed. When they were lying closely entwined, he said, "What made you change your mind?" She started to move away, but he pulled her back. "I wasn't complaining."

"I certainly hope not." She managed a small laugh. "I'd hate to think I was the only one who enjoyed myself."

"You know better than that." He smoothed the damp hair off her forehead and gazed at her tenderly. "You're very special to me."

"I'd like to believe that," she said wistfully.

"Good Lord, woman, what more can I do to show you?"

If only great sex was all she wanted, Alexandra thought despairingly. But she'd made her decision and she didn't regret it. This interlude with Chase, no matter how brief, was worth any pain she might suffer afterward.

Giving him a radiant smile, she said, "You can give me a repeat performance."

"Did you have any doubt?" He nibbled delicately on her lower lip. "It was tough to convince you, but you're mine now and I don't intend to let you get away."

"My, my, aren't we macho all of a sudden?" she teased.

"You wouldn't want me to be a wimp, would you?"

"I don't think you'd know how."

"I could learn, if that's what you want." He kissed her tenderly.

"No, I like you just the way you are—bossy and impatient," she said mischievously.

"Look who's talking!" he hooted. "You've been setting the rules since the day we met."

"I could dispute that, but there's something incongruous about two naked people lying in each other's arms and having an argument."

"True. I suppose we could get dressed." He slid a hand between her thighs. "Or we could find something infinitely more enjoyable to do than argue."

Alexandra tried to ignore the warmth that sprang to instant life inside her. "We've been gone for more than an hour. We really should go back for Willie and your mother."

"The party is still going on." His tongue slid across her lips until they parted. "Wild horses couldn't drag Willie away until it's over."

"Your mother might be worried about us," she said weakly.

"We're all grown-up now," he murmured.

Alexandra's conscience couldn't compete with Chase's seductive mouth and hands. She clasped her arms around his neck and arched her body into his with a tiny sound of pleasure.

"You're so wonderfully responsive," he said huskily. Scissoring his legs around hers, he kissed her deeply.

Their lovemaking was more leisurely this time. Chase aroused her with sensuous caresses and an intimate exploration of her body, feeding her desire until it escalated into passion.

Then he positioned himself between her legs and they entered a private world of mutual delight. When it was over, they curled up together in sated satisfaction.

Alexandra finally stirred, but Chase tightened his embrace. "Don't go," he murmured.

"We really have to," she said reluctantly. "What time is it?" When he told her, she gasped. "The party must be over by now."

"Don't worry. If it is, there are a lot of people who would give Mother and Willie a ride home."

"That's not the point. We should have been there."

He caught her hand as she started to get up. "Are you sorry?"

Her face softened and she leaned down to kiss him. "Only that we can't stay longer."

"Maybe we can. Mother would be happy to keep Willie overnight."

"No, that's not a good idea. He's had a very exciting day. If he stays at your mother's, he'll never calm down and go to sleep. It isn't good for a child his age to get overstimulated."

Chase sighed. "I suppose you're right."

"Call your mother and tell her we're on our way."

"Have you any suggestions as to why we're late?" He grinned.

"Be creative."

"I'd rather be truthful." He got out of bed and put his arms around her. "I'd like the whole world to know how lucky I am."

She rested her head on his shoulder for a blissful moment. It didn't get any better than this.

Alexandra and Chase were full of apologies when they finally showed up at Estelle's house. The birthday party was long over and someone had driven Estelle and Willie home.

"I'm sorry we're so late, Mother," Chase said. "It's all my fault. We were at my apartment watching the golf match on television and I wanted to see the end."

"It was just as much my fault," Alexandra said. "I was as interested as he was."

Estelle hid her amusement at the transparent excuse. The young couple had a radiance about them that told a different story. Had Chase finally met that special girl? his mother wondered happily.

"It's quite all right," she said. "I'm glad you enjoyed yourselves."

Chase cast a mischievous glance at Alexandra. "I'll have to admit it was an improvement over the birthday party." As her color rose and she gave him a reproving look, he turned to his mother. "Where's Willie? Is he still wired from the party?"

"It was pretty exciting for him. He'll sleep well tonight." Estelle laughed. "I don't think he'll eat much dinner, though."

"That's good, because I didn't have a chance to do any marketing this weekend," Alexandra said.

"Why don't we all have a little snack here later on?" Estelle suggested.

"I wasn't hinting for an invitation," Alexandra protested.

"I know you weren't, but it would give me great pleasure."

"Isn't Margaret off today?" Chase asked.

"Yes, but she left a casserole in the refrigerator, and I'm sure I can find something to go with it," Estelle answered.

"No offense, Mother, but you're not exactly Julia Child in the kitchen."

"That's not a nice thing to say!" Alexandra exclaimed.

"But it's true." Estelle smiled. "My sons could never brag about their mother's cooking. I'm capable of putting a casserole in the oven, however, so I do wish you'd stay."

"I'd love to, if you'll let me help."

"We'll all help," Chase said. "I'll start by making us a drink."

Dinner was a simple affair, quite unlike lunch the previous day, where they had been waited on and served on fine china. They ate in the breakfast room adjoining the kitchen, like a family.

It was the perfect end to a perfect day. Chase and his mother made Alexandra feel like part of the family. She crossed her fingers and hoped they were expressing more than just gratitude.

Chase's behavior was reassuring when he brought her home a little later. After they'd gotten Willie into bed, they returned to the living room and Chase immediately took her in his arms.

"I've been wanting to do this all evening," he groaned,

kissing the soft skin behind her ear. "It was torture not being able to touch you."

She turned her head so their lips grazed tantalizingly. "Wasn't this afternoon enough?" she asked provocatively, wanting to hear him deny it.

He did, in a very satisfactory way. "I'll never get enough of you," he murmured as his mouth closed over hers for a deep kiss that left her trembling.

She clung to him, returning his kiss with equal fervor while he caressed her body sensuously. They strained against each other with mounting desire for a few moments before Alexandra reluctantly drew away.

"Willie might not be asleep yet," she said.

"I know." Chase sighed. "I'm just making it harder for both of us, but I can't seem to stay away from you."

"Don't try too hard." She smiled enchantingly. "I've gotten kind of used to having you around."

"That's good, because I intend to show up regularly." He caressed her cheek, gazing deeply into her eyes. "Good night, sweetheart. I'd better get out of here while I still can."

Alexandra awoke the next morning with a smile on her face. It was amazing how one fateful afternoon had changed her life. Before then, she'd seen problems where none existed. Now the future was dazzling, with not a cloud in sight.

Danny and his vague, unpleasant threats were merely a minor annoyance. She forgot about him completely when Chase telephoned as she was getting out of the shower.

"I just wanted to say I miss you and wish you were here," he said in a husky voice.

She laughed breathlessly. "That sounds like something you say on a postcard."

"It's true, even if I'm only across town. I can't wait to hold you in my arms again."

"That might be a little difficult to accomplish." She glanced over at Willie, who was struggling to put on his shoes. "But come for dinner tonight and we'll hold hands under the table."

"It will take a lot more than that to satisfy me."

Her pulse rate quickened as Chase described what he had in mind. When they finally hung up, she was glowing.

Alexandra's building didn't have garages. Like many of the apartment dwellers on the block, she had to park on the street. Chase's phone call had delayed her, and when she and Willie went downstairs that morning most of the neighbors had already left for work.

The street was fairly deserted, except for a dark-colored sedan parked near the entrance to her building. A man was sitting behind the wheel, appearing to read the morning newspaper. When Alexandra and Willie came out onto the sidewalk, he started to get out of his car.

Before Alexandra could cross the street to her own car, she was joined by the two young men who had an apartment across from hers. They were college students attending school on football scholarships, and she'd gotten quite friendly with them. They were always willing to help out when she had a stuck window or something heavy to be moved.

"No school today?" Alexandra asked. They were dressed in jogging suits.

"It's spring break, remember?" the one named Sean answered.

"How do you expect me to remember back that far?" She laughed.

"Hey, you're just a kid. If I wasn't crazy about Cindy, I would have hit on you long ago."

As the students walked across the street with her and Willie, the man in the sedan got back in his car and started the motor.

Willie was in high spirits after his eventful weekend. On the way to Mandy's, he kept up a continuous chatter about everything from yesterday's birthday party to the circus Chase promised to take him to. Alexandra listened indulgently, dividing her attention between Willie and the Monday morning traffic.

She'd forgotten about the previous times when she felt she was being followed, so she didn't notice the sedan that stayed a steady distance behind hers. It inched closer as she slowed down. When she turned into the circular driveway in front of Mandy's apartment house, the car started to come in after her. But when the parking attendant approached and Henry, the doorman, came out of the building, the dark-colored car hurriedly backed out onto the street and drove away. None of them paid any attention. If they'd noticed, they would have thought the driver had simply realized he was at the wrong address.

"Hi, Willie," the doorman said, helping the little boy out of the car. "Did you have a nice weekend?"

"Yes, I went to a party and there were two clowns there."

"I've been to some of those kind of parties myself." Henry chuckled. "I'll take the little fellow upstairs for you, Miss Reynolds."

"Thanks, Henry, but I want to see Mrs. Winfield. You can leave the car here," she told the parking attendant. "I'll be down in a few minutes."

Mandy's housekeeper answered the door with a welcoming smile. She'd grown fond of Willie, and the feeling was mutual. He spent a lot of time following her around. Mandy came in from the terrace as Helga led Willie off to the kitchen for orange juice and a freshly baked muffin.

"Hi, Alex, how was your weekend?" she asked.

"Fantastic!"

Mandy gave her friend an interested look. "That sounds promising. What did you do that was so spectacular?"

"Oh...lots of things. We were busy every minute. Chase and I took Willie to his mother's for lunch on Saturday and to a birthday party on Sunday."

"That means Willie had a great weekend. What made it so special for you?"

Alexandra's mouth curved in a smile as she remembered Chase's impassioned lovemaking. The word "special" didn't begin to describe it!

Mandy's gaze sharpened. "I have a feeling you didn't spend all your time with Willie. You can tell me about it over coffee."

Alexandra glanced at her watch. "I really shouldn't leave Tina all alone in the office."

"Okay, whatever you say."

"You could show a little more interest," Alexandra exclaimed indignantly.

Mandy laughed. "I figured it would speed things up if I didn't coax you. I'm dying to know what went on."

When they were seated on the terrace with coffee and a plate of Helga's blueberry muffins, Mandy said, "I assume that glow on your face is due to Chase."

"Is it that obvious?"

"To anyone who knows you, it is. What's the story? It wasn't too long ago that you were complaining about how arrogant and unreasonable he was."

"We didn't know each other then," Alexandra said defensively. "He thought the same about me."

"But you've both obviously changed your minds. It must have been some weekend." Mandy grinned.

"It was," Alexandra answered softly.

"This sounds serious. He took you to meet his mother already?"

"That doesn't mean anything," Alexandra said reluctantly. "It was so she could spend time with Willie. Chase and Estelle are convinced that he's a Mainwaring, and I've come around to their way of thinking."

"I suppose that's the best-case scenario for Willie. He'll have a family to take care of him, one that really wants him. I can't imagine a mother deserting her child." Mandy was filled with indignation at the thought.

"We don't really know what happened."

"I guess I shouldn't rush to judgment. The poor woman might be lying in a shallow grave somewhere."

"It's certainly a possibility."

Mandy gave her a penetrating look. "But you have doubts. Why?"

Alexandra told her about the shadowy figure she'd seen watching her apartment one night. "I haven't seen her since, and I'm not even sure it was a woman. Perhaps I just wanted it to be Brenda—because she and Willie cared so much about each other. I want to think she's out there somewhere and she'll surface eventually. But that's probably wishful thinking."

"Maybe not." Mandy looked thoughtful. "A funny thing happened the other day. I took Willie out for lunch, and afterward we stopped in a toy store. There was a woman there who kept staring at him. I didn't think much of it at the time. He's a beautiful child. A lot of people comment on it. But what if the woman was Brenda? She was really fixated on him."

"What did she look like?" Alexandra asked excitedly.

"I can't honestly describe her. It was last Tuesday, I think—whatever day it rained. She had on a raincoat and a big, floppy hat that shaded her face. I can't even tell you what color her hair was."

"Did Willie see her?"

"No, he was too busy playing with all the toys. He finally picked out the one he wanted, and when I looked up again, the woman was gone. I could be imagining things, too. If it *was* Brenda and she cared enough to want a glimpse of her son, why wouldn't she come forward?"

"It's a real puzzler." Alexandra sighed. "I'm just glad that Willie has Chase and Estelle for backup."

"You've decided Danny doesn't have a valid claim to Willie?"

"It was hard to believe such a far-out story, but I thought I should give him the benefit of a doubt. The more I know about him, though, the shadier I think he is. I'm going to have as little to do with him as possible. When he finds out I'm backing Chase's claim, he's liable to turn nasty— or I should say, nastier."

"If he gives you any trouble, go right to the police and tell them he's harassing you. I don't want you taking any chances, Alex."

"I can handle Danny. He isn't dangerous, he's just a very unpleasant man."

Alexandra would have changed her mind about Danny's potential, if she'd heard the phone conversation he was having at that very moment. He'd called Nate Arcos on the other man's car phone.

"Why the hell haven't I heard from you?" Danny demanded. "You were supposed to snatch the kid when Alex left with him for the office. It's almost a quarter to ten. Don't tell me she hasn't gone to work yet."

"No, she left half an hour ago, but I ran into a slight complication."

Danny clutched at his hair. "I don't want to hear this! Can't you do one simple job without screwing it up?"

"If it's so simple, why didn't you do it, hotshot?"

"You know why! Alex could finger me. She doesn't know you."

"I agreed to pinch-hit, but I'm not going out on any limb for you. It has to be a clean snatch, with no chance of getting caught. Kidnapping is a serious rap."

"Okay, so what went wrong?"

"She came out of her apartment house a little late this

morning, which was good. There wasn't anybody around. I was just getting out of the car when these two young guys came out. They were great big bruisers, all muscle. What could I do but back off? It was three against one.''

"Four—you forgot the kid," Danny said sarcastically.

"Get rid of the attitude, I don't have to take this from you. Do your own dirty work. I quit!''

"Come on, Nate, I didn't mean it. This whole thing has me crazy! That damn broad has been trouble from the very beginning.''

"Couldn't get to first base, huh?'' Nate snickered.

"Who needs her? I've got all the women I can handle.''

"Yeah, sure. You're a regular Brad Pitt.''

"Knock it off," Danny answered furiously. "I'm on the spot here. Karpov wants the kid now, today. He won't cut me any more slack.''

"I wouldn't want to be in your shoes, pal.''

"Don't get too comfortable in your own, *pal*. You're involved in this as much as I am. Karpov might have put me in charge, but he won't be happy with either of us when I tell him I turned the job over to you and you blew it.''

"You're real pond scum, Danny, you know that?''

"Hey, it's a dog-eat-dog world out there and I'm not going to wind up as pet food. Let's knock off the insults and get down to business. This is what you have to do....''

Alexandra loved her work. It was rewarding to help people plan vacations, whether it was a weekend in the mountains or a glamorous cruise to far-off places. Everyone was so happy at the prospect. The time usually flew by, but that day she was so eager to see Chase again that the hours seemed to drag. She hoped he'd be prompt, so they'd have a nice long evening together.

"What's the matter with you?'' Tina finally asked in the early afternoon. "You're as restless as a cat in a closet.''

"That's what I feel like. It's too nice a day to be stuck in an office."

"I'm glad it's only spring fever. I was beginning to think you were either in love or catching something. The symptoms are the same." Tina laughed.

"You have a lot to learn about love," Alexandra told her in a vibrant voice.

"Ohh?" Tina gazed at her speculatively. "Is there something you haven't told me?"

"It was just an observation." Alexandra was suddenly cautious about voicing her feelings for Chase. It was too soon to spread the word.

"Too bad. I was hoping something had developed between you and that gorgeous hunk. Has he been around lately?"

"As a matter of fact, he's coming over tonight after work."

"That wouldn't have anything to do with your eagerness to get out of here, would it?"

"Maybe a little bit," Alexandra admitted, knowing her offhand manner hadn't been convincing.

"Why don't you knock off early? I can handle things around here. Go home and make yourself glamorous."

"Are you implying that would take hours?" Alexandra laughed.

"Don't get touchy. I only meant a guy like that is worth a little extra effort."

"He *is* pretty spectacular," Alexandra said softly.

"Then go home and start setting the stage."

It was a tempting thought, but Alexandra declined.

Business was slow, making the day seem even longer. But shortly before closing time, Alexandra got a phone call from a client who wanted to change her itinerary. The procedure was complicated and took time. When the arrangements were finally made to the woman's satisfaction, Alexandra was behind schedule. After finally cradling the receiver, she grabbed her keys and raced out the door.

The rush-hour commute delayed her even further. She wove her way in and out of traffic, muttering mild expletives, without a thought for the car following her.

Since Nate was fairly sure he knew where Alexandra was going he felt free to stay several lengths behind her car, where there was no chance of her spotting him. When Alexandra pulled into the driveway of Mandy's building, he waited on the street with his motor running.

Nate smiled grimly as Alexandra drove out a few minutes later. "This time I gotcha," he murmured with satisfaction.

Willie chattered animatedly on the way home. For a while he was content with Alexandra's absentminded replies, but they finally registered. "You're not listening, Alex," he complained.

"Yes, I am, honey. Helga let you help her bake cookies today."

"No, I asked you if Uncle Chase can take us out for ice cream again, like he did last time."

"I'm sure he will if you ask him."

"Okay, I will. Can we go tonight?"

"Maybe," Alexandra answered vaguely. She was looking for a parking place, always a problem at this time of night. As she cruised slowly, a car pulled away from the curb right near the entrance to her building. "This must be our lucky day," she declared.

"I want to get out," Willie said impatiently, after she'd parked and turned off the motor.

Alexandra was reaching in the back seat for the groceries and a few other purchases she'd bought during her lunch hour. "Just give me a minute to gather up all my packages."

"I wanna wait for you outside."

It was easier to comply than argue with him. "All right, but stand over there by the front door." She released his seat belt and unlocked the door.

Alexandra didn't notice the car that slanted into the curb in front of hers. By the time she faced forward, Nate was out of his car and closing in on Willie. After that, everything sped up like an old Mack Sennett comedy. But there was nothing funny about what was taking place.

By the time Alexandra scrambled out of her car, Nate had Willie by the arm. The little boy was more bewildered than frightened at first. He tried to pull away, but when the stranger yanked him back, Willie panicked and called out to Alexandra for help.

Their struggle gave her time to reach him. She pounded on Nate with her fists, causing him to lose his grip on the child momentarily.

"Run, Willie!" she shouted.

Nate swore coarsely and backhanded her across the face with such force that she fell to the sidewalk and hit her head. Alexandra willed herself not to lose consciousness as a red mist obscured her vision. She could hear Willie screaming and she managed to get to her knees, but it was too late. Nate was carrying the kicking, hysterical child toward his car.

The squeal of brakes barely penetrated her misery. She'd let Willie down. It was like a miracle when she heard Chase's voice. Lifting her head with an effort, she saw him snatch Willie out of the man's arms and deliver a powerful uppercut that sent the man sprawling.

"Thank God," she whispered.

After Chase made sure Willie was all right, he turned on his attempted kidnapper with murderous intent.

But Nate knew when he was outclassed. He scrambled to his feet and ran to his car, cursing Danny with every breath.

It had seemed so simple, when Danny outlined the plan.
Grab the kid and split, using the element of surprise. Even
if there were bystanders, they wouldn't be able to react
soon enough. Yeah, sure!

Chase started to sprint after the car as it burned rubber
pulling away. He soon realized it was hopeless, and that he
had more pressing worries. Taking Willie's hand, he returned to kneel beside Alexandra.

The little boy hurtled into her arms. "Don't die, Alex,"
he sobbed. "I don't want you to leave me."

"She's never going to leave us, son." Chase tried to
project confidence, but his face was pale under his tan.

Alexandra gathered Willie close and smiled at Chase,
even though it hurt her bruised face and every bone in her
body ached. "Uncle Chase is right, honey. I'm not going
anywhere. Everything I want is right here."

Chapter Nine

Chase wanted to call an ambulance or at least take Alexandra to the emergency hospital for a checkup, but she managed to talk him out of it. Willie was already traumatized. She didn't want to put him through the further ordeal of a hospital, with all its strange smells and accident victims. Chase reluctantly agreed, on the condition that she let him call a doctor.

After examining her, the doctor told them Alexandra hadn't broken anything. "You have a nasty bump on the back of your head, plus an assortment of bruises that will turn black-and-blue. But you'll be fine after a couple of days in bed."

"I can't go to bed!" Alexandra exclaimed, wincing as she struggled to a sitting position on the couch. "I have a child to take care of and a business to run."

Chase made her lie down again. "I'll see that she follows your instructions," he told the doctor in a firm voice.

"Good. Reaction will set in and she'll be a little shaky.

Have you reported the mugging to the police? It's disgraceful, the way these thugs prey on women. You're lucky you weren't seriously injured, young lady."

Alexandra and Chase both glanced at Willie. He had calmed down, but he refused to leave her side, and they didn't want him to be alarmed any further.

"It was just one of those one-in-a-million things," she said dismissively. "It could never happen again."

"I wouldn't be too—"

Chase didn't let the man finish. "Thank you for coming by, Doctor. I'll walk you to the door."

"Yes, well, don't hesitate to take those pain pills I prescribed, if you need them," the doctor said over his shoulder as he was being urged toward the entry.

When Chase returned from showing the man out, Alexandra said, "Do you feel better now? I told you there was nothing wrong with me."

"I'd feel better if I'd stopped that slimeball's clock— permanently!"

"My knight in shining armor," she teased gently. "What would I do without you?"

"You'll never have to find out." He smoothed her hair with great tenderness before asking unexpectedly, "Where do you keep your suitcases?"

Alexandra stared at him blankly. "What do you want them for?"

"You'll need a nightgown and a few other things I can't supply you with." His face relaxed into a smile for the first time. "It's fine with me if you'd prefer to sleep in the nude, but you'll need slippers, anyway. I wouldn't want you to catch cold."

"I'm not going to your apartment, if that's what you had in mind."

"I certainly don't intend to leave you alone, and it would be a little crowded if I moved in here."

"Nothing is going to happen to me. You're being overly protective, Chase."

"Maybe, but I'd rather err on the side of caution. Don't argue. I have a big day tomorrow and I need to get some sleep tonight. If you're not right there where I can check on you, I'll be up all night worrying."

Instead of answering, Alexandra said to Willie, "Will you bring me my red sweater? It's in one of the drawers in my dresser. Look through all of them until you find it." After the little boy had left the room, she said to Chase, "That was the only way I could get him to leave us. Willie is still in an emotional state over what happened tonight. I don't think his routine should be disturbed. He's never even been to your apartment."

"*We're* his security blanket, not some place he happens to sleep. But if that's all that's bothering you, Mother has plenty of room and Willie loves it there. She'll be tickled pink to have both of you."

"He's the one we need to worry about." Alexandra looked thoughtful. "That might be the solution—if Willie will agree to go. I'll admit I'm concerned for his safety. I'm not in the best shape to protect him, if that man comes back."

"You don't seem to get it. I don't intend to leave you alone until we find out who that guy was and what this is all about."

"He's after Willie, not me. I wonder if it's wise to involve your mother. It would be terrible if she got in the way, like I did."

"I wouldn't suggest it if I thought there was any danger. Mother's house is the best place for both of you. For one thing, it has a sophisticated alarm system. Nobody could break in without alerting the police. But to make doubly sure, I'm going to move in, too, temporarily."

"I wonder how Estelle will like running a hotel," Alexandra remarked wryly.

"Are you kidding? She'll love it, and so will Joseph and Margaret. Between the three of them, they'll spoil Willie rotten."

The little boy returned with Alexandra's sweater. When Chase told him about the plans, Willie responded cautiously. "Can Alex come, too?" After being assured that both she and Chase would be there with him, he got very excited.

It was a win-win situation. Estelle was delighted, and after her initial objections, so was Alexandra. How could she mind living with Chase—under any circumstances?

He wouldn't let Alexandra stir off the couch. Chase packed a suitcase for her and Willie, and even wanted to carry her downstairs to the car.

"There's nothing wrong with my legs," she protested.

"I'm well aware of that." He leaned down to kiss her. "In a couple of days when you're feeling better, I hope to see more of them," he murmured in her ear.

"I'm feeling pretty good right now," she answered softly.

Chase groaned. "Stop torturing me. I'm supposed to be taking care of you, and all I can think about is getting you into bed—like the doctor ordered," he added, becoming belatedly aware of the little boy.

"Are you real sick, Alex?" Willie asked anxiously.

"I'm not sick at all, honey," she assured him. "Grab Teddy and let's go. Auntie Estelle is waiting for us."

Alexandra didn't notice at first that Chase was driving erratically. He changed lanes frequently and cut through an alley for no good reason. She was about to question him, when he made a right turn off a busy street and stopped at the end of the block.

"Why are we stopping here?" Alexandra wasn't aware of the car that had also pulled over to the curb a short distance behind them.

"Lock the doors after me," he said.

As he got out of the driver's side door, she realized they were being stalked again. "Chase, wait! Don't go out there. Suppose he's armed?"

"Stay here," he ordered. With a face as hard as granite, Chase started toward the other car.

"What's wrong, Alex?" Willie quavered. The anxiety was back in his voice. "You said we were going to Auntie Estelle's. Why did Uncle Chase stop here?"

"He...uh...he wants to speak to somebody for a minute. Everything's fine, darling, don't worry."

Willie started to cry. "I want him to come back."

Alexandra felt the same way. Chase was taking a terrible chance out there all alone. She wanted to go after him to provide backup, but Willie mustn't be left alone. Her dilemma was solved suddenly and without her intervention.

The barely leashed fury in Chase's powerful body evidently convinced the other man not to tangle with him. The car zoomed past them and sped off down the street to the corner, where it made a screeching turn.

After staring at the retreating taillights for a moment, Chase returned to his own car with frustration on his face. "Gutless creep!" he muttered. "What kind of coward only picks on women and children?"

"I don't want you to leave us anymore," Willie said anxiously.

Chase forced a smile. "Anything you say, pal. We'll go straight to Auntie Estelle's now."

"How could you do such a dangerous thing?" Alexandra whispered furiously.

"I hoped I could put a stop to this terrorism," he replied in a low voice.

"It was a different car than the earlier one. Could you see if it was the same man?"

"No, he didn't let me get that close."

"Did you get the license number?" she asked. "I tried, but I couldn't see clearly through the windshield."

"You wouldn't have been able to make out anything. The plate was smeared with mud. He thought of everything."

"So we don't have anything to give the police," Alexandra said slowly.

Chase reached over and squeezed her hand tightly. "Don't worry, they'll get him. And until they do, you and Willie will be safe at Mother's."

She didn't mention it, but Alexandra wondered what would happen when they left their safe haven. Willie couldn't stay cooped up in the house day and night, and she had to go to work. That wasn't as great a problem, because she wasn't the one they were after—which didn't make Alexandra feel any better.

Willie's lingering anxiety disappeared once he was safely inside the Mainwaring house. He was overwhelmed with attention, not only from Estelle but also from Joseph and Margaret. They took the little boy into the kitchen with promises of anything he wanted for dinner.

Estelle was equally solicitous of Alexandra. "What a terrible experience for you, my dear! I'm so glad Chase brought you here. I've prepared his old room for you. Can you navigate the stairs? If not, we can convert the downstairs den into a bedroom."

"Thanks, but that won't be necessary," Alexandra answered. "I was shaken up a bit, but I'm fine, honestly. Willie is the one we have to worry about."

"This is all very puzzling," Estelle said. "Do you have any idea who would do such a thing?"

"I can't prove anything, but I think Danny Riker is behind both incidents. He was very abusive on the phone this weekend when I refused to let Willie stay with him for a few days."

"You didn't tell me that! I would have made damn sure he never bothered you again," Chase said grimly.

"That's exactly why I didn't tell you. Danny would love to have you thrown in jail for assault and battery. He'd have an easier shot at Willie, if you were out of the picture."

"I don't understand this at all." Estelle looked perplexed. "Why does he want the child so much that he'd try to kidnap him? By his own admission, he didn't even know Willie existed until Brenda disappeared."

"We're pretty sure his story is phony. Unfortunately we don't know what's behind it. I'd better call the police and make a report," Chase said. "Maybe they can find out."

It was a busy evening. The police came to the house and asked a lot of questions, but Chase and Alexandra didn't have any concrete evidence against Danny. The man who assaulted her had been someone else.

By the time the police left, Alexandra was too exhausted to eat dinner. Her head throbbed and her body ached.

Chase looked at her pale face with concern. "You should be in bed," he stated.

"Maybe I will call it a day," she conceded.

"That's an excellent idea," Estelle said. "Take Alexandra upstairs, Chase, and run a hot bath for her. It will help soothe away the aches and pains. I'll have Margaret bring up a tray later on."

The bed had been turned down in Chase's lovely corner room, and there was a bowl of flowers on the dresser. Alexandra was touched by the older woman's solicitude.

"If you're really going to move in here, you should have this room," she told Chase. "It's yours."

"When you're feeling better I'll share it with you," he said, kissing her cheek gently.

"I don't think that's what your mother had in mind when she put me here." Alexandra smiled. "It would also bring some interesting questions from Willie."

"Okay, we'll visit a lot. I'll be in the room next door," he said as he went into the bathroom. After turning on the water, Chase returned to the bedroom. "Get in the tub. I'll unpack for you."

It was an unaccustomed luxury to be this pampered. Estelle had even provided a cut-glass jar of bubble-bath crystals. Alexandra took off her sweater and bra, and winced as she stepped out of her skirt. A bruise on her leg was visible after she removed her panty hose. She was inspecting herself for other marks, when the bathroom door opened.

"I brought your robe and—" Chase stopped abruptly, staring at her.

Alexandra's body heated instantly, in spite of her aches.

As he moved toward her, he noticed the reddened marks on her shoulder and legs, and his expression changed. He touched her face gently, but his voice was charged with fury. "I'd like to kill him for hurting you."

"They look worse than they are," she murmured.

"I wish I could kiss them and make them go away." He lowered his head and touched his lips very lightly to her shoulder.

"That makes it feel better." She smiled.

"I'm glad." He knelt and clasped her hips while he brushed his lips in a whisper caress across the bruise on her thigh. "Does this help?"

"That depends on what you're trying to accomplish," she said with a breathless laugh.

"I want to make you feel wonderful."

His mouth slid over to the apex of her thighs for a burning kiss that set her on fire. Alexandra's legs trembled as his caresses became more penetrating. She had to anchor her fingers in his hair to keep her balance.

When she moaned softly, Chase stood and cupped her face in his palms. "My beautiful, passionate Alex," he said huskily.

She parted her lips for his kiss, but when he took her in his arms she flinched involuntarily.

He let go of her immediately. "I'm so sorry, darling! Did I hurt you?"

"It's all right. I'm just a little sore in spots," she said reluctantly.

"I'm an insensitive clod! You probably hurt all over."

"Not everywhere," she murmured with a smile.

"I wish you hadn't said that." Chase groaned. "Get in the tub before I do something stupid. I don't have unlimited willpower."

"It's one of your most attractive assets," she said impishly as she eased herself into the bubble bath.

"I'll remind you of that in a couple of days," he replied before going out the door.

"I expect to be as good as new by tomorrow," she called after him.

Alexandra's prediction wasn't quite accurate. She was still sore the next day, but she felt a lot better. She would have gone to work, if Chase hadn't raised such a fuss.

Estelle backed him up. "You really should take a day or two off. Can't your associate run the office?"

"I suppose so," Alexandra admitted. "All right, I'll stay home today, but I'm going in tomorrow," she said firmly.

"We'll see," Chase answered.

It was an unaccustomed luxury to have nothing to do. Estelle supervised Willie, Margaret cooked a delicious lunch, and Joseph hovered over Alexandra, ready to bring her anything she wanted.

"I'd better not get used to this." She laughed. "It will be a terrible shock when I have to return to the real world."

"You're not even to think about leaving until that terrible man is caught," Estelle said.

"Who knows how long that might be?" Alexandra's

laughter died. "We couldn't give the police much to go on."

"Their job is catching criminals," Estelle answered dismissively.

"I'm sure they're doing the best they can." Alexandra hesitated. "I don't want to alarm you, but having Willie here might be dangerous for you. The men who are after him won't stop at anything."

"This is the safest place he could be. My husband insisted on having the most sophisticated alarm system available. Nobody could break in without being detected. You have absolutely nothing to worry about, my dear."

Alexandra's fears did seem foolish as she glanced around the stately property. Estelle's home was like a fortress and high walls surrounded the lovely back garden where they were relaxing in pampered luxury. Nobody could get to Willie here.

Both women would have been a great deal less confident if they'd heard the conversation taking place between Danny and Nate.

Danny had started out by venting his anger and frustration at the other man for his latest failure, but Nate cut him off. "Yelling at me isn't going to do any good. That Mainwaring guy is the problem. I would have had the kid if he hadn't blindsided me in front of Alex's apartment. He almost broke my jaw," Nate said in an aggrieved voice.

"Okay, so you didn't see him coming. What about later that night? When you tailed them after they left her apartment. You had plenty of time to waste him before he got to you. Why didn't you?"

"Oh, sure, that would have been smart! Alex was locked in the car with the kid. They'd both have started screeching loud enough to wake the dead when I tried to get them out. Somebody would have called 911. There's always a cop around when you don't want one."

"You could have tried. I wouldn't have lost any sleep if Mainwaring had gone down," Danny muttered. "Or that uppity broad, either."

"Listen, dimwit, do you really want a murder investigation? The police would tie it in with the attempted snatch I made a couple of hours earlier."

"So what? Alex couldn't identify you."

Nate rolled his eyes toward the ceiling. "Has it occurred to you that the cops might figure out the kid is the key to all this? The first thing they'd do is take him into protective custody, and then we'd never get near him."

"I guess you got a point there," Danny admitted grudgingly. "So, where do we go from here?"

"This is your gig. When did I get to be the head honcho?" Nate asked ironically.

"You got to help me," Danny pleaded. "This thing is making me crazy!" His arrogance had been replaced by nail-biting anxiety.

"I'm not doing the dirty work anymore, but I figured you were in over your head. I put two of the boys on Alex. One is watching her apartment and the other is staked out near her office. There weren't any lights on in her apartment last night, but sooner or later she's bound to turn up at one of those two places."

"I suppose she spent the night with Mainwaring." Danny scowled. "That's a fine example to set a kid."

Nate laughed. "Don't take it so hard. At least you're getting turned down by a better class of broad."

"As if I cared! All I'm interested in is where Alex and the boy are. You say she didn't come to work today? Is the place closed?"

"No, she has a gal working for her, which means Alex will come in eventually. She's the boss. And when she gets to the office, we'll wrap this thing up."

"From your lips to God's ears," Danny said fervently.

"I can't keep stalling Karpov much longer. He's giving me real heat."

"You have to stop being such a wimp. Stand up to him. He'll respect you for it."

"Are you kidding?"

"Well, maybe respect is the wrong word." Nate grinned. "But it's time you spelled it out for him. Tell Karpov if the police think there's more involved than the disappearance of the kid's mother, he can kiss his diamonds goodbye. Explain what happened and tell him you're being cautious for his sake. If he wants to send up some L.A. muscle, say it's all right with you. Maybe you'll get lucky and he'll take you off the job."

"Yeah, lucky! I only hope he doesn't take me off permanently," Danny muttered.

The next morning Alexandra came down to breakfast early, dressed in a business suit.

"There was no need for you to get up," Estelle said. "Joseph would have brought you a tray."

Chase looked at Alexandra with a frown. "Why are you dressed like that?"

"You didn't bring me an extensive wardrobe. This is what I had on when you brought us here."

"I packed you some pants and sweaters," he said.

"They're not suitable for the office." She braced herself for the argument that wasn't long in coming.

"The doctor said you should stay in bed for a few days," Chase stated firmly.

"Doctors always say things like that when they can't find anything wrong. It makes people feel better about paying their bill."

"You do have a collection of bruises," Estelle observed.

"They're fading rapidly. I don't have to be handled with kid gloves anymore." Alexandra gave Chase a mischievous glance.

He smiled unwillingly. "I'm delighted to hear that, but it still wouldn't hurt to take a couple of days off."

"I can't afford to. I have a business to run."

Chase didn't give up easily, but Alexandra stood firm. When he realized he couldn't change her mind he said with annoyance, "All right, if you insist. Get your purse and make it snappy. I have a meeting first thing this morning."

"Are you always this grumpy when you lose an argument?" she teased.

His expression changed as he gazed at her. "I hope that's all I ever lose. I don't know what I'd do if anything happened to you."

"I feel the same about you," she answered softly.

They gazed into each other's eyes, oblivious of Estelle, who rose from the table murmuring something trivial.

When they became aware of her, Chase's brisk manner returned. "Are you ready?" he asked Alexandra. "I have a busy morning and I have to allow for the traffic."

"There isn't any traffic between here and my apartment." She expected him to give her a lift, so she could pick up her car.

"No, but there is around your office. I'm taking you to work. You can give me a call when you're through, and I'll come by for you this evening."

"That's absurd! Just drop me at home. I'll drive my own car."

They argued the point briskly. Chase finally gave in again—albeit reluctantly—when Alexandra convinced him that she needed time to go upstairs and pack more clothes than he'd brought for her and Willie.

"All right, but be careful," he warned. "If you think you're being followed, drive straight to the nearest police station."

She agreed solemnly, without telling him she had no idea where one might be. Alexandra was convinced that Chase was being slightly paranoid, but his concern gave her a warm, loved feeling.

Nate's men were professionals. Although Chase gave the street in front of Alexandra's apartment house a close scrutiny, he wasn't suspicious of the man engaged in a conversation with a woman down the block. They simply looked like two friends having a discussion.

Chase couldn't know the man was only asking the woman for directions. As soon as Alexandra disappeared inside her building, Chase drove away.

Alexandra was equally careful when she emerged with a suitcase a short time later. On the way to work, she kept an eye out for a possible tail. She was wary of a car that pulled into her lane, until she noticed the man was talking on his car phone, apparently paying no attention to her.

"She finally showed up at her apartment," the man reported tersely. "I'm on her tail."

Nate was lounging in a chair in Danny's office behind the sports bar. He sat up abruptly. "Is the kid with her?"

"No, she's alone."

Nate swore pungently. "Okay, what's the story?"

"A big guy in a fancy suit dropped her off. She went inside and came out about twenty minutes later with a suitcase."

Nate's hand tightened on the receiver. "Is she headed for the airport?"

"What's going on?" Danny asked in alarm. "Is Alex skipping out with the boy?"

Nate held up his hand for quiet and spoke into the phone. "I didn't hear you, Jerry. Is she going toward the freeway?"

"No, we're on our way to the Marina district or maybe to Fisherman's Wharf. In that general direction."

Nate relaxed. "All right, I can guess where she's going. Her office is on Union Street. Stay with her, but don't let her spot you. Charlie is staked out somewhere near her place of business—it's called Jet Away Travel. Touch base with him. I want both of you on the job. Follow her wherever she goes.''

"It doesn't take two of us, Nate. Have a heart. I've been up all night."

"Life is hard, pal. Just do as I tell you."

"Why do you need both of us?"

"Because I have to know where she goes, and I don't want any slipups this time. When she leaves the office I want both of you to follow her in tandem. Cut in and out so she doesn't suspect she's being tailed. Just make sure you don't lose her. And get back to me when she lands someplace." Nate cradled the receiver and turned to Danny with a look of satisfaction. "We've got her."

"I've learned not to count my chickens," Danny answered sourly. "We still don't know where she stashed the boy."

"We will by the time the day's over, and then we'll pick him up. Only this time we'll have a better plan. Trust me on this."

"It's that Mainwaring creep I don't trust," Danny muttered.

"You've let him psych you out, that's your trouble. He's no superman. He just happened to be in the right place at the right time, but everybody's luck changes sooner or later."

Alexandra spent a busy morning taking care of business. There was such an accumulation of matters needing her attention that she didn't have time to think about anything else. Mandy's phone call reminded her of the unsolved problems still out there.

"What's going on?" Mandy asked. "You rushed me off the phone Sunday night, when you called to tell me you wouldn't be bringing Willie over this week."

"I'm sorry. I didn't mean to cut you off, but we were at Estelle's house and dinner was about to be served," Alexandra lied.

"I understand, but what are you going to do with Willie all this week?"

"I thought I'd like to keep him with me. I'll have to turn him over to Chase soon, and I'm going to miss him."

That part was true, but as the occurrences surrounding Willie became more sinister, she'd realized it wasn't fair to involve Mandy, who was eight months pregnant. Anyone connected to Willie was in potential danger. While Alexandra knew the risks and was willing to take them, Mandy was simply a Good Samaritan, trying to help out. The less she knew about what was going on, the safer she'd be.

"Are you sure you don't want to leave Willie with me for half a day at least?" Mandy asked. "He's awfully good, but it's hard to get any work done with an active youngster around."

"Tina and I will manage to keep him busy."

"Okay, if you say so. How's the big romance coming?"

"Everything is just wonderful." Alexandra's happiness was evident in her voice.

"I couldn't be more pleased for you," Mandy said sincerely. "How does Danny feel about you and Chase? Or doesn't he know?"

"I didn't feel it was necessary to ask his permission," Alexandra said disdainfully.

"You know what I mean. You said he turned nasty when you wouldn't let Willie visit him. If he finds out you're taking the child to Chase's house, he's apt to get even more unpleasant."

"It isn't possible. Anybody that disgusting has to have reached his peak."

"I don't think you're taking Danny seriously enough."

"Don't worry, I'm taking him *very* seriously," Alexandra answered, with unguarded emphasis.

Mandy picked up on it immediately. "Is something going on that you're not telling me about?"

"No, I just meant I agree with you. I don't trust him."

"I have a bad feeling about this whole thing, Alex," Mandy said slowly. "What if Danny gets violent when he finds out you're on Chase's side? The newspapers are full of senseless crimes committed out of frustration. There's no telling what Danny might do to you."

"You've been reading too many tabloids in the supermarket checkout line," Alexandra said dismissively.

"I'm serious," Mandy insisted. "Maybe Willie should stay here with us until this thing is sorted out."

"No!" Alexandra quickly modified her tone. "I mean, it isn't necessary. Willie and I will both be fine."

"I hope you're right."

"I know I am." Alexandra tried to project assurance. "Stop being a mother hen. Don't you have enough on your mind with a husband, a teenager and a baby on the way?"

"I'll always have time for my best friend. I don't want anything to happen to you, Alex."

"I feel the same about you," Alexandra said fondly. "Stop fretting about me and take care of yourself. We're expecting a baby, remember?"

"If this is a team effort, why am I the one with the swollen ankles and the extra fifteen pounds?" Mandy asked dryly.

Alexandra laughed. "I meant, I'm expecting to be a godmother."

"Sure, you wound up with the easy job," Mandy grumbled.

"You wouldn't change places and you know it."

"You're right," Mandy replied softly.

Alexandra was smiling when she hung up, but the conversation with Mandy had reminded her of the uncertainties in her own life. After trying and failing to concentrate on the airline schedules on her computer screen, she dialed Estelle's number.

"Willie and I are having a lovely time," the older woman assured her. "You mustn't worry about us."

"I wasn't worried," Alexandra lied. "I just called to see if you wanted me to pick up anything on the way home."

"Not a thing, dear. And don't hurry on our account. Willie and I are very busy. He taught me to play catch, and now I'm going to teach him to play croquet. We were just about to set up the wickets on the lawn."

Alexandra felt better after she hung up. It was natural to be jumpy after everything that had happened, she assured herself. But Willie was safe now, so she could relax.

Any lingering uneasiness vanished when Chase phoned late in the afternoon. "This is the first minute I've had to call you, angel," he said. "I've been in meetings all day, but you've been on my mind. Are you feeling all right?"

"As good as new," she assured him.

"I'm glad to hear it. I didn't know whether to make plans for tonight," he said in a deepened voice.

"That depends on how strenuous they are." She laughed breathlessly.

His answering chuckle had a deep male sound. "It's something we can do lying down."

"In that case, I don't see any problem."

"Our problems are over, sweetheart. Tonight will be a time for celebration."

"I can hardly wait," she answered softly.

"That doesn't begin to express how *I* feel. See you soon, darling."

Fortunately the day was almost over, because after Chase's call, Alexandra found it difficult to concentrate on anything else. She even closed the office a few minutes early, something almost unheard of for her.

As she pulled away from the curb, Alexandra considered making a detour to her own apartment to pick up the new peach chiffon peignoir set she'd bought. It was almost sinfully seductive. Her mouth curved in a smile as she decided it would be a waste of time, considering the brief period she'd be wearing it.

The two men following Alexandra were very professional. Jerry trailed her for a short distance, then changed lanes. His place was taken by Charlie. To keep her from spotting them, they sometimes allowed two cars to get between Alexandra's and the one tailing her, but the other man was always in a position to close the gap if she got too far ahead.

It was a masterful strategy—but unnecessary. Alexandra's earlier uneasiness was forgotten and she had better things to think about. She never gave the surrounding traffic a second thought. When she pulled into Estelle's driveway and saw Chase's car already parked there, a little ripple of pleasure ran up her spine.

Jerry shared her pleasure, if not for the same reason. After noting the address as he drove by, he dialed Nate's number. "Your bird flew to the high-rent district," he said when the other man answered. Jerry gave him the address.

"Bingo!" Nate smiled broadly at Danny. "The kid's at one of those big mansions in Pacific Heights. Probably Mainwaring's place." He spoke into the phone again. "Good work, Jerry."

"Can I go home and get some sleep now?" the other man asked plaintively.

"Sure, get a good night's rest. I'll be needing you again." Nate hung up and said, "I told you we'd find her."

"What good's it gonna do?" Danny asked sourly. "Those big houses are alarmed like bank vaults. We'll never get Willie out of there."

"I'm getting damn sick of your whining," Nate said impatiently. "We don't have to go in. We'll wait until a nanny or somebody brings the kid out. Or else we'll snatch him out of the backyard," he continued, anticipating Danny's further objection. "They can't keep him inside forever, and their alarm system won't be worth squat outside."

"If you can pull this off, I'll owe you one," Danny said fervently.

"Don't think I'll let you forget it," Nate answered.

Alexandra found Chase in the garden, playing croquet with his mother and Willie.

"We're playing a game, Alex," Willie called to her. "Do you wanna play with us?"

"I think it's time to stop now," Estelle told him. "We all have to wash our hands for dinner."

"Come on, I'll show you where to put your mallet." Chase helped the little boy put the heavy wooden mallet in its stand by the back door.

"It's so nice to have everybody home this early," Estelle remarked as they all walked into the house. "You're a good influence on my son," she told Alexandra.

"You have Willie to thank for dragging Chase out of the office," Alexandra replied lightly.

"Somehow I doubt that." Estelle's eyes twinkled mischievously as she took the little boy's hand and led him upstairs.

As soon as they were alone, Chase took Alexandra in his arms. "How early do you think we can go to bed?" he murmured in her ear.

"Not for hours yet," she answered reluctantly.

He groaned and molded her body more closely to his. "I wish we could be totally alone someplace."

The warmth of his body penetrated hers, fusing them together. She moved voluptuously against the hard proof of his passion, making a tiny appreciative sound.

Chase's embrace tightened and he kissed her with pent-up desire. Sooner than she wanted, he released her, grasping her shoulders and putting her away.

"You're like a fire in my blood," he muttered. "If I don't stop now, I won't be able to."

It was as difficult for Alexandra to practice restraint. Every inch of her vibrated with the same need. She took a deep breath and managed a smile. "They say denial is good for the character."

"Maybe, but it doesn't do a whole lot for the rest of me," Chase said wryly.

An undercurrent of anticipation gripped both of them during the evening. Willie had an early dinner, with Margaret and Joseph hovering over him.

While the adults dined leisurely, he went into the den to watch television for a short time before going to bed. Joseph was removing their soup plates when Willie came racing into the dining room.

"You gotta come quick!" he said excitedly. "Mommy is on television."

They all exchanged a startled look before jumping up and hurrying into the den. The television screen showed a man and a woman sitting at a desk and talking. They were both glitzy Hollywood types, with perfectly arranged hair and high-style clothes.

"Is that Brenda?" Estelle asked, gazing at the blonde woman.

"Not her," Willie said impatiently. "She had a picture of Mommy. I saw it!"

Alexandra and Chase exchanged a glance. "Maybe it was somebody who looked like your mother," she said gently.

"No, I saw her. I did!"

"What program is it?" she asked Chase.

He picked up a television log lying nearby. "Something called 'Follow Up.' I believe it's one of those tabloid-type shows."

Estelle nodded. "Margaret watches it. They take unsolved police cases and report any new developments."

"But there haven't been any," Alexandra said. "The police would have told us."

"Let's listen," Chase said.

"Where the case stands now..." the blonde TV hostess was saying. "We'll show you her picture again. If anyone out there has information on this woman's tragic disappearance, please call the number on your screen and we'll follow up on it." A picture of Brenda appeared, with an 800 number below it.

"You see? It *is* Mommy. Is she coming home soon, Alex?"

"I don't know, honey," she answered soberly.

"Why not?" The little boy's lower lip started to tremble. "I want to see her again."

"We all do, son." Chase picked him up and sat down in a big chair with the child on his lap. "Your mommy wants to see you, too, but she can't right now, so she asked us to take care of you. You like it here, don't you?"

"Yes," Willie said doubtfully. "But when am I gonna go to my other house?"

"We have a lot of things to do first," Chase said evasively. "We haven't been to the circus yet or gone to the zoo. You'd like to do that, wouldn't you?"

"I guess so," Willie answered without enthusiasm.

Before he could talk about going home again, Chase had an inspiration. "I also need you to help me pick out a puppy. Do you think you could do that for me?"

The little boy's eyes brightened. "A real live puppy? Can I really?"

They all breathed a sigh of relief as Willie appeared to bounce back to normal. He was still hyper when his bedtime came, but Alexandra finally got him tucked away.

"Come have something to eat, dear," Estelle said when she finally came downstairs.

Alexandra wasn't hungry, but she picked at the warmed-over dinner while they discussed the television program.

"Where do you think they got that picture of Brenda?" Estelle asked.

"Those tabloid shows have better sources than the FBI," Chase said. "They have an incredible amount of money to spread around."

"Do you think they'll get any response?" Alexandra asked.

"It's possible," he answered noncommittally.

"I'd like to believe she's still alive, but why wouldn't she return to claim her son? It always comes back to that."

They asked the same unanswerable questions for what seemed like hours, still without finding any answers. Finally Alexandra said, "I give up. If you'll excuse me, I'm going to bed."

"I think I'll turn in, too," Chase remarked casually. "It's been a long day."

Alexandra's depression faded as they climbed the stairs together. Willie didn't need them any longer. The rest of the night was theirs.

Moonlight was streaming in the window of Chase's old bedroom when he closed the door and took Alexandra in his arms. The silvery light outlined his strong features and turned his blue eyes into glittering pools.

He kissed her slowly, savoring the sweetness of her mouth. While he caressed her body, she unbuttoned his shirt and pulled it out of his slacks. He did the same for her, and when her blouse was unfastened, he lowered his head and strung a line of kisses across her breasts.

Alexandra arched her back as his lips closed around one taut nipple. His tongue was warm and wet, and even more sensuous, somehow, through the lace covering of her bra. But still she longed to feel his mouth on her bare skin.

When she whispered in his ear he was quick to comply. Chase was reaching to unclasp her bra when a low wail broke the silence, seeming to come from a long distance.

It didn't penetrate their consciousness until the sound became louder and words were discernible.

"Mommy! Where are you, Mommy?"

Alexandra and Chase sprang apart and sprinted down the hall, hurriedly straightening their disarranged clothing. They burst into Willie's room and she took the little boy in her arms.

"It's all right, darling. Alex is here."

He looked at her in bewilderment. "You're not Mommy. Where did she go?"

"It was just a dream, darling, but Uncle Chase and I are here. Close your eyes and go back to sleep."

"No!" He clutched a handful of her blouse to keep her from leaving. "I don't like it in here all alone. I wanna sleep with you."

Alexandra's eyes and Chase's met ruefully over the little boy's head. Without hesitation, she said, "Of course you can sleep in my room, honey."

"I'll carry you." Chase hoisted the child in his arms. As they walked down the hall he murmured, "If this doesn't earn me a halo, nothing will."

Chapter Ten

Willie didn't refer to his dream the next morning, and the adults didn't either. After finishing his breakfast ahead of them, the little boy ran upstairs to play with his toys.

"Do you think he's forgotten about the dream?" Alexandra asked.

"I doubt it," Estelle said. "He just doesn't want to talk about it. Seeing that picture of his mother reminded him of how much he misses her."

"It's too bad," Chase said. "He seemed to be accepting the situation."

"This was just a minor setback," Estelle said. "Children are remarkably resilient. Willie might refuse to sleep alone for a while, but he'll get over that, too."

Alexandra and Chase avoided looking at each other. He pushed back his chair. "Well, I have to get to work."

"I do, too," she said.

They had both left their cars in the driveway overnight.

Chase walked Alexandra to her car and kissed her cheek chastely.

"I can't even kiss you properly out *here*," he grumbled, waving an arm at the street which was unusually crowded for that residential neighborhood.

A utility truck of some kind was parked across the street, with a dry cleaner's van behind it. Farther down the block, a gardener was unloading a lawn mower and other equipment from another truck.

"The whole world does seem to be conspiring against us," she agreed wryly.

"We'll find a way. All I want is twenty-four hours of your undivided attention. Is that too much to ask?"

"It doesn't sound like it to me. Keep a good thought." With a smile and a wave of her hand she backed out of the driveway.

Estelle made sure that Willie was kept busy that morning. He "helped" Margaret in the kitchen for a while, until she had to start preparations for lunch, and then Joseph told him stories while he polished silver.

The morning fog burned away about eleven o'clock and Estelle took Willie outside to play croquet. It had turned into a lovely day after the sky cleared.

She took a deep breath of the fresh air. "Isn't it nice to be outside? The flowers smell so lovely. Look, darling, there's a hummingbird."

Willie glanced in its direction, but he was more interested in the man on the utility pole. "What's that man doing up there?"

"He's fixing something," Estelle said dismissively. "Here's your mallet. You can go first."

They were in the middle of a spirited game when Joseph came to tell Estelle she had a telephone call. "Take a message and tell them I'll return the call," she said.

"I offered to, madame, but it's Mrs. Willoughby. She said you wanted some names and addresses from her."

"Oh, that's right, for the donors' luncheon. Tell her I'll be with her in a moment."

"Would you like me to bring you the cordless phone?" he asked.

"No, I'll take it at my desk, so I can make notes. I'll be right back, Willie."

As soon as she went into the house, the man started to descend the pole he was perched on. When he was level with the wall, he leapt onto it.

Willie wandered over, looking up at him with interest. "What are you doing up there?"

"I'm a friend of your daddy's. He sent me to get you."

The little boy's face lit up. "Where is he? Where's my daddy? I haven't seen him in a long time."

"I'll take you to him," the man promised, crouching down and extending his hand. "I have a car outside. Grab my hand and I'll pull you up."

Willie looked doubtful. "I have to ask Auntie Estelle first."

"No, you don't." The man jumped to the ground and started toward him. "Your daddy says you have to come with me." As Willie backed away, he lunged at him. "Come here, you little brat."

The sudden action startled the child, as well as the menacing tone of voice. It brought back memories of the other time a strange man had tried to grab him. Willie turned and ran toward the house, screaming at the top of his lungs.

The man sprinted after him, too intent on the child to see the croquet wickets in the lawn. He caught his foot in one of the wire loops and went sprawling full length on the grass as Joseph came running out of the house.

The butler assessed the situation in one quick glance. "Go in the house and tell your aunt to call the police," he told Willie, who obeyed without question.

The man had gotten to his feet and was advancing menacingly. He was young and muscular. Joseph was clearly
at a disadvantage, but he stood his ground.

"Get out of my way, old man," the intruder said contemptuously. "I'm going in there."

"You'd better leave while you still have the chance,"
Joseph answered, barring the way. "The police will be here
any minute."

"I'll be long gone before then—with the boy. You want
to try and stop me, Pops?"

As the younger man came closer, Joseph grasped one of
the croquet mallets from the stand next to him. Choosing
just the right moment, he swung it with all his strength.

The element of surprise was on Joseph's side, but the
younger man's reflexes were good. He swerved in time to
avoid a blow on the head, but the mallet struck his shoulder
with enough force to knock him down.

He was dazed for a moment. Then as Joseph stood over
him, poised to strike again, the man struggled to his feet
and ran back to the brick wall. Clutching the ivy for hand-
and toeholds, he hoisted himself up and over the wall.

Joseph stood guard until the police came a short time
later. They took down his description of the man and
looked around outside for footprints. Other than that, there
was little they could do. The intruder had vanished, along
with the truck that had been parked outside.

"We get these daytime burglaries sometimes," the officer told Estelle. "The crooks are getting bolder all the
time. I'd suggest you keep your back door locked, ma'am,
even when you're at home."

She agreed, without telling him this wasn't a simple burglary.

Chase and Alexandra arrived at the house within minutes
of each other, after Estelle's phone call.

"I didn't think there was any harm in leaving Willie

alone in the backyard for a few minutes," she said plaintively. "I should have been more careful."

"It isn't your fault, Mother." Chase's jaw set grimly. "You couldn't know what lengths these people will go to."

"If I'm right and Danny *is* behind all these incidents, he has a lot of help," Alexandra said slowly. "Joseph's description of the man today is different from the man who attacked me. And how did anybody know where to find us? Somebody must have followed me home, but I'm sure I would have noticed if it had been Danny."

"Why would all those people want to kidnap Willie?" Estelle asked in bewilderment. "And why can't the police catch them?"

"I don't know the answer to either of those questions, but I'm through relying on the police," Chase said.

"What else can we do?" she asked.

"What I should have done in the first place. I'm going to hire a bodyguard for Willie. From now on he'll be guarded every minute, night and day."

"You'll need more than one man for that," Alexandra said doubtfully. "And I'm not sure it will be a healthy atmosphere for Willie. He's already spooked by strange men. How will he react to a succession of them?"

"That isn't what I propose. We only need one man—the right one. He'll sleep in Willie's room, eat with him, go everywhere he goes until we catch whoever is terrorizing the child."

"Can you get someone to put in that many hours?"

"I already have somebody in mind. His name is Bob Gorsky and he's done work for me in the past when some securities were stolen. Bob is an ex-cop, like a lot of PI's, but he looks like a professional athlete. Willie's going to take to him right away."

Bob moved in that afternoon. He was everything he was touted to be, tall and muscular, with a direct gaze that announced he wouldn't back down from a challenge, should anyone be foolhardy enough to issue one. But he was also a very friendly, outgoing man. Alexandra and Estelle liked him at their first meeting.

Under different circumstances Willie would have, too, but he was automatically suspicious of strangers now. Bob's friendly overtures got him nowhere in the beginning. Even though the fiction was that Bob was an old college pal of Chase's.

"Why don't you show Bob your room?" Chase suggested casually. "He's going to sleep in your other twin bed for a few days."

"No, I don't want him to," Willie answered promptly. "It's *my* room."

"That's not very generous of you," Alexandra said. "You have to learn how to share."

"Why?"

"Because when you do nice things for people, they share with you, too."

Willie thought it over. "Okay, he can sleep in my room. I don't care. I'm gonna keep on sleeping with you."

Alexandra knew that trying to convince the child now would only make him more adamant. But she had to bite her lip to keep from laughing at the look on Chase's face.

Everybody but Bob was on edge for a couple of days after that, on the alert for the next incident, whatever it might be. But an uneasy calm prevailed. Perhaps because the police were a conspicuous presence in the neighborhood.

Alexandra had voiced her suspicions of Danny to them, finally relating all the unsettling occurrences she hadn't mentioned before. Although the police couldn't even question him without more to go on, they assured her and the Mainwarings that they were investigating him thoroughly.

Bob fit effortlessly into the household. His unflappable

cheerfulness had a calming effect on everyone. As Willie got used to him, his reserve lessened. Soon he was playing catch with Bob in the backyard, and listening with rapt attention to his stories about being in the marines.

The one thing Willie wouldn't do was return to his own room to sleep. He hadn't completely forgotten the scary events he'd been through. Sometimes in the night he would wake and call out for Alexandra. She was his security blanket. After she spoke soothingly to him, he would hug Teddy and go right back to sleep.

Once it was apparent that Willie didn't seem to have suffered any other ill effects, Chase's concern changed to frustration.

One night when he and Alexandra were alone for a few precious moments, he said, "I don't know how much longer I can go on this way. It's torture to know you're in the next room and I can't do anything about it."

"I feel the same way, darling, but all we can do is wait for Willie to get over his fear. It shouldn't take much longer," she said coaxingly. "Hiring Bob was a brilliant idea. Willie really enjoys being with him. It's only a matter of time until he's the same happy, secure little boy he used to be."

"I want that more than anything in the world. You know how I feel about the child."

"Then try to be patient." Alexandra put her arms around his waist and rested her head on his shoulder. "That's what I keep telling myself."

Chase's embrace tightened and he kissed the top of her head. "Patience is admirable, but we don't have to be martyrs. It's no longer necessary to keep our eyes on Willie every minute. He has plenty of other people doing that. Tonight we're going to have dinner at my place—if we get around to eating," he added with a sultry smile.

Alexandra reacted with enthusiasm that dimmed fast.

"There's nothing I'd like better, but Willie still wakes up and calls for me. If I'm not here, he'll get upset."

"Mother or Bob could go to him," Chase said, but his voice was tinged with uncertainty. "He's perfectly happy with them while you're at work."

"I know. You'd think by now he'd be more dependent on them than he is on me, but I'm the one he wants when he wakes during the night."

"I can certainly understand that," Chase said wryly. He gave a deep sigh. "All right, angel, I'll have to get by on cold showers for the foreseeable future."

At dinner that evening, Estelle and her son discussed some business matters. He headed the family foundation, but she still took an active interest.

"You haven't mentioned the stockholders' meeting in Los Angeles. Isn't it scheduled for this Friday?" she asked.

"Yes, but I'm not going," he answered.

"You have to go! The board is voting on new members. It's very important for you to be there. You're the chairman."

"It's more important for me to be here for Willie."

"Isn't that what you hired *me* for?" Bob asked. "I thought I was doing a good job."

"You are. We all feel a lot more secure with you here." Chase hesitated. "I guess I could fly to L.A. for the meeting, and fly back in the late afternoon."

"That's ridiculous," Estelle said. "You need to get away for a few days. I've never seen you this tense. Why don't you take Alexandra along and stay for the weekend. She could use a little vacation from Willie, too."

Alexandra's heart raced at the mere thought of an entire weekend alone with Chase. Unfortunately she had to decline. "I couldn't leave Willie. He expects me to be there when he wakes up at night."

"That's a problem I think we should address," Estelle said thoughtfully. "Willie's behavior was understandable in the beginning, when he was traumatized. But as long as he continues to sleep in your room, we're tacitly admitting he's in danger. Children sense these things. I believe he'd get over his fears a lot faster if he found out he's safe anywhere in the house.''

"You might be right, but I wouldn't want him to think I deserted him," Alexandra said doubtfully.

"He has to make the break sometime. The longer you let this dependency go on, the harder it will be for him to adjust.''

"That makes sense," Chase said slowly. "We don't want to feed his apprehension by being overly protective.''

Estelle's reasoning was probably correct, but Chase was the one who convinced Alexandra. No matter how much he wanted her with him, he wouldn't urge her to go at Willie's expense.

"You can stay in touch by phone, and L.A. is just an hour plane ride away," Bob remarked. "I agree with your mother. You need a little R and R.''

"Okay, you convinced me." Chase turned to Alexandra with dawning excitement. "How about it? Can you get away for a few days?''

"I don't see why not." She laughed breathlessly. "Tina has taken over for me so often lately that our clients already think she's the head of the firm.''

"Okay, it's all settled then," Chase said. "I'll make reservations at the Beverly Hills Hotel.''

Everybody except Willie approved of the decision. The little boy reacted strongly when they broke the news to him, even though they tried to act casual.

"No! I don't want you to go away," he said.

"It's only for a couple of days, honey," Alexandra said placatingly.

"I don't care. I don't want you to go.''

"You won't even miss us. Alex and I are away at work all day anyway," Chase said in a reasonable tone of voice.

"But she won't be here at night when I go to bed."

"Well, no, but Auntie Estelle and Bob will be."

"I want Alex," the little boy said stubbornly. "I don't like it when I wake up and nobody's there."

"I'll be there if you move back to your own room," Bob said. "It's kind of lonesome all by myself."

Willie looked at him uncertainly. "Grown-up men don't get lonesome."

"Sure they do," Bob said. "You've got Teddy to keep you company. I don't have anybody."

The others held their breath as Willie considered this new idea. Finally he said, "Okay, I guess I can come back after Alex leaves."

Chase breathed a sigh of relief. "Good. Now that that's settled, what would you like us to bring you when we come home?"

"A puppy," the little boy answered promptly. "You promised to get me one, but you didn't do it."

"That's right!" Chase exclaimed. "I completely forgot. Why didn't you remind me?"

"I guess I forgot, too. But I still want him."

"We'll go to the animal shelter first thing in the morning," Chase promised. "They have all sorts of dogs. You can pick out the one you want."

Once more, Alexandra was impressed by Chase's compassion. He could have bought Willie an expensive pedigreed dog, but he preferred to take in a homeless pup and give it the love it needed.

Willie's objections to being left behind were forgotten. He was so excited that it was difficult to get him to go to sleep, and he was up early the next morning.

Alexandra declined the offer to help Willie choose a dog. Chase and Bob could handle what promised to be a lengthy selection process, and she had a lot of details to take care of at the office before her trip.

"I hope you don't mind," she said to Tina tentatively. "I've been asking you to take over a lot lately."

"It's fun being the boss. I could get used to it." Tina laughed. "Have a good time and don't worry about a thing."

"I don't expect to, but I'll be at the Beverly Hills Hotel in case you need me."

"Wow! Chase really goes first class, doesn't he? I wouldn't mind having a guy like him."

"There isn't anybody like him," Alexandra answered softly.

The Beverly Hills Hotel was one of the most prestigious hotels in Los Angeles. It had recently undergone a multi-million-dollar renovation, but the original ambience had been carefully preserved. The famed Polo Lounge, the legendary meeting place for celebrities and movie moguls, looked just the same, and lunch was still served on the outdoor patio shaded by a towering tree.

Chase had reserved one of the bungalows by the swimming pool, a traditionally choice location, and commensurately more expensive. It had a luxurious living room and a glamorous bedroom with a king-size bed and silken draperies. A master bathroom adjoined the bedroom and there was also a powder room off the living room.

Alexandra looked around happily after the bellman had deposited their luggage and left with a sizable tip. "This really has all the comforts of home. If we had a hot plate, we could set up housekeeping."

"We have a telephone," Chase said. "You can order food and drinks twenty-four hours a day."

"That's even better." She grinned.

"The best part is that we're finally alone," he said fervently. "I can hardly believe it!"

"It was a real cliff-hanger," she agreed. "I kept expecting something to come up at the last minute, to prevent us from leaving.''

"Fate couldn't be that cruel," he murmured, taking her in his arms and kissing her with slow enjoyment. "I have too many plans for us."

"Tell me about them." She wrapped her arms around his waist and gazed up at him provocatively.

Chase held her tightly for a moment, before groaning and urging her away. "A little more of this and I won't make my board meeting."

"We could have our own meeting." She smiled seductively. "I'd vote yes on all your proposals."

His eyes began to smolder and he reached up to remove his tie. "How can I refuse a proposition like that? The board will just have to get along without me."

Alexandra caught his hand. "I was only joking. Of course you have to go to your meeting."

He paused indecisively, then sighed. "I suppose you're right. Once I get my business out of the way, the rest of the weekend will be pure pleasure."

She smiled happily. "I'm not even going to let myself think about it or I won't get through the day."

"Tell me about it! What do you plan to do today, angel?"

"I'll keep busy, don't worry about me. What time will you be back?" she asked.

"It's hard to tell, sometime this afternoon. I'll try to get away early, but I can't promise, unfortunately."

"It doesn't matter, we have all night." They kissed longingly, making hungry little sounds. Alexandra was the one who moved away this time. "Go!" she ordered breathlessly.

"You're right again." He smoothed her hair lovingly. "Have a good day, sweetheart."

After Chase left, Alexandra changed into white silk pants and a cropped blue silk blouse banded in matching blue satin. It was a Southern California outfit, unsuitable in San Francisco's fog but just right for L.A.'s warm climate.

She took a cab to fabled Rodeo Drive in the heart of Beverly Hills and strolled in and out of the famous-name boutiques, looking at outrageously priced shoes, dresses and jewelry.

A nearby toy store was more to her taste. She wandered through it happily, picking out gifts to take back to Willie.

When she'd had her fill of shopping, Alexandra took a taxi back to the hotel. It was still only early afternoon, so she changed into her bathing suit and went for a swim in the pool, practically outside their room.

While she was lying on a chaise, half asleep, she heard two women talking nearby. One was telling the other how marvelous the hotel masseuse was.

"Her name is Kirsten. You really must try her, Margo," the woman said. "I've never had such a fabulous massage! It was better than sex."

Alexandra stifled her laughter. The poor woman had obviously never met a man like Chase. As she raved on about the experience, Alexandra decided it was worth checking out. Especially since she had nothing better to do until Chase returned.

A phone call to the hotel health spa brought Kirsten to her room a short time later. She was a statuesque blonde, with magical hands. Alexandra groaned with pleasure as the masseuse kneaded her taut neck and shoulder muscles.

"I haven't felt this relaxed in weeks," she commented.

"People are too tense these days," Kirsten observed. "Everybody has problems, but it doesn't do any good to tie yourself up in knots over them."

"I don't have problems," Alexandra answered blissfully. "Not anymore."

"I'd guess from that smile on your face that you've met somebody special."

"Not just special—he's *perfect!*"

Kirsten turned her head when she heard the front door open, but Alexandra was too busy thinking about Chase to notice.

He walked toward the bedroom, shrugging off his light-weight jacket. When he saw what was going on, he put a finger to his lips.

Kirsten smiled and nodded. "Don't tell me, let me guess," she said to Alexandra. "Your special man is handsome, naturally. He has dark hair, a great tan and he's over six feet tall."

"That's exactly right!" Alexandra exclaimed. "How did you know?"

"Call it a lucky guess." Karen laughed as she pocketed the bill Chase held out to her.

He took her place beside the portable massage table. The masseuse left quietly, as Chase poured a trickle of scented oil on Alexandra's back and rubbed it in with long, steady strokes.

"Mmm, that feels wonderful." She felt like purring. "This *is* almost as good as sex."

Chase's mouth curved with amusement and his hands moved to her rounded bottom.

"That's what I heard some women saying out by the pool. I thought they were crazy, but it just shows you shouldn't knock something until you've tried it." She laughed.

His smile broadened to a grin as he parted her legs and slowly stroked the inside of her thighs with his fingertips. It was more of an erotic caress than a massage. Alexandra tensed slightly, but when his hands moved even higher and he probed her hidden secret, she turned over quickly.

"What are you—" the sharp exclamation died as she saw Chase.

"I'm disappointed that you'd choose a massage over sex," he said. "I didn't know times had changed that much. This isn't really my field, but I'll give it a try."

"It isn't nice to eavesdrop," she said with a mock frown. "Do you know a better way for me to find out things you never told me?" As Alexandra started to get up, Chase urged her shoulders back. "Lie still, your hour isn't up yet."

"I don't mind," she murmured. "I can think of something I'd rather do."

"I want you to get your money's worth. If you think that masseuse was good, you haven't seen anything yet." Chase's hands glided over her body, circling her breasts, then capturing her nipples between his fingers.

"That isn't the way you give a massage," she said faintly.

"It's the way I give one. Do you want me to stop?" He leaned down to kiss her navel, then dipped his tongue into the small depression.

"No, but I wouldn't want you to get oil on your good suit. Why don't you take off your clothes?"

"An excellent idea. I should have thought of that myself."

Their casual tone covered their mounting excitement. Alexandra watched Chase do a male striptease. Her pulse beat faster as he discarded his outer garments and only his briefs remained. When he removed those, the male perfection of his nude body was breathtaking.

She reached out to touch him as he returned to continue his slow exploration of her body. His buttocks felt firm and smooth, like the rest of him. Not an ounce of fat blurred the clean lines of his splendid physique. She wanted to touch him everywhere, as he was touching her.

Before she could gratify her wish, Chase climbed onto the padded table and straddled her hips. "You're so beautiful, my love," he said huskily. "I want to kiss every lovely inch of you."

Alexandra's breathing quickened as he began with her lips and continued from there. Pausing at her breasts to suckle each pink rosette, his mouth trailed a path of fire to her most vulnerable part. She cried out as his intimate kiss sent shock waves through her.

Tugging urgently at his shoulders, she gasped, "I need you, now!"

Chase moved up to cover her body with his. "Not half as much as I need you," he muttered.

They clasped each other tightly for an incendiary moment, sharing the same throbbing anticipation. Then he parted her legs and fulfilled the promise.

Their lovemaking was turbulent, a wild coupling that brought steadily mounting excitement. Their bodies arched and their muscles tensed as each escalating wave of sensation sent them hurtling toward completion. It came in a thunderous burst of pleasure that left them limp in each other's arms.

After a blissful few moments, Chase slid onto his back and positioned Alexandra on top of him. "Do you still think a massage is better than sex?" He chuckled.

"I didn't say better, I said almost as good as."

"That's still not the right answer. I guess I'll have to try harder."

"I can't imagine how you could better the performance you just gave." Her laughter died as she framed his face in her palms and gazed down at him tenderly. "What we shared just now was love, not merely sex, and nothing could surpass that."

"My precious Alexandra, how was I ever lucky enough to find you?" Chase slid off the table and carried her over to the bed.

They curled up together, murmuring soft endearments. Gradually their kisses became more prolonged and their gentle touches grew more sensuous. When Chase scissored his legs around hers, joining their loins closely, Alexandra was happily aware of his reawakened passion.

She stroked him erotically, feeding their escalating desire

until Chase groaned with pleasure. He captured her mouth for a deep kiss that set her on fire. Their sated passion flamed to life, demanding satisfaction. Alexandra arched her body as he entered her, filling her with limitless joy.

"Do you know how wonderful you are?" He smoothed the damp hair off her forehead when it was over. "I'll never get enough of you."

"I certainly hope not," she answered blissfully.

"Can you doubt it?"

"I suspected you were sort of fond of me." Her joking tone covered a deep longing. She wanted their relationship to mean more to him than merely exciting sex.

"Fond isn't the word I would have used," he said indulgently. "I don't know what I'd do without you."

"We can't go on living together forever," she said lightly.

"Not the way we have been, anyway." He grinned. "Willie isn't the only one who doesn't like to sleep alone."

Alexandra reluctantly faced the fact that Chase wasn't going to make a commitment. "Maybe it's time I went back to my own apartment. There really isn't any reason for me to stay on at your mother's. Willie doesn't need me any longer."

"How can you say that? You know the way he depends on you. We all do."

"Good old reliable Alex," she remarked ironically.

Chase levered himself up on one elbow and looked at her searchingly. "What's wrong, angel?"

"Nothing," she answered quickly.

"I know you better than that. Do you feel Mother is taking your place with Willie? Is that what's bothering you?"

"Of course not! I think it's wonderful that she cares about him so much. You can't look after him all alone."

"I wasn't planning to. I'm counting on you to do all the

dirty work—like disciplining him when he needs it," Chase teased. "You know what a pushover I am for that child."

"Sometimes I think he's the only person you love unconditionally," Alexandra said soberly.

"You can't mean that!" he exclaimed. "Not after what we just experienced together."

Chase had been generous with his body, but she wanted his heart as well. Unfortunately it wasn't something he could give because she asked for it. Alexandra reminded herself that she knew the score when she made her decision—and she didn't regret it.

Managing a smile, she said, "You were pretty spectacular."

"I'm not looking for compliments. I want to know why you doubt my feelings for you."

"I don't, darling!" Alexandra regretted her incautious words. The last thing she wanted was to spoil this glorious interlude. They'd both looked forward to it for so long. "This has been the most wonderful afternoon of my whole life."

Chase looked at her searchingly. "I'm happy that I can satisfy you, but it isn't enough to build an entire life on."

Alexandra's heart almost stopped beating. "I'm not sure what you mean."

"I'm saying that our marriage has to be based on more than just satisfying sex."

"You're asking me to marry you?"

He stared back at her with equal incredulity. "You sound surprised. I thought that was understood."

"Oh, Chase, you have a lot to learn about women!" Alexandra was torn between laughter and tears of joy as her dearest wish was realized.

"Did I only believe what I wanted to believe?" His expression was bleak. "Are you saying you don't want to marry me?"

"I never wanted anything more! I kept waiting and waiting for you to ask, but you never did. I was just about ready to give up.''

"Darling Alex!" Chase gathered her in such a tight embrace that she could hardly breathe. "Don't ever give up on me. I wouldn't want to live without you."

"Why didn't you ever say anything?" she scolded gently.

"Because I'm an idiot. But I promise I'll never take anything for granted again. Love of my life, will you marry me?"

"Yes...yes...yes." She punctuated each word with tiny kisses strewn over his face. "Tomorrow morning, if you like."

"Nothing would please me more, but we have to get a license first. That will probably take a few days."

"I wish we didn't have to wait." Alexandra's face clouded. "I'm so afraid something will happen to stop us."

"Nothing can ever come between us," Chase said tenderly. "We were meant to be together."

She relaxed in his arms. "You're right, I'm being foolish. It's just a little scary to be this happy."

"Get used to it, angel. I intend to devote my life to keeping you that way."

They whispered words of commitment between kisses and loving caresses.

"I suppose we should call and tell your mother and Willie the news," Alexandra said finally.

"We can tell them when we go home." Chase urged her head onto his shoulder. "We deserve a weekend without any intrusions."

"Enjoy it while you can. Little boys don't know the meaning of privacy."

"He's the only person I'd share you with."

Alexandra's smile dimmed. "I don't suppose there's any chance of Willie's mother coming back."

"I'm afraid not," Chase said soberly. "But I think

Brenda is watching over him somewhere, and she knows we'll give him the same love she would have if...if things had worked out differently.''

Sadness over the fate of the young mother tinged their happiness. They were quiet for a few minutes. Then Alexandra sighed and moved out of Chase's comfortable embrace. "Well, I guess we should get dressed."

"Why?" He reached out and drew her back.

"Because I don't know of any restaurants in Beverly Hills that are clothing optional." She laughed. "It's getting late. Aren't you hungry?"

"Only for you," he said, cupping his hand around her breast.

"I don't suppose there's any big rush about dinner," she murmured. "We can go out later."

"Actually I planned on keeping you right here all weekend. It's been a recurring fantasy of mine."

"You didn't have to rent an entire bungalow," she teased. "One room would have been enough."

"Stick with me, angel face. You'll go first class all the way." He grinned.

"I could be happy in a leaky tent with you," she said softly.

When Chase covered her body with his, the outside world ceased to exist for both of them.

Chapter Eleven

Alexandra and Chase slept late the next morning and then had breakfast in the living room of their bungalow. The sun shone through the sheer curtains and the swimming pool was a gleam of blue surrounded by green foliage and flowering plants.

Alexandra stretched luxuriously. "What a glorious day!"

"It's amazing how good you feel when you go to bed early," Chase remarked mischievously.

"I highly recommend it." She smiled. "Are you going to eat all your bacon?"

"Poor Alex, you didn't have any dinner last night. Tonight I promise to take you to the best restaurant in town."

"Where are we—" she broke off as the phone rang. "Who could that be? Your mother and Tina are the only ones who know where to reach us, and today is Saturday. The office is closed."

They stared at each other in concern for an instant before Chase reached for the phone. "We thought it might be you.

What's wrong, Mother?'' he asked, confirming Alexandra's fears.

"Everything is fine here," Estelle assured him. "Willie is having a wonderful time with King. The two are inseparable."

Chase's tense expression relaxed in a smile. Willie had insisted on naming his new puppy King, although the small dog was less than regal. He had a long plumey tail, floppy ears and a black circle around one eye that gave him a clownish expression.

"Willie insists on letting King sleep with him," Estelle continued. "I can't talk him out of it."

"His bed must be crowded," Chase chuckled. "Or did Teddy get evicted?"

"Oh, no, the three of them are always together. Willie now has two best friends—three, counting Bob. He's wonderful with the child."

"I have a lot of confidence in him. Bob is a good man to have around."

"That's why I urged you to go," Estelle said. "I knew it was just what you both needed."

"You're a positive genius, Mother."

Willie's voice sounded in the background. "Is that Uncle Chase? I want to talk to him and Alex." When Estelle handed over the phone, the little boy said, "You know what, Uncle Chase? Me and Bob are teaching King to do tricks."

"That's just great. What can he do?"

"He can roll over, but we have to give him a dog biscuit or he won't do it."

"That proves he's a smart pup." Chase laughed.

"Are you gonna bring me a present?"

"Didn't I just get you a dog?"

"Yes, but Alex said you'd bring me a present, too."

"Then that's what we'll do. I think she already bought it."

"Yea! When are you coming home?"

"Pretty soon," Chase said vaguely.

"I have to speak to your uncle now." Estelle retrieved the phone.

"Since Willie is doing so well without us, Alex and I just might stay a little longer," he said casually, smiling at her across the table.

"I'm sorry to have to spoil your plans, but I had a reason for calling," Estelle said. "I'm afraid you two will have to come home."

Chase frowned. "I just talked to Willie and he sounded fine."

"This isn't about him. There's a problem at Alexandra's apartment. The manager called to say a pipe burst in her bathroom or someplace. Since nobody was at home to report it, the leak went undetected for quite a while. There's evidently extensive damage."

"That's too bad."

"What's wrong?" Alexandra asked as Chase looked over at her. After he explained, she took the phone.

"I'm so sorry you'll have to cut short your vacation, my dear," Estelle said, after giving her more details.

"I am, too, but it can't be helped. We'll get packed and catch the first flight out."

"Why do we have to go home?" Chase asked as Alexandra hung up. "It was an unfortunate accident, but there's nothing you can do about it. Tell them to call a plumber."

"I have to go see what can be salvaged and what can't. The insurance company will want me to take a detailed inventory and give them a list of the damaged articles. I do hope my grandmother's antique rocker wasn't warped," she fretted.

"Okay, honey, we'll go back. What choice do I have?" he joked. "I wouldn't be able to get your attention now, anyway."

"I feel as badly about this as you do." She put her arms around his neck.

Chase parted her robe and reached inside to caress her warm body. "Just as long as you remember we have unfinished business."

She smiled impishly. "You could have fooled me. I thought we covered everything last night."

"Don't you believe it! We haven't begun to explore all the possibilities," he murmured.

"If you're trying to distract me, you're succeeding." She groaned with pleasure. "I'm almost ready to write off Granny's rocker."

He closed her robe reluctantly, kissed her cheek and turned her around. "Go get dressed, before my willpower fails."

Chase and Alexandra took a cab from the airport to her apartment, where he dropped her off. He wanted to come in with her, but she talked him out of it.

"I don't know how long it will take me to sort through the mess."

"Look on the bright side," Chase said. "Maybe it isn't as bad as you think."

"I hope you're right, but I want to take my time and look around carefully. You can help by going on home. If I know Willie, he's waiting impatiently for his present."

"You're undoubtedly right." Chase said indulgently. "Okay, honey, call me when you want me to come pick you up."

Alexandra braced herself as she opened her front door, prepared for the worst. It was a pleasant surprise to find the living room untouched, including her grandmother's rocker. The water hadn't penetrated this far.

Which meant the bedroom area must be a mess. The manager had told Estelle there was extensive damage. Alexandra walked toward the bedroom, frowning. Something didn't fit, but she couldn't quite put her finger on what was wrong.

The nagging thought flew out of her mind an instant later when she entered the bedroom. Danny was lounging on her bed, making himself at home. The morning newspaper was spread over the coverlet and a can of beer sat on her nightstand.

"What are you doing here?" she asked sharply. "How did you get in?"

"Are you kidding? An amateur could break into this cracker box."

"And you've had a lot of experience at breaking and entering, haven't you? I always felt you were a shady character. All that talk about being a prominent restaurateur was just a front. You're nothing but a common burglar," she said contemptuously.

"Watch your mouth!" Danny shot up from the bed.

"Don't try to deny you broke into my apartment before this. I could tell someone had been in here, pawing through my things."

"Why should I deny it? You knew you couldn't prove anything or you would have gone to the police."

"I can prove it now."

"What makes you think you're going to get the chance?" he drawled.

Anger had been Alexandra's first reaction to Danny's invasion of her privacy. His menacing tone made her reassess the situation. If he wasn't bothering to cover up his criminal activities, she might be in serious trouble.

"You could have saved yourself a lot of grief if you'd given me a break. But I wasn't good enough for you," Danny said bitterly. "I didn't stand a chance against that pretty boy and all his money."

As Alexandra was framing a careful reply, the bathroom

door opened and a big, beefy man came out, wiping his hands on one of her best linen guest towels.

"I know you!" she exclaimed. "You're the one who knocked me down!"

"That was no love tap your boyfriend gave *me*," Nate commented, glancing over her shoulder into the empty living room. "Too bad he didn't come back with you. I'd love to get another crack at him."

"You will," Danny promised.

Alexandra was definitely alarmed now. She eyed the two men warily, gauging her chances of making it out the front door.

Nate guessed her intentions. "Don't even think about it," he said, producing an ugly-looking revolver.

She froze. "Take whatever it is you're looking for and go. I didn't call the police before, and I won't this time."

"Unfortunately you don't have what we want," Danny said. "I made sure of that a long time ago."

"Then why are you here? Why have you been following me and standing outside my house? I'm sure I didn't imagine it."

"No, we had a tail on you, but you weren't the one we wanted. You were only a means to an end."

"Willie? What could you possibly want with an innocent little boy?"

"Not him, his mother."

"Brenda?" Alexandra asked in bewilderment. "But she's either dead or she's left the country. She came to me in the first place because she wanted tickets to London."

Nate shifted impatiently. "Cut the chitchat and let's get on with it."

"There's no hurry. Alex isn't going anywhere."

"Somebody might come looking for her."

"Her boyfriend?" Danny's smile was chilling. "I hope he does. You're not the only one who'd like a crack at him."

Alexandra's palms were damp. She dug her nails into them in an attempt to stay calm. Danny was paranoid about Chase. He would hurt him for the pure pleasure of it. Somehow she had to prevent that from happening—but how? The only thing she could do was stall for time, keep Danny talking.

"I'm sorry I didn't believe you were Brenda's fiancé," she said placatingly.

"He never got to first base with *her,* either." Nate grinned.

"Like *you* could." Danny scowled.

Nate shrugged. "I'm not into rejection. Anybody could see she was crazy about Bill."

"Was he really Chase's brother?" Alexandra asked.

"Yeah, but we didn't know it until Mainwaring showed up to claim the kid. It gave Danny quite a jolt. Bill never talked about his family. We figured maybe they were in the slammer." Nate laughed. "That was a big joke on us. Who would guess they were pillars of society?"

"Big deal," Danny muttered. "They had their black sheep just like ordinary people."

"Is Bill really dead?" Alexandra asked soberly.

Nate and Danny exchanged a glance. After a moment, Nate nodded.

"How did he die?" she persisted.

"He committed suicide."

Danny's sarcasm was lost on Alexandra. "That can't be. He was so young!" she exclaimed. "And he had everything to live for, a beautiful wife, a darling child. From the things Willie told me, they were a happy family."

"He should have thought of that before he got greedy," Danny remarked sourly.

"I don't understand." Alexandra looked at him in bewilderment.

"Oh, what the hell, it doesn't matter now anyhow. Bill worked for an organization that smuggles diamonds from

Russia into this country. He picked up a consignment, but he never turned it in. The boss didn't take kindly to being ripped off.''

"Bill was a damn fool," Nate said. "He might have gotten away with palming a few stones, but only an idiot would have thought he could get away with the whole lot."

"He was killed for stealing?" Alexandra asked in horror.

"We're not talking petty change here. Those rocks were worth a couple of million."

"But not a man's life! You didn't have to murder him."

"Hey, we didn't have anything to do with it," Danny said in alarm. "Neither of us was the one who wasted him."

"That makes you regular choirboys," she said sarcastically. "Terrorizing Bill's innocent wife and son is okay, is that it? Even though they're not responsible for his poor judgment."

"That's an interesting way of putting it," Nate commented dryly.

"Let me set you straight," Danny said. "Brenda is in this up to her ears. Bill knew he was a marked man the minute he decided to go into business for himself, so he passed the diamonds on to Brenda to hold for him. They planned to skip out, only she made it and he didn't. At least, she got as far as San Francisco. It won't do her any good, though. We'll catch up with her sooner or later."

"How do you know she isn't long gone?" Alexandra asked. "She must know you're after her."

"Sure, but she's just as greedy as her husband—and as stupid. Any sensible person would have taken the first plane out of town after she found out I was on her tail. But she thinks she can outsmart us and wind up with the diamonds *and* her son."

"You're wrong. If Brenda really does have the diamonds, all she had to do was contact me with some excuse about why she'd been delayed. I would have returned Willie to her.''

"And we would have been waiting," Danny said. "She knew that. We almost had her a couple of times, but she slipped through our fingers. This time her luck is about to run out.''

"If you think I know where she is, you're wrong," Alexandra said.

"It doesn't matter, we're through looking for her. Now Brenda will have to come to us," Danny said with satisfaction.

"You've impressed her enough with your brilliance," Nate said irritably. "Tell her to make the call.''

"Yeah, I guess it's time. I'm looking forward to seeing Mainwaring again." Danny smiled malevolently as he picked up the phone and handed it to Alexandra. "Call your boyfriend and tell him to bring the kid over here. Think of some excuse—and make it a good one."

Her nerves tightened. "What will that accomplish? Willie doesn't know where his mother is, either."

"But she'll know where *he* is. If Brenda is still around— and I'm damn sure she is—she'll come running like a tiger to defend her cub.''

"It's a good plan, but there's one thing you've overlooked." Alexandra tried to sound calm and analytical. "How will Brenda know that Willie isn't safe at the Mainwarings any longer? She can't be keeping him under constant surveillance. You've been doing that, and you would have caught her.''

"Willie's a lucky little boy," Danny drawled. "He's going to get his picture in the newspaper again.''

Alexandra was silent for a moment as Danny's plan became nauseatingly clear. He wanted her to trick Chase into bringing Willie to the apartment. As soon as Danny had his hands on the child, he would kill Chase and her. How could he let them live after admitting his criminal involvement?

Danny and Nate might not have killed Bill, but they were clearly capable of murder. Both were carrying guns they wouldn't hesitate to use.

A double murder would make a splash in the newspapers. Especially when it involved the disappearance of a child who was already an object of interest. Danny was correct: Brenda would know exactly what had happened. And she would respond as he anticipated.

"Get on the extension phone," Danny told Nate. "If she tries to get cute, cut her off."

Alexandra set her jaw grimly. "I'm not making the call."

"You'll do as you're told," he said menacingly. "I'm just itching for an excuse to slap you around."

Her lip curled. "I don't doubt it. You're a coward and a bully." She had nothing to lose. He was going to kill her anyway. But at least she could save Chase and Willie.

Danny grabbed her long hair and yanked her head back. "How'd you like a split lip?"

"Will that make you feel like a big man, instead of the little punk you really are?"

His face contorted with fury. "You've got a smart mouth on you, but I can fix that. When I get through working you over, your fancy boyfriend won't be interested in what's left."

As Danny raised his hand, Nate said, "All you'll get that way is satisfaction. It won't change her mind."

"What's wrong with satisfaction?" Danny snarled. "She's been asking for this, and I'm gonna give it to her."

"Stay focused," Nate said disgustedly before turning to Alexandra. "You can be a hero, but you can't win, babe. If you don't get the kid over here, we'll find another way to flush Brenda out of hiding. Don't force us to use drastic methods. If you cooperate, nobody will get hurt."

"You must think I'm simpleminded," she said indignantly.

"No, I'm giving it to you straight. Make the call, and you and Mainwaring will be okay. We'll just tie you up and clear out, that's all."

"Are you crazy?" Danny shouted. "She'll go straight to—" He subsided as Nate gave him a warning look.

"The boy won't be hurt, either," Nate continued. "All we want are the diamonds. After Brenda returns them, we'll let her and the boy go."

"It's a very generous offer, but I'm afraid I'll have to decline." Alexandra knew he was lying. Brenda and her son would be dead minutes after these two thugs got what they were looking for.

Nate's face hardened. "I'd reconsider, if I were you. Unless you want to be responsible for the deaths of everybody in the Mainwaring house. We don't necessarily need the boy alive. A firebomb would help us locate Brenda just as easily. She'd want to see if her kid was alive or dead."

Alexandra looked at him incredulously. "You'd kill a lot of innocent people who had nothing to do with any of this?" When he simply stared back at her impassively, she knew it had been a foolish question.

Her mind started to race furiously. There must be a way out. Not for her, but she couldn't let all those people die. She'd just have to shout out a warning to Chase before Danny shot her. Then the police could put him away for murder, and Willie and the Mainwarings would be safe.

"Well, what's it going to be?" Nate asked.

"All right, I'll tell Chase to bring Willie here," she said slowly.

Danny looked at her suspiciously as he handed her the phone. "Don't try any funny business, understand? Nate and I will both be listening in."

She didn't bother to reply. Her heart was pounding as she waited for Chase's voice, knowing this was the last time she'd ever hear it.

"Hi, darling," he said. "Are you through already? It couldn't have been too much of a mess."

"No, it's not so bad. Did Willie like the toys I picked out?" she asked, to prolong the bittersweet moment. Danny had his ear close to hers, listening in, but he could fume all he wanted. She was entitled to say goodbye.

"He was crazy about them. Even Teddy and King took a temporary back seat."

"I'm glad," she said wistfully.

Danny put his hand over the mouthpiece and hissed, "Get to the point!"

Before she could comply, Chase asked, "Was your grandmother's rocker damaged? I know you were worried about it."

Suddenly Alexandra had an inspiration. There might be hope after all! "The wooden rockers were soaked, but I think Bob Gorsky can refinish them. He's the best cabinetmaker in town."

Danny grabbed the phone out of her hand. "What the hell do you think you're pulling?"

"I'm supposed to have had water damage," she said rapidly. "Chase would be suspicious if I wasn't concerned about it."

"Okay, but watch it," Danny said grudgingly.

"Alex? Are you there?" Chase asked.

"Yes, I'm still here, darling."

"You want Bob to repair your rocker?" Chase asked slowly.

"He's the most experienced man I know of for this sort of thing." Alexandra could tell Danny had been pushed to the limit. "I'm all finished here," she told Chase quickly. "You can come and pick me up. Oh, and bring Willie with you. He needs to get out of the house more."

"Yes, I suppose you're right," Chase said.

Danny took the phone out of her hand and hung up. "That's enough," he said firmly.

Nate returned from the living room. "Good job," he told Alexandra. "You played it smart."

She shrugged. "You didn't give me any choice."

"Let's have a drink to celebrate." Danny's mood had changed to one of jubilation. "I know where she keeps the liquor. You're coming with us," he said to her. "I want you where I can see you."

She accompanied the two men silently, scarcely hearing their gloating comments. Her thoughts were focused on Chase. Did he understand her message? He must have, or he would have argued about the wisdom of taking Willie out for such a trivial errand.

But what if he didn't understand? They'd both thought all their troubles were behind them. What if the unthinkable happened and he came and brought Willie with him? Would she have time to call out a warning before they were inside the apartment?

Nate shoved a glass in her hand. "Come on, have a drink. It'll make you feel better."

"Sure, it'll all be over soon," Danny chuckled.

Nate gave him a disgusted look, which was unnecessary. Did he think she didn't know what they had in store for her?

"Look on the bright side." Danny continued to goad her, ignoring his partner's warning glance. "It could have been worse. A pipe really could have burst, and all your stuff would have been ruined. The old lady at Mainwaring's house got real upset when I called to tell her."

Suddenly Alexandra knew what had been bothering her earlier. Nobody knew she'd been living at Estelle's, so the manager wouldn't have known where to reach her. Why hadn't she and Chase realized the phone call to his mother must be bogus? Because they'd made the fatal mistake of letting down their guard, she thought despairingly.

As the minutes ticked by, Alexandra's nerves tightened almost unbearably. She hoped Chase had called the police, but it probably wouldn't do her any good. Danny and Nate would use her as a hostage. She knew Danny wouldn't hesitate to shoot her out of sheer vindictiveness for thwarting his plans.

The waiting was the hardest part. Danny felt the same way as time passed. He wasn't good under pressure. "Where the hell are Mainwaring and the kid? If you tipped him off in some way, you're gonna get yours," he told Alexandra.

"Calm down," Nate advised. "You heard her conversation. She played it straight."

"Maybe. I didn't like the part where she—" They all stiffened as the doorbell rang.

Danny pointed his gun at her. "Tell them to come inside. We'll be right behind the door. If you try anything stupid, you'll both get it—starting with your lover."

Alexandra's legs felt leaden as she walked to the front door. Would Danny and Nate start shooting when they saw the police? Or would they expect her to get rid of them? If the police asked her if everything was all right what could she say, knowing two guns were trained on her?

Her heart sank even further when she opened the door and saw Chase standing there. He hadn't understood her message after all. Or had he? Willy wasn't with him. But Chase didn't know he was walking into a trap. Before she could shout a warning, he entered the apartment.

Danny looked past him. "Where's Willie?"

"I asked him if he wanted to come, but he declined the pleasure of your company," Chase drawled.

"I told you she double-crossed us!" Danny said to Nate. He swore viciously, pointing the gun at Chase. "You and your girlfriend aren't as smart as you think you are, hotshot. I'm gonna enjoy blowing you away, but first you get to see her die."

"Don't be a fool, Riker." Chase's face was pale under

his tan. "You can't get away with this. Do you think I was dumb enough to come here alone?"

"Yeah, it's just the kind of macho thing you *would* do to impress a broad. Too bad all it got you was a double funeral."

As Danny raised the gun, Chase said quickly, "Don't do anything stupid. The police are on their way."

Alexandra prayed that he wasn't bluffing. But if Chase had called the police, where were they?

Danny shared her doubt. "You always were full of bull," he said disgustedly. "Maybe now your girlfriend will believe me."

Nate hadn't taken any part in the confrontation, but he was getting increasingly restless. "Cut the chatter. I think we should get out of here."

"As soon as I take care of a little unfinished business," Danny said.

"What's the point? He didn't bring the kid."

"You want to let them spill their guts to the police?"

"They don't have any proof. It would sound like they've been watching too much television."

"Maybe so, but this is one they owe me. Now who's chicken?" Danny taunted as his partner prepared to argue.

Nate frowned at the sound of a distant siren. "Okay, then get it over with. I don't—" He broke off abruptly. "What's that noise?"

When he and Danny turned their heads momentarily, Chase sprang at Danny and grabbed his wrist. Chase was the more powerful of the two, but Danny was unexpectedly wiry. Both men were fueled by fury, which evened the imbalance.

Nate didn't wait for the outcome. He moved quickly to help his partner. Without a moment's hesitation, Alexandra picked up a vase and hit him over the head. The gun flew out of his hand as he crumpled to the floor with a surprised look on his face.

When he didn't get up, she turned her attention to Danny, but Chase had the situation under control. Danny yelped with pain as Chase twisted his wrist viciously. After the gun clattered to the floor, Chase delivered a punch that floored the other man. He was pulling him upright, preparing to hit him again, when the police entered from the back door.

"We'll take over now," one of the officers said. He glanced at the two prone men and chuckled. "Looks like you didn't need our help."

After Danny and Nate were taken away in handcuffs, reaction set in and Alexandra began to tremble. Chase took her in his arms and held her tightly.

"It's all right, darling, I'm here for you." He smoothed her hair tenderly. "I'll always be here."

"I was so afraid you didn't understand what I was trying to tell you." A tremor ran through her. "Especially when I opened the door and saw you there."

"The police told me they'd handle it, but I couldn't stay away. There was no telling what those thugs would do to you before the police got inside." Chase's embrace tightened. "You'll never know what I went through, when I realized you were in danger. I'd have killed Riker with my bare hands, if he'd hurt you!"

"He's no threat to any of us anymore." She smiled brilliantly at the realization. "We can all live normal lives again—especially Willie."

Chase and Alexandra agreed to play down the danger they'd faced, to spare Estelle from worry. But the afternoon newspaper carried the story. The details were sparse, since all the facts weren't known yet, but Danny and Nate were pictured as major criminals. The article alluded to mob connections and made vague references to money laundering and diamond smuggling, among other activities. It hinted at an imminent arrest in Los Angeles of a big-time rack-eteering ring.

Estelle looked at Chase in bewilderment. "How could Bill get mixed up with these people?"

"We'll never know," he sighed. "My guess is it was a gradual descent. Bill always liked the excitement of living on the edge. I suppose he finally went too far and couldn't find his way back."

"It's such a waste. He was so vital, so full of life." Estelle's eyes were sad.

"He'd want us to remember him that way. We'll tell Willie all the good things about his father."

They had been too engrossed to hear the doorbell. Joseph came into the library to announce, "There's a lady to see you, madame."

"I don't think I can talk to anyone right now," Estelle said. "Who is it and what does she want?"

"Her name is Brenda Clark," Joseph said. "She didn't state her business, but I'll tell her to call back another time."

Brenda appeared behind him. "No! I have to speak to you, Mrs. Mainwaring."

Alexandra was the first to react. She jumped up and rushed over to the other woman. "Brenda! Where have you been all this time? We thought you were dead."

"Is this Willie's mother?" Chase was staring at her.

"Where is he? Where's my son?" That was Brenda's only concern.

"He's upstairs," Alexandra said. Willie was helping Bob pack, since the bodyguard's services were no longer needed. "Before we call him down, you have a lot of ex-plaining to do. Sit down and start talking."

Brenda perched on the edge of a chair, casting a longing look at the stairs. "Is he all right? I've been so worried that one of Danny's attempts to kidnap him would suc-ceed."

"You knew about those?" Chase asked.

"I've never been far away." She turned to Alexandra. "I'm sorry to have caused you so much trouble, but I didn't have any choice. I realized Danny was following me when I got a few blocks from your office that day. If I'd tried to come back for Willie, I would have put him in terrible danger. I thought I'd gotten away from Los Angeles safely, but Danny picked up my trail somehow."

Chase's face was stern, as he remembered the danger Alexandra had been subjected to. "Riker was after Willie only to get to you. If you were that concerned about your son, why didn't you just return the diamonds?"

"I don't have them!"

"That's a little hard to believe. If you're telling the truth, where are they?"

"I don't know, but he wouldn't have believed me any more than you do," she said with a sigh.

Chase stared at her with indecision. "Did Bill really steal those diamonds?"

"Yes, but he was going to give them back. It's true!" she insisted, when the skepticism on all their faces was evident. "Bill did a lot of foolish things when he was younger, but he changed after we were married. He was trying to get his life in order, but they wouldn't let him." Brenda eyes filled with tears.

Estelle squeezed her hand and gave her a tissue. "Are you all right, my dear?"

Brenda nodded and continued her story. "Bill was a big gambler when I met him, but he changed after we got married and had Willie. He wanted to start over, so he borrowed money to pay off his gambling debts, not realizing he was dealing with a loan shark. A man named Karpov controlled the loan-sharking business in Los Angeles. After Bill was hopelessly in debt to him, he suggested Bill join his organization. Karpov was into all kinds of illegal rackets.

"Bill didn't have any choice. He wasn't afraid for himself, but when he refused Karpov threatened to hurt Willie and me. Bill went to work for him, but he hated it. He tried to pay off his debt so he could get out, but Karpov kept adding interest charges. There was no way Bill could get free of him."

"So that's why he took the diamonds," Alexandra murmured.

"It was an act of desperation. Bill thought we could go somewhere and start a new life. He realized almost immediately that it was wishful thinking. Karpov would track him down wherever we went. He would have been willing to chance it for himself, but he couldn't put us in that kind of jeopardy. Bill loved Willie and me more than his own life," Brenda said sadly.

"Why did they kill him before they got the diamonds back?" Chase's voice was husky with emotion.

"They ambushed him, not knowing he intended to return them."

"But surely they searched his body."

"He didn't have the stones on him. Bill was fairly sure Karpov would have him killed afterward, so he planned to tell him where to find the diamonds if he'd let us leave town. Bill didn't expect them to kill him without even listening to him," Brenda said bitterly.

"Where could he have hidden them?" Alexandra asked. "Did you have a safety-deposit box?"

"Yes, but there was nothing in there of any great value. Before leaving town I closed our bank account and sold my jewelry—everything except my wedding ring." Brenda gazed down sadly at the wide gold band on her finger.

"Karpov must have sent someone to search your house," Alexandra remarked. "Just like he instructed Danny to search your hotel room and my apartment. Those people are very thorough. How could Bill have hidden the diamonds so successfully that professionals couldn't find them?''

"They weren't on him, but they had to be someplace he could get at easily," Chase mused. "Maybe they were in something of yours," he told Brenda. "Is there anything you always carry around with you?"

"Just my purse when I go out of the house. But it's a different one all the time, depending on my outfit."

"It has to be something like that," Chase muttered.

Alexandra looked at Brenda with dawning excitement. "There's something else you always take with you when you go out—Willie!"

They all gave her a puzzled stare. "So?" Chase asked.

"So, what does Willie always have with him?"

"His teddy bear!" all three chorused as her hunch became clear.

"Wait here while I do a spot of stealthy bear-napping," Chase said. "We'll have to perform minor surgery, and I don't want Willie to see it."

As he bounded up the stairs, Alexandra said, "Willie told us he lost his bear once, and his father found it for him. I had no reason to think it was important at the time."

"That was just before Bill died, and I didn't attach any importance to it, either," Brenda said.

Chase returned with the toy bear and they all watched avidly as he slit open the seam up its back. It was a letdown when all he pulled out was wads of stuffing.

"I was so sure," Alexandra sighed.

A smile spread over Chase's face as he reached deeper inside the bear. "Bingo! Who would have thought Teddy was the richest bear in town?" He drew out a small suede bag. After untying the drawstring, he poured a stream of large, glittering diamonds onto his palm. His smile faded as they all stared soberly at the sparkling stones that had caused such tragedy.

Willie came running down the stairs followed by a small

white dog. "Guess what?" he called. "Uncle Bob gave me a whole dollar."

"Uh-oh." Chase thrust the bear at Estelle. "See what you can do about this, Mother."

She hid it in her skirt and left the room to give it to Margaret for a quick repair job.

Willie's face lit with joy when he reached the library and saw his mother. "Mommy, Mommy, I knew you'd come back!" He raced into her waiting arms.

"My darling boy." She held him as if she'd never let go. "I missed you so."

"Why did you go away, Mommy? I missed you, too."

"I'll never leave you again, I promise. We'll be together from now on."

"Daddy, too? When are we going home to see Daddy?"

Brenda hesitated. "Daddy had to go away for a while, honey. We aren't going back to our old house."

Estelle had returned to the library. "Where will you go?" she asked her. "Do you have family you can be with?"

"No, I don't have anyone." Brenda squared her shoulders. "But Willie and I will be fine. We have each other."

"You're very fortunate. I live alone in this big house."

"Bill used to talk about growing up here." Brenda glanced around wistfully. "He had very happy memories of those days."

"Yes, that's the way I always think of him," Estelle said quietly. "Having Willie here was almost like having my son back. I'll miss Willie dreadfully." She paused for a moment. "Since you'll be looking for a place to live, would you consider moving in here with me?"

"That's very generous of you, but you don't know anything about me."

"I know my son loved you, that's all I need to know. You and Willie are not only welcome here, you would be doing me a great favor."

Tears filled Brenda's eyes. "That's the kindest thing anyone has ever said to me. Willie and I would be pleased to accept, Mrs. Mainwaring."

"I can't tell you how happy that makes me, my dear. But I'd rather you called me Estelle. Two Mrs. Mainwarings in the same house would be rather confusing," Estelle said with a bubbling little laugh.

Brenda smiled through her tears. "Why don't we compromise? Would you mind if I called you Mother Mainwaring?"

Chase took Alexandra's hand as the two women embraced emotionally. "Let's leave them alone to get acquainted."

"It won't take long," she remarked as they strolled into the garden. "They already have a lot in common."

Chase's expression sobered. "I wish Bill could have lived to see it."

"I like to think he knows," she said softly. "And I'm sure he's pleased that his family will all be together."

"It's a blessing for Mother, after being alone all these years."

Alexandra glanced covertly at him. "I know you're happy that Brenda turned up safely, but you planned on raising Willie as your own son. It must be a little difficult for you to step aside."

"Not any harder than it will be for you. Willie was beginning to think of you as his mother."

"It won't be the same without him," she admitted with a sigh. "I'm so used to all of his cute, little ways. A child steals your heart when you're not looking."

"There's a solution to that." Chase's eyes kindled as he took her in his arms. "We'll just have to have our own children."

"I was kind of counting on it," she murmured.

"Darling Alex, love of my life, will you marry me?"

"You already asked me," she reminded him.

He laughed exultantly. "I know, but I like to hear you say yes."

"No matter how many times you ask, my answer will never change," she said tenderly.

Alexandra gazed with starry eyes at the man of her dreams, the one she wanted to spend her life with. As their lips met, she knew her dreams would come true.

* * * * *

**This summer, the legend
continues in Jacobsville**

A LONG, TALL
TEXAN SUMMER

Three **BRAND-NEW** short stories

This summer, Silhouette brings readers a special
collection for Diana Palmer's LONG, TALL TEXANS
fans. Diana has rounded up three **BRAND-NEW**
stories of love Texas-style, all set in Jacobsville,
Texas. Featuring the men you've grown to love from
this wonderful town, this collection is a must-have
for all fans!

*They grow 'em tall in the saddle in Texas—and
they've got love and marriage on their minds!*

Don't miss this collection of original Long, Tall Texans
stories...available in June at your favorite retail outlet.

LTTST

And the Winner Is...
You!

...when you pick up these great titles
from our new promotion at your
favorite retail outlet this June!

Diana Palmer
The Case of the Mesmerizing Boss

Betty Neels
The Convenient Wife

Annette Broadrick
Irresistible

Emma Darcy
A Wedding to Remember

Rachel Lee
Lost Warriors

Marie Ferrarella
Father Goose

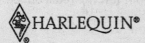 

Look us up on-line at: http://www.romance.net   ATWI397-R

ERICA SPINDLER

the bestselling author of
FORTUNE and FORBIDDEN FRUIT

Outrageous and unconventional, Veronique Delacroix is an illegitimate child of one of the oldest and wealthiest families in New Orleans. A gambler by nature, Veronique can never say no to a challenge… especially from Brandon Rhodes, heir to one of the biggest business empires in the country. Thus begins a daring game of romantic roulette, where the stakes may be too high….

"Erica Spindler is a force to be reckoned with in the romance genre." —*Affaire de Coeur*

CHANCES ARE

Available in May 1997 at your favorite retail outlet.

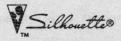